GROUNDWATER

The Last Good Man

GROUNDWATER

THOMAS MCMULLAN

BLOOMSBURY PUBLISHING
LONDON · OXFORD · NEW YORK · NEW DELHI · SYDNEY

BLOOMSBURY PUBLISHING
Bloomsbury Publishing Plc
50 Bedford Square, London, WC1B 3DP, UK
29 Earlsfort Terrace, Dublin 2, Ireland

BLOOMSBURY, BLOOMSBURY PUBLISHING and the Diana logo are
trademarks of Bloomsbury Publishing Plc

First published in Great Britain 2025

A catalogue record for this book is available from the British Library

ISBN: HB: 978-1-5266-7802-7; TPB: 978-1-5266-7803-4;
EBOOK: 978-1-5266-7804-1; EPDF: 978-1-5266-7801-0

2 4 6 8 10 9 7 5 3 1

Typeset by Integra Software Services Pvt. Ltd.
Printed and bound in Great Britain by CPI Group (UK) Ltd, Croydon CR0 4YY

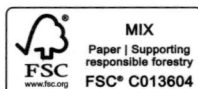

MIX
Paper | Supporting
responsible forestry
FSC
www.fsc.org FSC® C013604

To find out more about our authors and books visit www.bloomsbury.com
and sign up for our newsletters

For product-safety-related questions contact productsafety@bloomsbury.com

For David and Miriam, my parents

ONE

'WE CAN'T CUT THE chair in half,' she said, planting both hands on the wood in a movement that was flippant but abrupt and all of a sudden John felt himself an intruder, as if she held genuine fear that he would seize the antique and cleave it in two. Surely she knew how much he enjoyed its ornate carvings, the central panel of the backrest with the figure he took to be a shepherd, a small oval face worn away, wrapped without expression in carved wooden leaves. She gripped its ridge. The four other chairs, the cheap set, waited like pieces in some obscure game. With the antique there were five. Six were needed. The family were on their way and here was the feeling that they had nothing of their own to offer.

'I saw a stool by the lake,' he said.

Liz pressed her tongue against the inside of her cheek. Her gaze was fixed on the furniture and he could not bear it, tapped the table and she looked up with brow furrowed. Already they were altered by their new surroundings, he felt. In London they'd moved around each other with a fineness that had been honed by routine but here they were untethered. A faint cry came up to the window and he turned to see what it was.

Nothing.

He went outside to look for the stool, found it by the water's edge, beside an old tin of paint and a noise of weeds, small yellow flowers open and interested in the passing bees. Flecks the colour of spoiled cream covered the wood, left by the previous inhabitants. They'd never met in person but he had the impression they were elderly and from the evidence they'd not kept themselves in good condition. He knew there was no point being resentful but he just couldn't help himself, the spread of the clutter, disrespectful the way it was scattered about with no real effort to remove their presence. Yesterday he'd found a full ashtray and a pile of old newspapers in one of the upstairs rooms, the garden had been left overgrown, there were broken hangers in the bedroom, old plastic bags in the kitchen, used bottles of shampoo in the bathroom. It made it impossible to see the house as theirs, all these signs in the stains and scuff marks.

He decided then that when Liz's sister had been and gone, he would build a bonfire on that spot, a statement of intent set on the edge of their home. He meant to gather the dead vines and fallen branches that had collected in the walled garden. He promised himself that he would bring them here, a good distance from the windows, and burn them. He would throw away the old tin of paint, pull up the weeds and build a tower of flame, smoke in a column that would no doubt be seen for miles around, and there was something comfortable in that thought, as if he were writing his signature at the bottom of a deed. There was no point feeling over-whelmed because the house was theirs and he needed to stop forgetting that fact. Their lives were still in the air but it wouldn't be long before they were brought down and when that happened they would be at home in this place, not swept up half-thinking by the deep pull of eddies, brought in and out of rooms by unfamiliar tides.

Another cry, louder, more urgent, and now John could see something crouched in a bank by the edge of the lake. With the wooden stool in hand he walked towards it, picked up pace at the sight of a fawn strug-gling on four thin legs, falling back in the dirt. When he was near, it raised its head at him, black eyes fear-ful. It bucked its head and cried out, the sound almost human. He took a step towards it, careful not to star-tle, but even that small movement caused the animal to panic, raising itself onto its legs and stepping a few feet in the opposite direction before collapsing. One hoof was touching the water and he was worried it would stumble further so he backed away.

He could see no wound from where he was standing. There was the lake to one side of them and the house to the other, the treeline close by – so it was likely the animal had come from that direction, and he searched for a sign of movement, a mother keeping distance, but everything was motionless. There were white dots on the fawn's brown hide, like it too had been splattered with paint. It was the closest he had been to a wild animal and he felt underprepared. He tried to show that there was nothing to be afraid of, made a shushing sound, smiled, hoped that animals could make sense of smiles. He placed the stool on the ground, took a step forward and the fawn bleated again, rose to its legs and this time stood without falling. He offered his hand.

This was it, what they had spoken about, a harmony with nature, a closeness. That was what they had wanted after the last couple of years, they'd agreed on that.

The fawn breathed warm on his fingertips, its black eyes considered him and in them he searched for understanding, liked to think that it was there. The fawn moved its head, cried, turned and limped away. He stayed where he was, watching the animal until it disappeared behind the treeline.

Back inside, when he considered the way the light cut straight across the wooden panelling, he found himself staring. The stool wouldn't look so bad with a cushion. The delivery could still arrive that day and if it did, he would take it back outside. The last time he'd seen his nephew and niece they were giddy and grinning, happy to be doing anything at all. They could have been asked to sit on a sack of flour for all it mattered but no doubt they had grown conscious in the way children can of unfairness, the world perfectly level and any rolling one way or the other an unconscionable crime. Irresistible, then, came the thought of the fawn nudging its moist mouth against an injured leg. John considered going out in search of it and he tried to recall the feeling of hot breath against his fingertips.

4

He looked through the window out at the lake, at the short jetty that extended with its dirty old fishing boat, also left by the previous inhabitants. A tightness grasped his chest. It was as if he had been climbing a ladder without realising and, turned by a gust of wind, he saw the distance below. The lake, the hills beyond, and only the two of them there for miles around. If he listened carefully, he could make out the sound of Liz cutting apples down the hallway. Aside from the chopping, the house was quiet. Let it lie, he thought. It won't be long until it's swept out the door, not long until they finally get what they want and then they'll talk about the times when the house used to be so quiet. He was confident these new surroundings would be the key to things. They say that it's important to feel at ease, that it's remarkable the effect relaxation can have on the reproductive system. The fresh air would do nothing but good, returning their bodies to some more natural state, each breath fixing what was weathered by years of crossing the Euston Road. He pulled the chairs into position around the dining table, letting himself linger on the antique: the panel on the backrest, the wooden leaves, the figure, its face without features. He'd always imagined it listening, as if in a hut at night, the sheep dreaming but the shepherd with one ear to the dark. It had looked so artfully out of place in their flat, but there it was as if it had been made for the house, the only thing of theirs that was.

'I saw a baby deer,' he said.

Liz stopped cutting apples and wiped the backs of her hands on a T-shirt. His words carried with them a childlike delight as he entered the kitchen and her first instinct was to welcome them with a smile, not taking the meaning but thinking instead of the cupboard door by her hips that would only close when lifted. Earlier she had stooped to inspect the hinge, loose in its screws. She tried to remember if the door had closed without a problem when they'd put in the tinned tomatoes and the stock cubes and the rice and the potatoes, all without order, and she wanted to speak to him about that, the jars as well as the door, but here now was something else, pressing with force on those thoughts so that they were squeezed out of view. He would think she had broken the door. Already she was prepared to argue, a heat across her forehead at the prospect.

'Limping, the poor thing,' said John. She could feel the expectation to engage, turned to the window, stood on her tiptoes to get a better look. Nothing. Liz liked to think she had a way with animals, one of those things she believed about herself that had come into being when she was very young and hadn't budged. When she was eight, she spoke to a magpie, had whole conversations. The bird had a nest on the roof of their building; it would come down to their balcony from time to time, hop about, inspect the few plant pots there for anything to eat. She started with raisins on a plate, her mum let her leave them out overnight and in the morning they were gone. She remembered it perched on the railing and she'd say all sorts of things to the bird. *Eat up your dinner. Tell me about your day.*

'Should we leave it some food?' he asked, looked around.

'I need the apples for the pie,' she said and scanned the treeline once more through the kitchen window. If a cute little animal could wait until her sister was here, yes, that would be perfect. They'd already talked about what they would choose to show Monica first: the fireplace, the bannisters, the view looking out from the back of the house at the lake and the woods beyond that rose into a ridge of hills.

There was the sound of the fridge closing behind her. John had pulled out a plastic bottle of semi-skimmed milk and was pouring it into a bowl. Oh God. Next he came to her counter, picking at a few of the pastry offcuts. She carried on with the knife, chop chop, cut a pip in two by accident and so a delicate manoeuvre was needed to gouge the remaining half with the tip of the blade. She felt him watching her do so, knowing he wanted to say that it would be easier with another knife, not one for meat, the small one. Where was that? Just try and find it, she'd say. Not in the drawer, oh no, not in any of the cupboards. If only we hadn't unpacked things in such a rush, put the tins in no order, the pans and plates in places that didn't make any sense.

'Are you looking for something to do?' she asked.

He picked up a slice of apple.

'She'll be jealous for sure,' he said and hoped it was what she wanted to hear, not taken to mean that jealousy was her petty intent. Sometimes it was hard to see the love for the competition, but he didn't blame her, given the way her sister sometimes acted, careful to present a version of life sanded to a fine, smooth surface. Last year he'd seen the hurt in his wife's eyes when she'd opened herself so sincerely, the New Year's fireworks exploding unseen in the mist. What could she do to stop the black dog from haunting her dreams, she'd asked, and there had been real vulnerability on the balcony with the momentum of their celebrations petering out around them.

*The poor dog, desperately
scratching against the floor.*

Liz was watching him now from the corner of her eye as he gathered the bowl and the pastry pieces. You cast these side glances, he thought. You used to look straight forward. You used to look direct, straight ahead at me.

He went outside with the milk and the pastry and the slice of apple. She watched him through the window as he set them on the edge of the veranda and part of her felt warm towards him even as another part grew resentful. *He's making more work for himself when there is already so much to do.*

She realised he was trying to say something to her but she could not hear it. He motioned for her to open the window.

'I said, we better enjoy the quiet before Harrie's knees.'

He mimed snapping sticks.

She forced her smile down. She would not let it be an easy win, not when he had irritated her with his sweeping in and out of rooms.

'Don't get at him.'

'Ah come on, I'm not getting at him.'

'He tries hard.'

With the pie in the oven, they cleaned the living room of the few remaining boxes, tidied the ornaments on the mantelpiece and tried their best to fluff the limp pillows on their knackered old sofa. A new one was on its way but when it would get there was anyone's guess. John binned a long-dead bunch of roses and Liz returned an edition of medieval maps to the bookcase, thought better, left it on the coffee table. Where had their belongings gone, she wondered, noticing how bare the walls seemed. Where was the painting they had brought with them of the ship in the harbour? She wanted to gather back all of the things they'd spent days unpacking, pile them up, the tins from the cupboards, the bed sheets with the plant pots, fill the room with their many shapes and show anyone who would care to see the objects that they had accrued. There would be the evidence, she thought. There amongst the duck-down stuffing and stainless steel, the knives and forks, the spoon they kept as a joke. There would be the proof.

She thought of telling him this, giggling at the image of all their things in a great big heap. He was neatening the throw on their old sofa and she opened her mouth to talk but couldn't find the words. She pictured a ball of phlegm lodged in her chest. A great black and sticky ball. She let her eyes rest on the window, and it was only then that she noticed a man standing by the edge of the lake, his back to the house. The man could have been a statue for how still he was, tall, dressed in a dark jacket, a wide-brimmed hat.

A few clouds had come in but the sky was still blue and bright, the late summer air not yet stifling. Liz watched from the window as John approached the stranger. The trees made a wall on either side of the lake. They went on for miles. She wished they hadn't seen that report about California. Unprecedented fire conditions. There was no point putting on your running shoes. If you saw the flames from your kitchen window, if you needed to get out of there, you'd think it would be possible. You'd think you could run, but the flames could outrun you. She turned on the tap, filled a glass of water. She wished they hadn't seen it. All that burning, a thousand things dying. She watched her husband swing his arms, aimless, self-conscious. He'd be putting on the voice he used for plumbers.

We have not been fruitful, she thought. Despite our best attempts.

She took a deep breath. We have time on our side, we have been seized by hope, by a love of nature. Most people would envy a free second under a ray of sunshine at the feet of the rolling hills. She focused on the warmth coming through the window. She pictured fire lapping at the hem of her trousers. Monica will be jealous. The uninterrupted views. She will say *this is something else.* Liz drank her glass of water, cool and quenching. When John got back to the house, he told her that the man's name was Jim Sweet, that people just called him Sweet, that he was a warden for the area, took care of wildlife and the paths, and he seemed nice enough, said he may be over again, and when she asked him what he wanted, John could only shrug his shoulders. The man knew the people who used to live here and they were apparently fine with him cutting across the shore.

What work a warden must do, he thought, looking out at the lake and the hills differently in the knowledge that someone else was there. He should have told Sweet about the fawn, but he was worried he'd done something wrong by putting his hand close to the animal's mouth. He'd heard once that you shouldn't touch wild baby animals because you could leave your scent and then their mother would reject them. He brought his fingers to his face. There was the faint smell of apples.

Liz lay on the sofa, half her face pressed against the armrest.

'If we don't like him being on our land, I'm sure we could ask him to go another way.'

A faint smile spread across her lips. 'Our land,' she echoed, and he could not tell if she was mocking or enjoying the words. Hearing them back they sounded unreal, but it was the truth. The documents outlined their ownership right up to the water's edge and so it was theirs, the spot where the man Sweet had been standing, the grass and the shingle, the soil beneath. There were no other houses to border, no neighbours for fences, but that stretch between their home and the lake was theirs. He was buoyed by the feeling and he wanted Liz to open her eyes so he could share his pleasure. *Let me in.* He moved to the sofa, knelt on the floorboards, and when this did not stir her he put the back of his forefinger against her cheek, stroked the skin with what he meant as tenderness. For the briefest of moments the grey irises were pressed, awoken from a bad dream. 'I could fall asleep,' she said, her voice flustered, the words shaken like dice in a hand as if anything could have been said.

*

A door opened and Ciara and Finn ran into the kitchen, their mother touching their heads as they passed the counter. 'Nothing but criminals,' said Harrie in his Dutch accent, lifting a leg, bending it at the knee until an almighty crack resounded. John tried to share a look with Liz but she did not meet his eye. Through the back door he could see Ciara take off her shoes, throwing them on the ground, joining her brother in dangling her legs off the jetty. He thought of the rooms above them, the air motionless, mute. 'The way they handled the whole thing from start to finish, nothing less than a travesty,' said Harrie. 'I don't care how difficult the situation was, they should have done better.'

John let it be known he agreed. They all did, nodding their heads, and the sight of their shared feelings must have satisfied Harrie because he took a deep breath, blowing the air into a full stop.

The tent poles and almond fingers were left in the car but John helped bring in a few bags that had been separated for the night's stay, up to the study that had been turned into a guest room, next to a box room for the kids. Weeks before, when Monica had got wind of their moving date, she'd announced that she would be driving up with the whole of her family. *All of that nature and the children are gagging for some space.* The expectation was that John and Liz would host them for a week and a half leading up to the August Bank Holiday. In the end, Liz had to tell her outright that it was too much. They would've only just moved and, as much as they would love to see her, as much as they'd missed them, couldn't they do it another time? But Monica was set on escaping London. *While we still can.* The restrictions had been lifted and she wasn't going to wait around. The compromise was a stopover in the house before the family drove to a camping spot not too far away, still within the area of natural beauty. They could go back and forth.

Some dark clouds had come in but the weather could fall either way and it was agreed that they would go for a walk. There was the path Liz ran that wound around the lake's perimeter. Since the move she'd taken up running again, had found a route that circled the water and lasted half an hour, which was a good marker for her fitness. The plan was to build up to two circuits, then three. She'd taken to waking up early and slipping wordlessly into her running clothes. John had also considered getting back into running but Liz never mentioned the possibility of his joining her, so he didn't bring it up. That morning he'd been awake when she set off and had watched her from the window as she did her stretches, as she disappeared beyond the treeline. He'd considered lingering until she resurfaced on the other side of the house but it made him feel more unemployed than he already was so he'd toasted a crumpet, liked a picture of Ali's kids, tapped the *Guardian*, read a story about the withdrawal from Afghanistan that felt distant, from a different time.

After university he'd travelled, ended up in Budapest. He'd never taken to languages before but he'd stuck with Hungarian because he had a girlfriend and she wanted him to be able to speak with her family, and, after all that was done with, he was good enough to get some work out of it back home. Total Translations had given him a steady stream of freelance jobs, mostly internal business documents, some academic papers and the occasional bit of copywriting. He'd enjoyed the work, each document a puzzle to fix and square away. He'd tried his hand at a few short stories and poems, and Liz had encouraged him to apply for British Council funding to set up some kind of Hungarian–English publishing venture, but it was the Total Translations work he'd always come back to and, frankly, it was in those jobs that he found the most pleasure. He could feel the functionality of the translation as he was doing it, like one rail running parallel to another.

But the office hadn't sent him anything for months. When he'd tried to find out why, they'd been evasive. He could read between the lines. For some reason or another they didn't want him translating for them. While technically he was still employed on a freelance basis, there had been no contact on either part for several months. Naturally he assumed that he had mistranslated a document. If he had, it must have been to an offensive degree for them to stop using him. He'd looked back over his work but at first couldn't find anything that might be misconstrued. There was a rogue indefinite conjugation in a financial report for a pharmaceutical company but that was the worst of it. He tried to be satisfied but the thought of a mistake stayed with him. What had he put into the wrong words, he wondered. On occasional nights he would dwell on it, unable to sleep.

He'd looked further backwards, at files he had sent months before. It became a habit, checking old emails and attachments, assuring himself each time that everything had been in order. Then, one night, he found a mistake in an image caption for a photograph of a black dog swimming across a wide river. *The dog is in the river.* A kutya a folyóban van. He had written folyosón. A kutya a folyosón van. *The dog is in the corridor.* The job was almost a year old. He told himself that if this was the culprit, something would have been mentioned sooner. But he had done something wrong, regardless of whether it had been picked up. He had fumbled.

They put on their shoes and stepped outside. Given the time and the distance, they estimated an hour for the loop at a gentle stroll, a tour of a clock face, and as they started out John pictured a minute hand following their movements from the centre of the water.

'Yes, lucky with the inheritance,' he said back to Harrie, who had come to his side, who had opened his arms at the landscape in front of them much like a conductor presenting an orchestra. Harrie didn't push on the money, to John's relief, but only called the place beautiful and John agreed, although he felt he was lying to himself, or at least ignoring the tightness in his chest at the distance between them and the horizon, the rain falling far away on the hills making their limits difficult to trace, bled out and wavering between land and sky. The peaks were concealed in a shroud of captured light. He let his eyes rest on the surface of the lake, sliding on its wind-rippled forms in search of something to hold him in place, finding only a grey reflection of the heavens, and he felt for a moment mesmerised, his own life and those around him subsumed in dim and uncertain depths. Harrie asked if there were fish and John said there were, or so he'd been informed. Bream, carp. There was the fishing boat on the jetty in view and Harrie suggested they go together later that day. He hadn't gone fishing since he was a boy.

At that moment Finn threw a stone into the lake with two hands, the splash making him and his sister shriek in delight. 'I have a flask of good scotch,' Harrie said, lowering his voice. John had always felt a degree of contrivance in their interactions, both of them forced into an intimacy that would otherwise not exist, if it were not for the fact that their wives were sisters – and yet something was exposed in the way Harrie looked then beyond him, through him, even, to the settling water, as if he too were mesmerised. *He tries hard.* Liz didn't need to tell him that. Of course he tries. They all try, that much is a given. To stop trying would be to admit things and nobody wants that. Better to try, to make an effort. Harrie glanced behind him to Liz and Monica, to make sure they had not been listening, thought John, and then he looked back to the water, to the daylight whisked into mirrored trenches.

If it were just the two of them, Liz thought, it would be easier to clear the air. It was always easier to speak when walking, she found. If it was just her and John, they could talk and talk and somewhere in it would be the sticky black ball, coughed up, no longer a block between them. She'd always thought of herself as having a way with words but in the past few days... She used to write short stories, still thought of herself as a writer of short fiction even though she hadn't finished one for at least five years. She'd been in *Best British Short Stories*. She remembered going to see it in the bookshop with him, they can't have been going out long, he'd made a big deal of it which was sweet but also a little much, the way he'd made her pose with it so he could take a picture. She'd thought it would've been more satisfying to see her name on the contents page, there in the big Foyles on Charing Cross Road, but she'd mostly felt a little silly. She'd wanted to leave even though he'd wanted to have a coffee and a cake in the cafe and so he'd been in a sulk afterwards, when they'd gone to the National Portrait Gallery and she'd felt a dark unravelling when she'd stood in front of a picture of John Donne with his broad hat and his delicate hands and his long face looking out and beyond.

Her work now with the animal charity was fulfilling. She was developing a system to monitor the black rhinos in a national park in Kenya, north-east of Nairobi. It was a partnership between the park and the startup. She was the product manager. Some of her developers lived in the UK, some in France and Germany, one in Singapore. Everyone was remote. Her team had just delivered an alpha milestone build to the founders and it wouldn't be long until she heard their judgement. There had been mutterings about the direction of things, second-hand anxiety. One of the founders flirted with her and that counted for something but still there was the worry she was facing a wall and with John not getting jobs, the costs of the move, it could soon become precarious.

She hadn't been to the national park herself. The founders had. They'd taken a lot of pictures standing close to the animals and the men who kept watch over them. There was one picture of a rhinoceros that she'd saved on the desktop of her laptop, one of the few pictures that didn't have the founders in shot. The rhino was standing at an angle, looking at the camera. Its eyes were expressive. Kind, she thought. She found herself looking at it whenever she had to remind herself that all of this was for a purpose.

There was a splash as Ciara threw a big stone into the lake.

'King and Queen of the seven seas!' shouted Harrie.

John still wondered where it had come from, Liz's pity, if it were pity, snipping the harmless mockery that was stitched into the entirety of their relationship right from the start? Harrie and the noises he made, his foolishness, all of it fair game because of the dominance he pressed on each and every situation. By the time they had made it halfway around the lake, the sun had broken through the clouds. They could see a house across the water and he realised it was theirs. It must be. There were no others. Harrie extended his arms once more. 'The life you're going to make for yourselves,' he said. 'The house needs a bit of love. But to have all of this.'

It was then John noticed the great many cigarette ends on the ground beside his shoe. Harrie followed his gaze and whistled through his teeth. The ends were close to a tree stump, left by one of the previous inhabitants, John imagined. 'Need to come out here with a bin bag,' he mumbled, embarrassed at having to explain. Then little Ciara came over to see what the men were looking at, hugging her father's leg until he picked her up and carried her on his shoulders. On a damp November evening, years before, Ciara had to stay the night in the hospital and Liz couldn't stop thinking about her there. *Only a small thing*, she'd said. *She doesn't know what's going on. She doesn't know why she's hurting.* When they'd made the trip to Tottenham after the operation Liz was frantic with love, keeping watch when Monica went to shower, and John remembered the look on his sister-in-law's face when she came back into the room, surprised at the way Liz was bent over with her hands on the sides of the crib, observing every breath from the girl. Monica and Harrie still treated their daughter delicately even though she was as fine as any other eight-year-old. Liz always asked about her first when the children were mentioned. How's Ciara? The air of an offhand question, and each time they would say she's fine. *Playing, fine.*

John felt bad for Finn. He made it a mission of his to show an interest, ask the boy questions, make him aware that he was seen as much as anyone. Finn would be looking at a book of planets and John would gasp in wonder and even his nephew seemed to think he was laying it on a bit thick, losing interest, so that more than once John was left alone, squatting with his hands on his knees.

'It *really* suits you,' said Monica, glancing at Liz from the side of her eyes. She nodded by way of emphasis, brows high and lips drawn thin into a closed smile, looked skyward at the canopy and made a pleasurable sigh, then brought her arms across her chest as they walked on, the temperature not easy to define as warm or cool, the lake passing in and out of view, and maybe it did suit her, Liz thought. Maybe it was the peace of it, the space.

'It's so authentic.' Monica pronounced the word as if she were handling it with gloves. 'John's neighbour, was it?'

Liz had known this was coming, was actually surprised it hadn't come sooner.

'Did he know her well?'

'As a child.' And then, because she felt the need to justify it further: 'John would help in her garden.'

Monica nodded sagely.

'It must've been a nice surprise.'

'We weren't expecting it.'

At one point the path was blocked by a fallen tree and they took it as an opportunity to sit and eat shortbread, unwrapped from kitchen towel paper and finished in no time at all. There John watched the children play by the lake. They had about them the unspeakingness of animals, he thought, searching for stones, heads bowed, aware of each other and somehow coordinating their efforts but with no words, no fingers pointed. He caught his wife watching him, Monica too, something whispered with a tilted head that caused Liz to pretend a smile. He made out as if he hadn't seen, focused instead on Harrie as his heavy frame was pulled by his son's hand to the water's edge, told to stand and observe as the boy threw a stone, the splash catching the sunlight in a dozen glass beads.

'She was saying she could see you with a baby,' Liz told him, later, when they had resumed their walk. A lattice of leaves the size of hands arched above. A thousand shades of green. Sunlit green, thought John. Stale green. Peat green. A wet green grazed by a child's hand in a rock pool. A young green. A cracked green. Beyond: the hills. He longed to see them, searched for them as he walked with his hands clasping the straps of his backpack, as if balance could be broken at a moment's notice. Luminous green. Inarguable green. Frozen green peas. Brittle green glass in a church window. A saint's gown, the sun shining through. He wanted to see the hills. Beyond assurance he wanted to see them, but the green leaves filtered everything from view.

*

Liz opened a bottle of sauvignon blanc that had been on offer when they'd done their last big shop. It was well into the afternoon and they had earned it, she said. An unusual energy was in her, the corner of her lip curled like paper in a fire. John was glad to see her happy but he was thrown by the intensity, not knowing whether to take it as truth or play. He tried to match it, closing his hands in a clap, suggesting they go outside to enjoy what was left of the day, which she chimed was a brilliant idea, *brilliant*. Something in the way she ran a nail against the rim of her glass kicked up an urge to take her away from the others, to speak to her in private and ask what was in her head.

'It's turning out fine,' she said.

'You don't have any more chairs, do you?' Monica stood at the doorway to the veranda, her face turned back for the question. *Who doesn't have chairs?* Liz laughed it off, explaining the delay of the furniture delivery.

John said he would get some from the dining room. And there it was, the stillness that had broken at the arrival of the others. A mist of butterflies settled on a bough. He let himself sink, sitting for a while on the wooden antique with the carving of the shepherd, what he took to be a shepherd. For the longest time it had stood in his granny's living room, facing the TV, swaddled in pillows and blankets so that it was only years later, when he had helped to clean out the small flat in the sheltered accommodation complex, that he discovered it was old and ornate with that fine wooden carving. A wainscot chair, he'd discovered. English oak.

Too late then to ask her whether there was a story, if it was some kind of heirloom or just something she'd picked up from a car boot sale. He liked to think he remembered it from his grandparents' house, when they had a house, but it might have only been the pillows and the blankets he remembered. He knew it as a seat for visitors, remembered when his father had perched on its edge watching his granny sleeping even though they were meant to be watching a Western.

He looked across the room to nothing in particular, to the wooden panelling on the walls and the fringes of the ceiling. If Liz came in then to see him sitting, he would reassure her that he was only resting after listening to Harrie go on, as if the world relied on his speaking not to vanish. A memory came of sitting in the hollow of a tree. He couldn't remember when or where but he felt the pressure of his knees against his chest and the stillness of the wet bark and it was as if he had stopped existing altogether. Was that something that had happened to him? He stacked and carried the cheap set of four chairs, leaving the stool and the antique, the creamy spots of paint on one and the carved figure on the other. Outside they drank on the chairs while the children played in the shallows of the water. Monica and Liz were side by side. How similar they looked, he thought. How their faces changed, orbited one another, at times so distant but at others in perfect alignment. Years ago, in the dark of a concert hall, he had mistaken Monica for her sister, had put his hand on her forearm and she had let it stay there, the music above their heads, and neither had mentioned it then nor since, but he thought of it still, at times.

'I can't remember the author's name,' said Harrie, clicking his tongue. He jabbed a finger in the air. Liz offered something about a book she had read but Harrie only repeated: 'What was his name?' And so they waited. His vanity to hold them captive, she thought. His spluttering attempts, worth their time and no doubt in him about it. He clicked a finger as if it might spark an engine. 'What was it? Klaszna-, Kaszna-' She saw it in the founders, the three men that would soon deliver their judgement on her work, their way of being that took up space, meant to take it up, more than needed, how they would lean back in their chairs, arms up, hands on the back of the head. Even on Zoom they found ways of taking up space, their little boxes somehow always feeling bigger than the others. Where did it come from? Passed on from father to son. Her own mother collected metals, a chemist by training. Copper shavings in small glass jars. Mercury under water.

Monica made a sharp intake of breath and pointed a little further along the shore to a man walking towards them. It was the warden, the one John had spoken to earlier. Jim Sweet, Liz remembered. A pleasant name. Monica called for the children but John told her not to worry. 'He works with the land,' he said. Sweet walked right up to the veranda, no sense of a boundary crossed.

He apologised if he was interrupting. He didn't know they'd be having guests and was only there because he remembered on his way back that he'd said he would come. He liked to keep his promises. Harrie asked if he wanted to join and Sweet said that would be nice.

'We're drinking wine but would you like a beer?' asked John.

'We have Heineken,' said Liz.

'Whatever's easiest,' said Sweet.

By the time John returned with a beer bottle and the stool Harrie was standing beside the warden and laughing loudly. John sat down but the other men remained where they were. Monica asked Sweet what he did and he explained in a convoluted way that he helped to maintain the public paths, mind the wildlife.

'We had a problem on our path today,' said Liz. 'There was a fallen tree.'

John caught her eye. 'What?' she mouthed.

'That's no good,' said Sweet. 'I will see to that.' And for a moment there rang a pause, broken by Harrie who said that it was the way of the countryside. Sweet gave an awkward smile and said that they had had strong winds not so long ago.

They got to talking about the lake, how nice it was to have that on your doorstep, all to yourself, and Sweet said it was a sight and a half. It was a kind of sinkhole, in fact, with a network of the caves that go on for miles because of the limestone. He grew animated as he spoke. Liz had no idea there were caves. John said he'd heard something but didn't realise it was such a big feature. He was lying. They'd never been told anything about caves.

Did it attract many divers? 'Does it get busy?' Liz was aware an urgency had crept into her voice. No, no. Only a handful a year, only accessible since the land had passed from the Forestry Commission and it's not on signs or maps. Sweet scratched the blue stubble on his jaw. You never know how these things go, it could pick up, become an attraction. They went pretty far, the underwater caverns. He'd sometimes considered taking a diving course so he could go down there for himself but you'd probably need some high-level certificate.

'There might be treasure,' said Harrie.

Monica made a cooing sound.

'Do you get many pirates around here?' asked John.

'No,' said Sweet, matter-of-fact.

'There's a famous sinkhole in Mexico, next to Chichén-Itzá.' Harrie was swirling the wine around his glass. 'When they dived down there they found gold, tools, weapons, jewellery. Jade idols. Sacrifices.'

Liz could see that he liked having the attention back on him.

'What a waste to throw things away like that,' said Monica.

Harrie cleared his throat. 'Haven't you ever thrown a penny in a well?'

'There's not much jade around here either,' noted Sweet.

At some point Monica left without saying anything and John watched her walk over to where the children were busying themselves on the veranda. He saw Liz notice his attention, glancing over before returning to her conversation with the men. Sweet took Monica's empty chair and pulled it towards the pair to form a close triangle. John had to lean forward on his seat to feel a part of things but even then he was distant enough from the others that it was a little awkward. They were talking about how it was only a matter of time before some property developer discovered this patch of natural beauty and decided to build more houses around the lake, at least that's what Harrie believed, but Sweet shook his head and said there were protections to stop that from happening. Besides, Liz rejoined, it was so remote that it would be impractical. She added defensively that it worked for them but it wouldn't work for everyone.

'If this was the Netherlands there would be a camp-site here. Cabins, water sports, some lovely restaurants.' Harrie was getting enthusiastic, wagging a finger at Sweet, and if there was any offence taken it wasn't shown by the warden, who politely asked Liz if she planned to grow anything in their garden.

'John has some ideas for making it nice.'

'I have some fertiliser I can bring around, if you like.'

That got Harrie going off about Hackney City Farm, the garden and the pigs, which John really didn't have the energy to listen to and in any case the air was getting cooler, the sky grey, so he stood and paused to see if Liz would glance at him again, but she didn't.

Across a slanted portion of the veranda were objects the children had collected from the shore of the lake: many small stones, a length of blue fishing twine and what looked like hooks for curtain rails. There were pinecones and pieces of wood, an empty wine bottle and a lime-green cigarette lighter. Monica was leant against a railing, watching Finn and Ciara deal with the objects, Ciara arranging them into distinct piles while her brother was lost in a flat stone that had been weathered right through, a neat hole in its centre into which he stuck his forefinger.

'Nice to have a change of scene,' he said.

'Very nice,' said Monica.

'Get away from London.'

'Hmm.'

Finn carefully put down the stone on the veranda. He observed it there, with its hole in its centre, and then he picked it up again.

'How are things?' asked John.

'Yeah, all right.'

She looked upwards. As soon as a topic became too much for Monica, veered too personal, she would tilt her head back, mouth shut, absorbed by the heavens. The effect was sudden and unambiguous. When her head went back down she would never respond to what had been said, instead start on something else.

'We've hired our bikes already,' she said. 'Not bad for a couple of weeks, if you wanted to do the same. You're more than welcome to leave them with us.'

'I think Liz said we're just doing a couple of days with the bikes.'

'Just a couple days?' She looked disturbed.

'I think that's the plan.'

She watched the children, didn't say anything, then knelt and picked up the bottle and the lighter before excusing herself. Ciara was not diverted by her mother's interference, focused on the task of lining up the small stones one beside the other. They reminded John of a row of faces.

He had once met an architect at a party who, after several drinks, had shown him a stone that he carried around in the inside pocket of his jacket. It was small enough to fit in his palm and there were two small grooves on its surface that gave the impression of a face, one without a nose or lips, only two vague spaces where the eyes would be. The architect had shown it to him with a sense of pride, he remembered, much like it was a photograph of a loved one. John had asked him why he was carrying around a stone and the architect had told him he'd carried it with him for at least twenty years and was waiting for the chance to build his ideal palace. The way the architect left a space for John to ask what he meant made it clear that he'd shown his stone to many people at many different parties. The architect had told him about a French postman from the nineteenth century, surname Cheval, who had a dream in which he had built a palace. One day, the postman tripped on a stone during his rounds that was so striking he picked it up and knew, there and then, that it would be the first piece of his vast construction. In the thirty-three years that followed, on his long walks through the French countryside to deliver the post, he would collect all manner of stones, first in his pockets, eventually in a wheelbarrow, and over time he cemented them together to build his ideal palace. This palace, which still stands today, is like something from another world, the architect at the party had insisted. In places it looks like a forest or an underwater kingdom. There are parts that resemble a Hindu temple, others that are like the walls of an Ancient Egyptian mausoleum, despite the fact that the postman Cheval never travelled beyond the region in which he lived. These references were things he would only have seen in the periodicals and postcards he delivered on his rounds, and that was the detail that had stuck most in John's mind: this postman, dreaming about pictures he'd seen on the backs of postcards, picking up rocks.

John later discovered that Cheval's daughter had died in the years when he was constructing his palace. How his grief must have intermingled with those dreams of faraway temples. Cheval had carved many inscriptions on his walls. On the north facade, above a small sculpted bird, are the words 'D'un songe j'ai sorti la reine du monde'.

Out of a dream I have brought forth the queen of the world.

On the veranda, John knelt down beside the children. 'Do you know what I saw today? A baby deer.' They did not react. 'It was there,' he added, pointing beyond them. Finn turned his attention back to the hollow stone in his hand. Ciara straightened a pebble in her row and John was just about to leave them to it when she stood and strode to where John had gestured.

'Baby deer,' she called. 'Where are you, baby deer?'

It was, in fact, after the party attended by the architect when John and Liz had found the dog on their doorstep. At first he had taken it for a coat, one of Liz's, left by a neighbour she'd lent it to, and he'd been angry at the idea someone could so carelessly dump some of their belongings on the floor outside their flat. Then he saw the face, its tongue drooping, the body on its side and the faintest of shivers running through one of its back legs. Liz had gripped his arm and the sudden movement must have alerted the animal because it had tried to move, its legs scratching against the hallway floor. They'd been frozen to the spot, unable to breathe, unable to move even a finger as the dog convulsed and it was terrible, the sight, in a way he could not entirely put into words. It was as if the whole world had withered, their life shown for the bad act it was, the streets and the buildings no more real than painted wood. They had watched it die, not knowing that was what they had witnessed until it was too late and only then did they kneel beside it, only then did he touch its stomach, still warm, and he had felt then a terrible unclasping, as if he had slipped from a bar that had supported his weight. He was unable to find his voice. If someone had asked him then who he was he would not have known how to answer.

Thinking of the encounter, he felt reinfected by it. The same terror was discernible, a lump in his throat. He tried to put it out of mind, forcing attention on the lake, its colour, the ripples, the fresh air drawn through his nose. 'Baby deer,' shouted Ciara. The other adults watched her with interest from their table. The black dog had not belonged to anyone in the building. They were told it must have wandered in to get away from the cold, although why the stray had climbed the stair-case and why it had chosen their door to die in front of was a mystery, at least that was how it was seen by the building's management, which had disposed of the body but denied any responsibility. John and Liz had laughed about it. What else could they do? But Liz had had nightmares about it for months afterwards.

In his own dreams he was high above a pool of black fur, nowhere to go but into its depths.

Sweet left them a torn scrap of lined paper with his phone number written clearly in blue ink. It was a nice gesture, Liz said, to recognise that they might need some help adjusting to the area but not to impose instructions, dos and don'ts, nothing of that, which was a relief because as soon as he had started talking about the Forestry Commission, her skin had prick-led at the prospect of regulations. But no, they could fish if they wanted, explore the surroundings to their heart's content and if they did notice any broken fences, disrupted paths, they should phone that number and let him know. In return, help was there if they needed it. He'd offered to bring over some compost and wasn't that a kind thing to say, Liz said, her face flushed. Wasn't it nice for him to go out of his way to make them feel welcome? And John had to admit that the man had made an effort to be a positive presence, even indulging Harrie when Christ knew he must have rolled his eyes at some of the things coming out of the man's mouth about the ways of the natural world, the life cycles of bees, the problems facing farmers with today's climate. 'He must get lonely,' she said, as she put on a red cardi-gan. They would make him a meal, they would show him their generosity, their warmth of spirit. It would be nice to have a friend in the area. Someone handy.

'You should have invited him for dinner,' said Monica.

'The chairs—' John started and did not finish because she waved a hand in the air.

'Prune,' said Harrie as he came into the kitchen. 'It's starting to rain.' He noticed John, his face for a moment motionless. 'I'll help to get the things in.'

Prune was a nickname Harrie had given Liz. It came from the time she'd lived with them in Clapton Pond, when she would have long showers in the evening, long enough to stop anyone else getting into the bathroom, and Monica made a comment one day about how her sister soaked up all their water supply, how they paid the bills to keep her fingers and toes as wrinkled as prunes. Harrie was unfamiliar with the expression but after that would knock on the door saying *Prune, Prune* whenever he needed to brush his teeth. He rarely used it around John. When it did slip out, Harrie acted as if it was a secret he wasn't meant to tell. It made him feel like a big brother, John guessed, although in truth he sometimes felt uncomfortable hearing it. Nobody else said it.

Soon after that it came down heavy. At one point John stood at the back door and watched it fall over the shore and the lake, obscuring anything beyond. After a while he realised Ciara had joined him. She was staring out intently and then it dawned on him that all the children's pebbles, so carefully ordered, were being swept away by a river of water flowing across the slanted boards. 'It's only rain,' he told her, meant as a comfort.

After that, a fog hung low on their faces as they sat indoors. Monica and Liz chatted on the sofa while Harrie lingered close to a window that overlooked the garden. Finn sat cross-legged beneath the window, his head supported by one hand, watching the rain. His sister lay flat beside him, face up, blowing puffs of air for no obvious reason. The children are bored, thought John. They spent a long time putting those things in order. The row of pebbles like a procession of faces. 'It's a shame we didn't take a picture.'

'Children forget,' said Monica, rolling her eyes. They'll get over it, was her meaning, although the way she put it seemed harsher: children are always forgetting, their minds unformed, don't expect any of this to stick. She liked to speak about things they didn't know, couldn't know, at least not yet. Just wait until you're woken at three in the morning; just wait until the teeth come through and you're at your wits' end – and it got to Liz, it frustrated her that there was this door through which she had yet to pass. *Sometimes I don't know what she'd do if she couldn't patronise me*, she had said once to John and he had assured her that her sister would find something else. Just you wait until they're standing, pulling knives from the drawers; just wait until they're old enough to talk back; one door would lead to another, and a shadow of a smile had appeared on his wife's face that made him consider whether the distance in experience was always unwelcome. He had no siblings of his own so the closest thing in his mind was a parent and what is left there if the doors are swung open, all the weakness plain as day? But perhaps an older sister is nothing like that and perhaps he is only guessing at things, putting his own shapes on the lives of the women who sat then talking side by side.

He once found his mother crying in her bedroom. She covered her face when he came close and he knew he should have wrapped his arms around her but he was afraid of the way her voice sounded when she told him it was nothing so he went back outside, to the other children and the ants' nest they had found on the street, with its many black and shiny creatures that were spilling around the edges of a loose paving slab, where small sticks had been pressed in an attempt to work them into some kind of frenzy. Somebody had gone to boil some water and those that remained watched the ants knowing that they would soon be dead, and the pavement was orange and pink with heat.

Liz changed in front of him. Nothing visible had shifted. There had been no movement in her posture and yet, the light from the table lamp struck her differently, as sunlight will look different on water ruffled by wind. He was certain then that something between them was wrong. Liz closed her eyes. She stayed like that for a few seconds, lost in thought, her nostrils widening at the deep and steady intake of breath, a flutter of movement beneath her eyelids.

Black paws,
struggling to right themselves.

She opened her eyes, met his gaze. Whatever was wrong could be fixed, he told himself. When the right moment came, he would ask her what had happened, what he had done.

'Do we need to book the bikes?' she asked her sister.

'For a couple of days you should be fine, I'd imagine.'

Monica straightened herself on the sofa, as if she might get up, but she stayed where she was. Liz could feel her stiffen.

'I didn't think we'd use them the whole time, if we're coming and going.'

She'd felt the need to explain herself.

'Sure,' said Monica.

'We'll barely be on them.'

'It makes sense.'

Liz sometimes thought of her sister as a particular kind of actor, someone who'd played a role when they were young and nothing she'd done since had defined her to the same extent. If they could only speak like they used to, with the lights out in their little room and their voices alone keeping them from sleep.

'We could still go fishing,' John suggested. Harrie hadn't mentioned it since the walk and so he brought it up out of mercy, feeling responsible for the mood that had descended since the weather turned. He longed to dispel the murk that had gathered about them and perhaps, if he showed willingness, it would put right whatever had been knocked off course.

Harrie took one look through the window and said it was coming down too heavy. 'Not that I wouldn't like to go with you,' he added, 'if there's time,' which made the whole thing seem like it was John's idea, to his annoyance.

Monica heard Liz wanted to take up an instrument. 'To have the time for *that*,' she said. '*Bliss.*' She had perked up. 'And all this space, no one to bother except poor John.'

Mutual laughter.

'And what instrument would you like to learn?'

'I'm not sure yet.'

'You can't go wrong with a piano.' Monica pointed to the corner of the room with sudden gusto. 'You could put one there, against the wall.'

Liz nodded unevenly. 'Maybe the guitar, I don't know.'

'No, no, the guitar, lovely,' said Monica with an intensity that could be taken for genuine encouragement.

'I used to play the guitar,' said Harrie. 'I could show you some chords.'

'We don't have one with us,' said Monica in a stage whisper.

'We could make a family band,' said John.

Harrie clicked his fingers. 'Ciara is very musical. She has a beautiful voice.'

'Maybe a clarinet,' said Liz.

'That's a bit...' Monica searched for the word. 'You can't have a singalong with a clarinet, can you?'

Liz sipped her wine.

'You might look silly, out here with a clarinet.' A mean smile had emerged on Monica's face. 'It is very you though,' she said. 'A clarinet in the woods.' She mimed playing a flute.

Liz looked at John, widened her eyes.

'It's very Elizabeth,' said Monica, then pointed again to the corner of the room. 'But a piano there, yes.'

He went to start the fire. The wood was already in place, laid on a bed of kindling, cradled on a cast-iron grille above a heap of shredded newspaper. He had been looking forward to this moment, the match lit and pressed against a headline about feigned national amnesia that ignited immediately. Harrie was standing above him then, arms folded, and together they watched the fire spread, drawn up into the wooden pieces, scratching at the logs until the bark oranged and curled in places. The sun had grown weak behind the rain clouds and, later, when the food was ready and they took their places at the dinner table, the flicker spread on their faces, on the wooden panelling of the walls, on their clothes and the chairs. They were living in an ancient kingdom, John thought. Ciara took the antique and Finn the stool, Monica making the decision and no argument in return. In the light of the fireplace they were ghosts, strung together with silver wire. Something was about to disappear, he felt, and caught sight of the lake through the window, its surface catching what was left of the day.

'I'll need a few hours for work,' Harrie said in a low voice, turning a fork that he'd pinched by the neck.

'Oh,' said Monica.

'Just an hour or two.'

She turned to Liz. 'I tell him he needs time to relax.'

Liz responded with some hesitation. 'You're on holiday,' she said; a harmless statement of fact.

Harrie tapped his head. 'No rest for the mind.'

Monica glared at her plate. Liz had once been told exactly what area of research Harrie was occupied with, but it was honestly not interesting enough to remember.

Something about ontology. There was something about God in there. She recalled that much because at the same party where he'd explained it all to her, someone had whispered in her ear, a little too close, that it was old-fashioned, the God stuff, a bit of a walled garden. It had been a man and he had been trying to impress her, she thought, but his hair was awful and greasy and his breath smelled of crab and, at the time, the overall impression made her want to be *more* enthusiastic about her brother-in-law's work, if anything. But the image of a walled garden had stuck with her and the more she got to know Harrie, the more she thought of his work as, most likely, pointless.

'It's important,' he hissed. His voice was uncharacteristically sharp. Whatever Monica had said, she did not follow it up, instead dabbing the corner of her mouth with a piece of kitchen tissue. John found himself for a moment forgetting where he was, reminded only by the mention of fresh air that there were miles of nothing around. He had drunk more than he'd planned and Monica could see he was tipsy. She kept glancing in his direction and it was making him self-conscious. 'You're speaking quite loudly,' Liz told him, later, when they were washing the dishes. He asked her straight out if he had done something to upset her and she said no, but maybe he could go upstairs and say goodnight to the children. They love their Uncle John, she said. He wanted to stay there with her and help. She said there was only a saucepan left to do.

For the children they'd picked a little room that could one day be a nursery, with a single high window and a few stacks of unpacked boxes against a wall. They'd found a fold-out mattress that would do for the night. Finn and Ciara were accustomed to separate beds but the excitement of being away from home meant that it didn't matter, and both were tucked in by the time John found them, Monica knelt beside, speaking softly about the things they'd seen. They had gone for a walk, she said. They had thrown stones into the water. Both of the children listened, soothed by hearing their own actions reflected back at them. John was careful to be quiet as he sat down, clocked by Monica who stared at him in the same way she had done at the dinner table. He felt too drunk to be there and had to be careful not to knock over a hooked wooden pole that was leant against a wall below the window. Finn asked him if they were going to catch fish in the morning. 'If there's time,' he answered and Monica said the fish needed to sleep, that they were tired too, and John imagined a thousand little fishes in a thousand little beds. That fish could sleep was strange to consider, as he had always thought of life in the depths as forever stirring, never staying still, even in death, falling and bitten, swallowed by others who would go on moving and on and on, always swirling in the dark. Monica glanced at him and he thought of the concert hall, his hand accidentally placed on her forearm and the fact she had let it stay there. The children had fallen asleep but the adults remained for a while longer, the sound of breathing so light and slender.

*

There was a thud and then another and I realised it was the boat against the jetty. It sat on the water, embarrassed in its moorings, as if it had been caught tiptoeing when the kitchen light had been switched on. My love was filling a glass of water from the tap and I stood at the open doorway, enjoying the sound as the boat thudded against the jetty, a rubber tyre bound to the hull, pressed with force, something else knocking against the side within. I imagined a hand rapping its knuckles. Quite happy, I'm sure, I would have been to lean like that and listen, not minding anything else, but I find myself angsty if I stay still for too long. So when she had finished with her drink, we set off to the water.

I soon found the source of the knocking: an empty bottle of Plymouth gin that must have come loose from its nook in the cabin, in that moment rolling back and forth with the swaying of the boards. Despite not knowing how long it had been in the boat, I'll admit we shared the last drops between us, the taste strong and lingering as we sat opposite one another beneath the moonlight. I would've taken us out a little if not for the noise of the engine. The family was sleeping inside the house and, as much as it was a relief to be away after a day of hosting, we didn't want to wake anyone. Instead we sat there unspeaking, rocking gently and listening to the rubber tyre thud against the jetty.

There was something I wanted to say but I didn't quite know how to put it.

Soon we saw a thing on the water, not yet knocking against the side: a mirror, circular, framed in wood, the kind you might have on a table, a dresser. Two stubs stuck out on either side, presumed to be held in place, to be rotated, to change the angle. I leant over the edge of the boat to fish it up, held it in both hands and looked at myself.

Have you ever looked into a mirror in the dark? Let me describe it for you.

TWO

T HE CHILDREN'S CRIES CLEARED the breakfast table, the crusts on the plates, the open pot of
strawberry jam and the dregs at the bottom of the silver
cafetière. The colour fell from Monica's face as the adults
turned without exception towards the open window.
'Ciara,' Harrie shouted when they were running down the
hallway. 'Ciara, my baby, what's the matter?'

The fawn was dead on their doorstep, its head over the
threshold to the kitchen, and it struck John that it must
have perished with its face pressed against the keyhole.
Ciara was distraught and had to be brought inside by her
father. Finn watched the scene from behind the kitchen
counter. John's first thought was to pull the fawn by its
legs, at least a little, so that its head was no longer across
the threshold to their home, but when he reached down
Liz grasped his shoulder and asked whether touching
a dead animal was the best thing to do. 'Disease, John.'
Monica clicked her tongue and stepped inside, where she
gathered Finn and whisked him away. John knelt to take
a closer look at the fawn, eyes open but lifeless, body neat
on its side. A sense of guilt was on him then, he wanted to
go back inside, follow Monica, return to the dining room,

close the window, close the door and finish his slice of toast. It was Liz who suggested they call the number Jim Sweet had left them.

'Surely this is the type of thing he takes care of,' she said.

He called Sweet and after three rings the call was answered. The warden was on his way to church, he said. Had there been a dog? No dog, said John. Sweet sounded disappointed by this. Dig a hole, was the long and short of it. Put the fawn into the ground. Sweet was calm and sure in his instruction so that it was only after hanging up that John felt the weight of having to deal with the task at hand. This was how things were in the countryside, he assured himself, and while Liz joined the others, he found a shovel in the overgrown garden caked in dry mud.

'Would you like something to drink?' she asked in the hallway, where the family had grouped around the bottom of the stairs, Monica perched with Finn's face against her neck, Ciara beside her father, calmed, it seemed, more interested now in her brother's distress.

'I'm good for coffee,' said Monica, serene and shushing Finn's almost inaudible whimper. Liz felt unnecessary in their presence. She would put the kettle on, her own father all over, to look for purpose in boiling water.

In no time at all, Harrie had put out a small stack of academic texts on the dining table. He worked in an A4 notebook, pen hovering above the unlined page, dipping to write a few words, then returning, then dipping, all the while his attention on the opened book that lay so close one of its corners was hanging in the air. When Liz put down his Earl Grey and honey, he didn't look up at first, only after she had gathered a few of the dirty breakfast plates.

'Does John need a hand?'

His pen was still writing.

'I'm sure he's fine,' she said.

Monica and the children were elsewhere, it was only Liz keeping him from his work and she took longer than she needed to collect the things. On the way out she stubbed her little toe on the doorway, a wonder she didn't drop the plates. She pictured the fawn and thought of the dog. What a thing to happen, right on their doorstep, and its whine all the worse for the cheap white walls. John had been so dismissive, brushed it off as one of those things, nothing really to do with them. When she'd been shaken, he had been understanding, but only went so far, sitting at the foot of the bed. *There, there.* He did that much. But a day or two and he got bored of hearing. Monica's voice sounded from the guest room. 'King and Queen of the seven seas.' Little laughter. She'd wanted to put something in the ground. A letter, she'd suggested at the time. Something written, nicely put, and it was a girlish idea but she wanted to do it. The roll of his eyes. She'd lost serious sleep. He'd said he understood but he didn't understand. And that was the first time she felt something unspeakable between them, when he looked so tired of hearing about the stray dog they'd found in the hallway and the sound of its laboured breathing, like wind blowing through a passage that curls around, down stone steps leading deeper underground until it gives way to a dim chamber.

The children were on the floor, drawing in notebooks. 'He's under pressure,' Monica started, when Liz told her how Harrie had occupied the dining table. 'There's a lot on his mind and you might have to be a bit more forgiving.'

Through the window she could see John working with the shovel.

He considered marking the grave with a stick but in the end decided there was no real point. When he was finished, he knelt and touched the soil, first with his fingertips then with his palm, patting it down. The idea of the body had already lost its solidity, out of sight it loosened and he focused his mind on the weight of the shovel, the texture of the wooden handle.

By the time he returned to the house, a row of bags were in the hallway. Although no time of departure had been specified, the fawn had upset the children and so Monica explained they would probably head off to the campsite. Better to be there early and get a good spot. Harrie loaded the bags into the boot and strapped the children into their seats while Monica kissed her sister on both cheeks, John on one, saying they had a beautiful house, she was very jealous. It was agreed John and Liz would visit them at the campsite in a day or so, once the family had settled into things. 'Why don't you stay?' asked John, and for a moment no one knew how to react. An urge had risen in him to keep them there. Something indistinct had been disturbed by their visit, he could feel it, and there was the hazy impression that if they stayed, perhaps it would pass as quietly as a stomach ache. But no, Monica said, they had everything arranged with the campsite and, as nice as the offer was, they knew it was too much to expect John and Liz to shelter and feed them for the rest of the holiday. There was a look between the sisters. Besides, they would see each other in a couple of days so it wasn't really a good-bye at all.

When they were gone, the quiet returned. Liz wanted to lie down. 'Nice but exhausting,' she said, and even though part of him wanted to ignore whatever was between them, he knew it was better not to let things fester. If there is rot, let it be scrubbed, so they went together to the bedroom and there she lay on top of the covers.

'What's wrong?' he asked.

She threw up her hands and blew a raspberry.

She'd been expecting his concern, had seen it coming in the glances, the awkward way he'd stood when their car pulled away, but now it was here she was in no mood to face it, not on his terms. There was a palpable expectation that she would be the one to do the work of putting it into words when it was as much him as her, just as much. Why should it be on her to dig her fingers beneath the weight, draw it out? The feeling again of something unspoken between them. Here was the chance to try and shape it, talk and see what came out of her, but she found herself unable.

He put his hand on hers, fed his thumb under her fingers and held it there. 'It's been a lot.'

'You're right. The move and then playing host. And that poor animal.'

'We're still us,' he said, and from the way she looked at him saw he had exposed something of himself. He was the same and so was she, that much had to be true, and he stroked the back of her hand with his forefinger as he had done when they lived in London and as he liked to think he would in the future, as if they were walking hand in hand through a river and all the water might rush around them but they were never changed. He said things would settle now they had time to get to know the house, and maybe they should have put their foot down about Monica coming but at least it was done and out of the way.

He was relieved that it was the stress of the move that had put Liz out of sorts. It brought them back to the balance of the previous months: him the convincer, her the hesitant, open to be talked around.

'You're right, I'm just drained,' she said, and there was an easing in her manner that pulled them further back onto solid ground. 'Being around the children is tiring.'

'You're going to be such a good mother.'

He did not know why it came to him, out of a corner in his mind that had been spinning its own circles. He thought about the implantation bleeding, the three or four days that had felt loaded with possibility, the period that had come heavy and how it had knocked them with such a terrible force. She raised her chin. 'It might not happen for us,' she said. Immediately he reassured her it would. They had only been trying a year and a half, maybe a little more, and that was perfectly normal. Monica had tried for a couple of years.

'One year,' she corrected.

He tightened his hand on hers to show that he had not meant it as a provocation and perhaps it was pity or perhaps it was discomfort but she stroked his finger and slipped herself free.

She forced herself back, pressed against a wall in the Tower of London. It was a moment she travelled back to when she needed to be certain of things. The strength of feeling. She is the same person from five years past, at heart the same. And him. She can see how he's older but he's still the same. A few lines, a sterner look. Inevitable really. What else would you expect? No great mystery, no source of trouble. A quiet room in the Tower of London and she was so wet.

'Harrie is having a bit of a crisis,' she said. 'Did you know he had a falling out with the head of his faculty?' She rearranged herself on the bed, straightening the pillow against her back. 'Some students complained about him.'

John wasn't sure whether or not he should drag them back to talk of trying. Why repeat the same thing over again?

'The head of faculty has cooled on him and Harrie feels a little betrayed,' said Liz. 'They used to be friends. They'd been to each other's houses for dinner.' She looked at the window, losing interest in her own story. 'That's a whole thing, isn't it, when you've got that going on.'

'Sounds tough.'

She looked at the sky through the window. Her attention was no longer in the room. The clouds were high and wispy. A quiet room in the Tower of London. She resolved to be upbeat for the rest of the day. No reason to dwell on things. The air was warm and it might even be weather for a swim. Whatever it was that lay between them would come out eventually, you can trust in the thought to find its way. When it arrived, it would be seen to, deftly handled between them, turned this way and that to find its flaws. The problem identified would be fixed. It's what they had always done, they were good at doing it, good at communicating, finding hairline fractures.

*

They worked together to collect the dead vines in the garden, many of them easy to gather, and it didn't matter if some of the paint came off the walls because they planned to expose the old brickwork eventually. The gardening, done together, was an effective distraction from whatever feelings in which they'd dipped their toes. As soon as they were in the rhythm of uprooting the plants and piling them up in a wheelbarrow, the spin of John's thoughts disappeared, or at least faded from view. The work absorbed him to such an extent that it was easy to forget where he was.

How long, if left to its own devices, would it take for the woods to encroach on the garden? A hundred years? Fewer? Perhaps the previous inhabitants had decided it was futile to maintain this patch of ground when there was wild nature only a stone's throw away. There was something in that, no doubt, but John thought it was a weak way to see the world. This was their property, they would shape it to fit their habits, and he felt then a sense of mastery over their surroundings, at least the potential for mastery. He thought about the life they would bring into the house and the bonds it would tie between them, the lake and the woods and the hills, a landscape that would belong to their child. He pictured new eyes looking through an open doorway at a world taken as known. Small steps on fresh wet grass. A child at home in the woods, naming trees, cutting pathways to lead to pockets of their own making. He viewed these thoughts as if from a great distance because what occupied his mind more than anything on that late morning was the shovel and the effort of pulling up roots, piling the dead vines and branches and other things onto the wheelbarrow.

When Liz asked him if he wanted to take a break for lunch the tension was gone from her voice. When they sipped their tomato soup and talked about Harrie's problems at the university it was like they were themselves again, the trouble of the morning vanished into thin air. They had only planned to spend a little while in the garden, enough to make a start on things, but when John suggested they go back Liz agreed. She seemed eager to occupy herself and when they moved things to the wheelbarrow, when they pushed the wheelbarrow to the shore and when they piled things high, it was as if time was passing away from them, beneath them, under a thick layer of ice.

It was Liz's idea that they swim in the lake, leaving their dirty clothes on the shore. She was faintly aware that there was every chance Sweet would pass through their land, as he had done the day before, but she was determined that the warden would not influence their behaviour and before she knew it, they were in the water, wading out until their feet barely touched the bottom. The lake was cool and their nakedness had happened so quickly that it felt like a dream. If only they had done this before Monica and her family had arrived. Then there would've been no strangeness between them, no mistaken feelings. *It might not happen for us.* And she was close to him, then, laughing at their bodies touching underwater. One of his legs was between hers. How long would it take for the woods to grow over their house? How many years before they were swallowed by the treeline? She kissed his lips, warm and wet with the water.

*

She adjusted the angle of her table mirror to get a better look at her chin. Midday and still no word from the founders. She shouldn't be checking emails in the first place. Perhaps they were waiting for her to get back from leave. So why then this feeling of bad news awaiting her? If she wasn't outside of London. If John still had his job. She busied herself with a box in the study, using the shortest of the keys in her pocket to cut the tape, slicing along the top until the cardboard flaps could be pulled apart with a pop. Inside were novels she'd studied for her master's. A small pile of used notebooks. Moleskine, imitation Moleskine, black and blue and green. She would have liked to squeeze them until the ink ran out into a glass bowl.

Sweet walked up with three bags of compost in his arms, chin resting on the top of the load, appearing in that moment a floating head, serious and unsmiling in his labour. His expression loosened when he caught sight of Liz at the door. 'I had them spare so it's no problem.' A place was found in the shed where they kept the tools, and when they were down she could see the sweat beneath his collar. She showed him where John had buried the fawn and he didn't have much to say about it. He would stay for a cup of tea, two sugars, and while the kettle boiled she didn't know what to say except that it was not so bad today, warm, and he looked around him at the cabinets and the fittings.

When they were back outside she told him they were drawn to the beauty and she hadn't meant beauty but couldn't think of the word.

'Can't have been cheap.'

'It wasn't bad at all,' she said, trying not to sound defensive.

He sipped his mug of tea.

'You'd get a two-bed flat for the same money in London,' she said.

'Hmm,' he said.

The cereal bowl John had left on the veranda was still there, she noticed. All the milk had long been washed out by the rain.

'I went to London a few years back and someone in the hostel stole my shoes,' said Sweet. 'They took them right from my bed when I was sleeping and it was an embarrassment, asking the people at the desk if they had any spare shoes because I was meant to be meeting an old friend and who turns up to a reunion without shoes? They only had these plastic flip-flops.'

He trailed off and sipped his tea.

An arrow of birds flew in formation above the lake, the distance between them perfect and straight so that it seemed to Liz unreal, their flight, only a float- ing of direction and its reflection, a show of intention in their silent organisation. They were alone against the sky and it made them all the more inscrutable, like a letter of a forgotten alphabet. 'Do you live nearby?' she asked.

Sweet waved a hand absent-mindedly towards the woods.

'Alone?'

'That's right.'

She nodded solemnly. He looked at her with what she thought was amusement.

'I have a favour to ask, now we come to it. There's work I'll be doing next week not far from here, very early start, and it would be a big help to me.'

He did not go on but waited for her response.

'Okay,' she offered tentatively.

'A sofa would be fine, if you don't have a room to spare.'

'Oh.' She was aware now of what he was asking. 'I suppose that would make it easier for you,' she said.

'The Palmers would do it for me every now and then. It ended up being a nice routine.' He smiled warmly. 'Say no if it's an intrusion. I wouldn't want to put you out.'

She shook her head. 'Of course not. We wouldn't dream of putting you on a sofa. There's a room upstairs. It's no problem.'

'A week from now.'

'No problem at all.'

John came down and said his hellos, but Sweet said he had places to be so he bid them adieu awkwardly and said he hoped the compost would help. It would be nice to see the garden in better shape, after it had been left in such a state.

Only when Sweet was gone did John kiss her on the cheek. He made a sound like he was kissing a granny. When he asked her if she wanted to do something together, she said she wanted to go for a run.

On the way upstairs to change into her Lycra, she caught sight of her reflection. She saw a head on shoulders, a body in turn, stacked up on a pair of legs. There were plenty of things she couldn't stand in the mirror, but she was proud of her legs. They were muscular, which had once been a source of shame. Ashamed of muscles, she thought. Can you imagine? No longer. These days she loved them, in fact. Their hardness, knock on wood. She could set out from the door and be around the lake in twenty-five minutes, putting those pork chops to work. And she was never more herself than when she was sweating, nothing on her mind but the rhythm of breath, the inessential fallen off, empty, in a way. And of course there'd be someone who'd disagree, who'd say she is so much more. Her humour, he'll say, that fine look of hers when the light is right. But that's only his version. Him, with his compliments, his way of categorising her in the shape of a loving list. It is not her. She is one leg falling after the other, nothing besides. Around the lake in twenty-five. That's the measurement.

John found himself staring at the leaves in the pile, brown and brittle, pockmarked with grey blemishes. It was not long until autumn would cover the ground with these colours and even though it would be beautiful, he hated the idea, did not want it to come. The wind picked up around the trees and he thought what a horrific thing, the late summer and its unstoppable slide into the dark and the cold. If only they had moved there in the spring, when the green was all ahead of them.

She hadn't gone for a run after all, only lain in bed checking her phone, so he suggested they continue with work in the garden. Together they pulled up the weeds that had grown around the edges of the flower beds, turned the soil and collected the dried leaves. He focused on the task and before he knew it the light had begun to fade. After an easy dinner of green beans and chicken they carried on in their different ways, the minutes moving in stops and starts. Later, in the bedroom, they had nothing to say but something inside him wanted to go on, and so he told her he would call the delivery company first thing in the morning. Her eyes were so tender that he felt them unveil him. She hummed an agreement and it was a sweet, musical sound. She was not someone to panic, could always take a breath, pause, reflect, put some distance between the thought and the feeling. It let her see the light in any situation and he loved her for it. Certainly, she would never become gloomy looking at a pile of leaves. *It might not happen for us.* He wanted her to know that it would. 'It's probably stuck in some warehouse somewhere,' she said, her voice far away, and John was only faintly aware that he was drifting off, in his mind a vast building filled with sofas and tables and chairs.

*

I awoke in a sweat, my love no longer beside me. For a horrible moment I was convinced something terrible had happened, something truly unspeakable.

Forcing myself to calm down when I found the rest of the house empty, I went outside in search and found her by the water, sitting on a stone as the lake lapped close to her feet. Not far from us was the bonfire heap we had begun to make from the garden detritus. In the dark it looked like some kind of animal. Not yet wanting to return to bed and still some hours to go before the sun would rise, we decided to take the boat out. Soon we were far enough for it to feel like we had drifted into another kind of sleep, the waters barely lit by the moon and the solid wood of the gunwale a final barrier to the weight of the lake's yearning.

With the engine turned off we drifted in silence, both of us looking back at the house, at least what we could make out of it in the dimness. She made the start of a word but abandoned whatever she meant to say and instead leant over, looking downwards at the water. I was about to ask her what she wanted to say to me when she pointed to something just out of reach, an object made of glass that bobbed up and down, flickering between a thing and nothing at all. A glass decanter, soon fished out and passed between us. There was not a chip on it, as far as I could tell.

First a mirror, now a glass decanter. I pondered the connections between the two. I put my nose to the rim. Stagnant water. Ripe. I tipped the decanter upside down, listened to the liquid splash back into the lake. My love was holding the stopper, a great glass hive of interlacing triangles. She turned it one way, then the other. I imagined a parlour with dark green walls, smoky air, a drinks cabinet. Two people were standing reflected in a mirror on a wall. You can't help the mind roaming where it wants. Was one of those people me? Could I make out my shape? I'll say it was me. It's easier that way. Me, pulling down the wooden top of the cabinet that doubles as a shelf, a clever little mechanism, supported on either side by brass chains. Me, picking up the tumbler. Me who scoops three cubes of ice from a clouded container, me who pulls the stopper from the glass decanter and me who pours. I am a mouth in the dark, straining to speak. My love handed me the stopper and I fitted it to the top with a clack. You can tell a good decanter if you can lift it by the stopper. I did so then. The glass aloft, the water below.

THREE

I T COOLED HER BRAIN to be travelling with speed, the trees arched above her and the sight of clouds above that. The uneven road made her judder and she had to stand on the pedals to stop the sense being shaken from her skull, stooping to avoid the branches that whizzed within inches. Liz sped downwards, the surroundings appearing to curve towards the path as if it were a basin for all that travelled in the woods.

When she reached the bottom of the hill the route opened up and she could see Finn on his little bike some way ahead. She sped to catch up with her nephew, suggested they wait for the others and together they came to a stop beside a patch of wildflowers. Monica soon turned the corner behind them, then John. Finn asked if they could keep going. John began to remind him they were waiting for everyone to catch up when Monica said it was alright if he wanted to cycle on with Auntie Liz. So they did, just the two of them.

She picked up pace but Finn met it, not saying a word. He was a quiet boy, thoughtful, with his tendency to furrow his brow, to stand and stare. What kind of man does a boy like that become, she wondered. It depends on the bullies. They don't like a quiet boy, don't like the idea of him. She knows how it goes, she's been on both sides. All that ahead of him. She felt a strong desire to protect him from it, hold him separate and away from the world with its endless bullies.

Finn rang his bell at nothing, cackling at the sound.

Hold him like a baby, she supposed, a little baby, all mouth and vowels. No doubt her sister would say she was broody. Maybe she's right. Maybe she is. She'd always assumed, ever since she was a girl. They get you with the dollies, rock and change, wipe-down plastic. She'd had a little girl with wiry curls. Always assumed, thought Liz. Only a matter of time. And there was still time. All this could be silliness still.

She glanced behind her, the others no longer in view.

Her dolly was called Beth and would whistle if squeezed. It gave out a high-pitched wheeze from her mouth hole, no bigger than a pencil lead.

They cycled on and she let Finn lead the way.

John stayed behind with Monica to wait for Harrie and Ciara to reach the bottom of the hill. There was a din of crickets in the grass. Sticky heat. Monica leant to one side to try and get a better view at the path. It seemed her bicycle might topple so John reached out to balance her handlebars. She looked amused by his hand on the bar. He let go. 'I heard about Harrie's trouble at work,' he said, grasping at something to cover his embarrassment. It was the first thing to his mind and there was something dark and pleasurable in mentioning it, a twinge of satisfaction at the look on her face. She didn't respond immediately, leant again to get a better look up the hill and this time he did not try to steady her bike. Instead of falling, she got off the seat, threw her leg over the frame and let it drop into the wildflowers as she paced to the other side of the path.

'They're lucky to have him,' she said from across the way, arching her head to see the hill path through the trees. 'You should see the amount of work he does for the university. The amount of prep.' Apparently unable to see anything from her new vantage point, she walked back to her bicycle and pulled it upright. There was a spikiness to her movements. John felt bad for stirring the pot. He suggested they walk back up the hill and she started off, over the stones and the dirt. Did she know that he sometimes made fun of Harrie, he wondered. Because she should be aware that it came from a good place. He was fond of him, only made fun of his accent and cracked knees because there was an understanding they were a constant in each other's lives and he wouldn't be surprised if Harrie did the same behind his back, picked at his posture, the habit he had of hitting his cutlery against his teeth. He wouldn't blame him, wouldn't hold it against the man.

'It's all political,' she said. 'They're playing their little games and Harrie is too kind-hearted to see it.'

He made a small, sympathetic hum.

'Doesn't matter to them that their staff might have reasons. Perfectly valid reasons.' She glanced over. In that moment something small and uncertain shone, her eyes on him in a way that felt close to panic. She switched her attention, looked up the hill and they pushed on in silence, the wheels crunching the grit, and there was something in the way she took a sharp intake of breath that made it seem like she was about to say something more. But then she didn't.

'Did something happen?' he asked.

'Well, he's fainted a couple of times over the past two months.'

John thought of his father, collapsed against the back door. The wind rustled the leaves above them. He imagined an enormous hand, running through the woods.

'They didn't find anything,' she said, her attention on the handlebars.

'That's good.'

'No, of course.'

She rang the bell for no reason.

A sudden wish, to see the row of pebbles that the children had arranged on the veranda, a field of faces, the crowd of onlookers, silent in their observation.

They found Harrie and Ciara at the very top, sitting side by side amongst the roots of an oak tree, perfectly content beneath the dappled sunlight. It would've made for a good picture, he thought.

'She fell,' Harrie explained, and John noticed the graze on his niece's leg, bleeding a little beneath her knee. Any tears had already been wiped away.

'I thought something had happened to you,' said Monica, directed at Harrie with a rawness that made her husband look uncomfortable. Sunlight fell through a gap in the trees. John closed his eyes, felt the warmth on his skin. He could be anywhere, any time, as long as there was sunlight and birdsong.

*

They'd set up in a quiet corner of the campsite. There was only one other group that shared their small clearing: what looked to be a trio who had been there for some time, said Harrie, judging by the way they hung their washing on a blue line tied between two trees. A single pair of white tennis socks was suspended above a set of plastic milk bottles full of water. John could see one of the group, a young man on a camping chair with dark shoulder-length hair and a plain red T-shirt, reading a folded paperback and smoking a roll-up. There was another man and a woman, he was told. 'And they all share the same tent,' said Harrie, voice lowered.

Monica was taking a nap. When they had returned from their cycle she'd informed the group she had a nasty headache and needed to lie down. Liz, on the other hand, was even more energetic than she'd been on the route. As John and Harrie sat around she played with the children, a Frisbee thrown in a wide triangle between them. She clapped her hands when one of the children made a good catch and if the plastic blue disc flew too far, she would run and gather it up. Harrie was talking about the future of Europe but John was only half listening, preoccupied with watching his wife. Finn threw the Frisbee high and, instead of letting it sail away, Liz leapt into the air with both hands outstretched. It flew right above her fingertips and her landing was unbalanced, falling in an over-the-top way so that she rolled onto her side on the grass. The children loved it, screaming in delight. She was clowning for them and that had to mean that things were alright, John thought. Their little talk in the bedroom must have done them good. *It might not happen for us.* If that's what she wanted to think, if that's what she wanted to believe, but he knew they were splashing about in time, still young. There would come a day when they were forced to be frugal with their days but it was not there yet. They were still at that perfect age, lying suspended, strong enough to swim in any direction and unafraid of caverns beneath.

The young man in the red T-shirt was also watching the Frisbee being thrown, observing the scene over the top of his paperback. After a moment he gave up on the book and reached for a pouch of tobacco that had been stuffed into his chair's netted drinks holder. He leant forward as he rolled another cigarette and maybe he caught John looking at him but when he was finished, he tucked it behind his ear, smiled in their direction, stood and moved to the washing line where he took down the socks, then disappeared from view.

A ladybird landed on John's forearm and he watched it crawl over his hair. He wanted to get up and join Liz with the children but he was unable to move. He heard a dog barking beyond the trees.

Sitting on the ground Liz massaged with one finger the skin around a knee, pushed at the soft meeting place of bones. She extended her leg out, flat in front of her to the pricking of grass. The skin gathered in a saggy pinch of flesh, looser than when she'd rolled it between a thumb and finger in bed that morning. It could be the light, the angle. Fantastic, she thought. Fat folds. When she's standing in her shorts she'll feel their eyes on her knees. She'll feel him glance down at fat folds. She was already tense at the thought. Who is he to judge? Doesn't he know the way things go? He can hardly talk, the way his sides are turning out. *You think I believe you, how you look at me? I can see the parts you dance around.*

'Of course, Mutti's been doing the rounds,' said Harrie, rolling his eyes. He looked pale, thought John. Or was he imagining it? Monica told him they hadn't found anything. That could be that; the end of it. There are things that happen, scary things which on closer inspection are perfectly innocent. It could be a shortage of magnesium. Diet has a lot to answer for. It's never nice to find yourself on the ground, to scare your family, but if nothing was found, if nothing was there... John could've told him then that he'd heard the bad news. Not bad news. The events. He could've said something supportive, but what would he say?

69

'She thinks she can sort out the Crimea before she buggers off.'

'Right,' said John.

'Good luck with that,' said Harrie.

'Mutti mummy,' said Harrie.

A moment passed as they sipped their beer.

'I think it'll be fine,' said Harrie.

Harrie had once told him that there was a time when a person could have known all there was to know. They'd been in his study and John had thought at the time it was bullshit. He'd seen a documentary about the library of Alexandria, which held such a vast collection because the city officials had a special law. Ships coming into the harbour would be searched and any texts confiscated for copying by the library's scribes. He didn't think any one person would've been able to read all those pieces of parchment, even then. Maybe Harrie had meant long before, in the walls of a cave, nothing more to know except survival. John remembered looking at the books in Harrie's study, which included at least five copies of Harrie's own. It was going to be put on the reading list for a course at Stanford. Had John been to San Francisco? Very impressive, the fog. Harrie had carried on about the seafood, folding layer upon layer over the pea of his pride and it struck John that this must matter a lot, to have his work taught to young minds. It was a legacy, he supposed. A contribution to the generations of thought.

Did he worry, as John imagined all academics worried, at least in the humanities, about the point of their toiling? Whether it was any more than a game played by a small and short-sighted team? Did Harrie bore Monica to tears with his uncertainties, his crises in confidence, so selfish and entitled?

John had at one point wanted to do a PhD, had been accepted but hadn't got any funding. He had the idea in the back of his mind that he'd one day apply again. *These days nothing is forgotten*, Harrie had said to him. *When we were growing up you didn't have this, couldn't have this.* Clicked finger. Harrie had meant cables beneath oceans, warehouses of servers in the Arctic Circle. The library of Alexandria, thought John. Stone pillars, flaming cauldrons. What empty words. Nothing forgotten. Nothing lost. When John was a boy he'd sat on a wooden pew and the priest had forgotten his sermon, lost his train of thought, completely gone, and John could recall the impression that it should've been funny, that if his friends were there they would have creased up laughing, but it had been the opposite: awful, something fallen away, all the worse when the priest tried to start again and the heart was out of him, the truth of his words left somewhere in the perfumed air. The library of Alexandria. Scrolls piled high. No wonder it had burnt down, he thought. In the study, Harrie had wanted to show him the photograph of Ciara and Finn, taken when they were small enough that he could hold one in each arm.

*

'Should we ask them to join?' Harrie nodded to the other tent. His eyes were mischievous. 'It might be fun.'

Soon they came together, the sun getting low, the children eating barbecue sausages on paper plates while the adults talked. Monica had re-emerged, the sleep having done her good. The woman in the trio was called Alma. The man with the red T-shirt who had been reading was called Richard and the other man, who seemed the most unsure about being there with them, was called Tariq. They were students in Glasgow. They'd been travelling for the whole of their summer and for the last week or so they'd been camping in the site.

Liz noticed that they were sitting close to one another: Alma, German, sandwiched in the middle between the two men, both Scottish, muscular in different ways. Tariq, squatter, studied history; Richard, thinner, art history; Alma, physics, with astrophysics, she noted, with the easy enthusiasm of someone who knows this is a conversation starter. Harrie began to tell them about an observatory he had once visited in the Swiss mountains. One of the highest in the world. From up there the clouds looked like an ocean, he said. Alma and Tariq's knees were touching. What do they make of us, Liz wondered. How much younger were they? Ten years. Twelve. 'The Sphinx!' Harrie remembered. 'Oh, it's beautiful. The silver dome where they keep the telescope. Do you know it?'

'I probably should,' said Alma with a small smile.

'No, no, not at all,' said Harrie. 'I'm sure you know much more than *me* about these things.'

'Brain fog.' Alma turned to Richard with mock fear. 'Oh God, this summer. I've forgotten everything.'

'It's been a long holiday,' Richard explained to the group, laughing warmly, opening the conversation back out in a way Liz appreciated. He had expressive eyes, charming, they caught the light.

'Don't,' said Monica. 'I've only been here a couple of days and I've already forgotten my PIN once.'

'Really?' said Liz. Perhaps she'd sounded a bit too repulsed.

Her sister furrowed her brow. 'It happens.'

'I doubt the university wants you to remember every telescope on the face of the earth,' said Harrie. Alma laughed a short laugh with lips closed. 'The sphinx between the mountains,' he went on. Richard rolled a cigarette. Before he lit it, he asked if it was okay to smoke, interrupting Harrie, who hesitated, glancing at the children eating their sausages, but Monica said it was fine, fine, and that was very unlike her, Liz thought. 'Jungfrau,' said Harrie. 'I think that was one of the mountains.'

'Tariq has forgotten how to swim,' noted Richard.

'See, Lizzy. It happens. People forget things.'

'Have you really forgotten how to swim?' asked Ciara, horrified, ketchup all over her chin.

'I think so. Maybe I've forgotten how to move my arms.' Tariq wiggled his arms above him. Both of the children found it hilarious.

Monica was looking at Richard, sizing him up, Liz thought. Why? She used to be able to read her sister like a simple story. There was the same beginning, middle and end. Monica's tempers, her boredom, the lines she'd pick up from TV, the music she'd play in the bathroom. It fitted in place and that was all there was to it, unthought of, taken along with the knowledge that *she* herself was made of multitudes. She would love to still be able to read her sister, would give her right leg to fit her back between two covers.

'Can that really happen?' asked John, all concern. 'Like, poof, gone?'

'I haven't been swimming for years. Then we went to a pool in Southside and I just couldn't do it. I splashed around and couldn't coordinate myself or anything.'

'It'll come back to you,' said Monica.

'Yeah, Tariq. It'll come back,' said Richard, the lightness in his eyes warming the transparent tone of mockery.

Tariq shrugged. For some reason the children found this funny too.

Liz slapped a mosquito on her leg. She has fallen quiet, thought John. The energy of the afternoon seemed to have left his wife and she sat on the ground with her legs folded close to her chest, absent-mindedly watching the others. He wondered what she was thinking.

They were young, he assured himself. Still young. When Tariq asked them where they were pitched in the campsite, he explained that they were only visiting, that they had a house in the area and that they'd only just moved there. 'You live in the woods?' asked Alma, eyes wide, as if they were talking about a gingerbread house. Liz explained they made the decision to get away from London after everything that had happened over the past few years. They could both work remotely and they liked the idea of being in the middle of nowhere.

'It's about the same price as a flat in London,' John insisted.

'It must be a nice place to live,' said Tariq. 'All this natural beauty.' There was a mutual nodding of heads. Harrie stared at his children. Let him come and take the attention away, John thought. Let him talk of mountainous observatories. Let him speak of whatever he desires.

'It must be romantic, to be just the two of you.'

John looked out at the darkening woods. Whose voice was speaking then? He lost his concentration, words for a moment failed, the space was black between the trees, oily black between the trees, the words failing again. Where did that sound come from, the one that beat like a stick on a drum? He had fumbled. He thought of the dog in the hallway, the great black dog. How many killed in the past few years? That voice again. How many dead? A simple splutter. Words fail, naturally they fail, pushed to their limit against the bark of the trees, held to hear nothing but the coursing of water within. He scratched beneath his right eye. What is born there, in that empty space?

Richard asked Monica if she would like a cigarette and she said she would.

He saw Alma glance at him.

He thought of skeletons dancing.

It was late by the time they drove home.

*

My love was perched once more on a stone. He looked out at the water and I was tempted to walk away, leave him to whatever pensiveness he'd put himself in since returning from the campsite. I'd left the back door open behind us and a sizeable part of me was worried about what would enter our home if we left it unguarded. He didn't seem to make much of me there and I wasn't in any mood to carry his grumbles into the open, but I stayed all the same, neither sitting nor pacing but standing still beside the stone. Call it persistence. I am nothing if not persistent. After all the day's movement, all the conversations, I am the one that remains by his side.

I listened to the boat tapping against the side of the jetty, watched the lake fade into nothing as the light from the house ran out of reach. No moon that night, no hope of seeing the woods or the hills. There was something to say, if I could find the words. Not just any words but the very best of them. I noticed a shape on the shingle. An object had washed up in front of us. How much more can one body of water hold, I wondered. Leaving my love on the stone I went to inspect, stooping to the waterline to wrap my hand around a length of smooth wood, a blunt metal end. A hammer; the truth of it. I held it aloft to show him. I'll admit I felt some pride at the discovery. He reached out and I placed the heavy end in his palm.

I pictured its movement in the water, a balance between the wood pulling upwards, the metal falling down. The handle was dark and worn, the metal tarnished. A few hard knocks could send the head spinning. I made a triangle in my mind. A mirror, a decanter, now a hammer. There were implications. Violent suggestions. For what purpose, I wondered. Was some cataclysm being counted down?

FOUR

'**M**ONICA IS JEALOUS.'
Even though the way she said it was mocking, there was something else in her eyes.

'Do you think they'll try to move here?' John asked.

'Are you joking?'

'They could be our neighbours.'

She squinted, as if trying to work out if he was making fun of her. When he'd told her about Harrie's fainting she'd done her best to hide the hurt. Monica hadn't said a thing about it to her. Not a peep. She'd made an effort to shrug it off. We don't go telling each other every fall, she'd said to John. There'd be nothing but worry.

'Where would they even live?' she asked him.

'I'm sure they'd find somewhere.'

'You're messing.'

He hummed.

'Jesus.' She picked up her phone. 'Can you imagine?'

For their first anniversary they'd stayed by the coast in Margate. Even though the weather had been terrible they'd gone for walks by the sea, hung out in the arcades, Liz taking pictures constantly and sending them to her sister. The two were closer then. John recalled posing in a fish shop, holding a wooden fork above a battered cod as if he was just about to eat, which was all he wanted to do, but he'd been blinking the first time and someone else was in shot the second. He'd felt embarrassed that other people were beginning to stare at them but Liz said he looked handsome. Monica had messaged she was jealous. It was as if she was there with them, he'd said. *Don't be like that. She's feeling lonely. Having children can be lonely.*

He started on the room Ciara and Finn had slept in, the one with the high window and the hooked pole. There were a few boxes remaining against one wall and he set about using his keys to cut through the tape, look at what was inside, decide whether it could be unpacked, consolidated, or left until they knew what to do with the limbo things, the old birthday and anniversary cards. The DVDs. Nobody needs DVDs any more. Some were still in their plastic wrapping. They could keep the Artificial Eye ones, put them on a shelf. How they had managed to get three copies of *Wedding Crashers* he had no idea. He made a series of piles on the floor, made happy work of separating one thing from the other, got to a card with a cartoon dachshund on the front and the words 'I like your sausage'. Inside was a message from Liz that he remembered reading in bed years before, on Valentine's Day, the ink thick and blue, signed off with a name they no longer used for each other. He put it in the pile of things to throw away. And so he went on, cutting the tape from each box and flattening it out when it was empty before moving onto the next.

As the boxes depleted it became clear that something was drawn on the wall behind them. He didn't know how he could've missed it before, when they'd first moved all the boxes there: the outline of two figures drawn faintly in pencil. He pushed their things aside to get a better look. The figures were life-sized, could have been sketched from memory although the continuous line led him to think whoever made them must have stood with their backs to the wall, maybe taking turns to draw around the other. He took one to be a man, one to be a woman, assuming it to be the work of the previous inhabitants although why they had taken the time to draw these figures was a mystery to him.

They stood side by side, arms lowered, no detail other than the pencil line that traced their borders. They reminded him of prehistoric paintings. He thought of ghostly hands, thousands of years old, illuminated in some cave in France. He searched the two figures for a name or a date. They were unaccompanied by anything, no captions, no sign that the previous inhabitants had done this before or ever again. His mouth was dry. The fact the children had slept in this room. He imagined the previous inhabitants standing where he was standing and there again was the pinch, the feeling that he was trespassing. It wouldn't take much to scrub them from the wall, he thought. The pencil line really was thin, almost as if it had been sketched to be completed at a later date. Maybe it was there to guide a painter's hand who would fill the empty space. He had cleaned up the cigarette ends and the empty bottles. This was no different. Some soapy water. If he took a couple of steps back, he could barely see them at all.

He thought of his father measuring his height on his birthday, the chosen place beside the fridge. His father would mark a line with a pencil pressed against the top of his head, captioned with his age. Did all parents feel an obligation to do this? For him it had been an achievement, not only in growing taller but in his body leaving a mark. He remembered the pressure of the pencil flat against his hair, the anticipation of a neat horizontal line. After his father had finished John would step away and stare grinning at the new measurement.

'We should talk about settling up,' she said when he came downstairs.

He stood in the doorway, collapsed boxes in his arms.

'I thought we said we'd wait a bit.'

'You owe me quite a lot now.'

'No, I know.'

'When do you want to talk about it?'

He hesitated. 'When I have an idea about work.'

He moved to lean the boxes against a wall in the hallway.

'Can't we do it today?' she asked.

One of the boxes slid from place onto the floor. He stooped to pick it up and several more fell over. She knew he would be feeling a wash of anger. She was too patient with his moods, too mindful that he would act as if she had backed him into a corner. Infuriating, this evasiveness, done with the manner of calmness. There was an implication that it was her making demands. She hadn't pressed him when they'd been moving. His work had dried up so it was only fair she should shoulder more of the burden; only fair, she'd said, given they wouldn't have managed the deposit in the first place without his old neighbour's inheritance. But she'd seen the hit to her savings and did not like the way it was becoming unacknowledged. He managed to balance the boxes back up against the wall, keeping his hands held out like a magician to keep them in place. 'It's all manageable,' she said. 'One length at a time.'

A swimming pool on Caledonian Road. He would go after work, twice a week. He didn't keep up a lot of things in those days but he kept that up, Mondays and Wednesdays, forty lengths, the time going in a blur and that was what he liked most, the way the world would fade so that there was only foreground, only patterns of breathing, arms and legs, beyond them the vague expanse of struggle in water. He would go to the pool in the evening and sometimes he would see the same people. There was an Italian sous chef around his age who was friendly with him but angry about a lot of things, such as how some swimmers would leave their shoes on the benches in the changing room. One time the sous chef shouted at a young guy with an underbite who left his shoes on a bench, threatening to do a shit in his Adidas trainers if he ever put them there again. There was another man, much older, who would change out of a three-piece suit, and who had an incredibly realistic tattoo of a baby's face on his chest right over his heart. He didn't say much and John liked that because it was exhausting to speak when all he really wanted was to get into the water and not to think about anything.

As well as the men in the changing room there was a woman who often shared his lane. Liz. More than once they'd taken a breather against the side of the pool at the same time. When this happened, they would acknowledge each other, smile and nod in their clouded goggles, but he hadn't heard her speak until, one evening, he was sitting in the small sad cafe at the front of the complex and she came up and asked if he wanted to get a drink in the pub across the road.

He'd been quite drunk by the time he got the bus home to Hannah, his girlfriend at the time. When she'd asked how his colleague was he'd forgotten for a moment that he had lied to her. But he didn't feel guilty about it, he told himself, and decided they might as well have been work friends, the way he and Liz had gossiped about the other people at the swimming pool.

The next time he swam the world did not fade away but he did not mind. He knew Liz was waiting for him at the end of the lane. They hung close against the tiled wall. A little closer and they would be touching. In the pub he mentioned Hannah in passing. They'd been talking about online radicalisation and he'd said that his girlfriend worked for the government, which he convinced himself he would have said in any case, even if he was there with someone else. Liz nodded slowly then said she needed to go to the ladies. When she got back he asked if she wanted another drink, a half, but she said she was meant to meet someone. It had been really nice to have a chat and she was glad she had made friends with another swimmer at the pool.

When he saw her the next week he tried to make conversation. He said he was tired. She said he just had to take it one length at a time. Neither of them suggested a drink, not that time, not the time after. Things would probably have stopped there if Hannah hadn't needed to see her parents for a weekend. To stop them getting lonely, she'd said. John was going to stay in London because he had a lot of work to do, which was true, but he also got it into his head that he would ask Liz from the pool if she wanted to do something. The zoo, he suggested, when their backs were touching the cool white tiles. She hadn't been to the zoo in years.

The collapsed boxes stayed in place against the wall. Would he still act like this when they had a baby, she wondered. Would he still duck and cover when bills needed to be settled? It's not as if she wanted to talk about money. She won't let him cast her as the collector of debts. How would it change what they had, when a baby came and its full weight was laid between them?

There again she needed to check herself, the assumption easy to slip into, as smooth as polished stone.

He was stooped in the hallway, inspecting something out of view, hands on hips in a pose that made him seem older. She imagined the ties between them as golden strands, a suspension of bright threads that ran from her to him. What weight could it carry? How would it bear the load? She thought again of Harrie, his fainting.

John had noticed a dent in one of the hallway walls. It was small, only a little bigger than a thumbprint, high as his knee, easy to miss. He wouldn't have seen it at all if he wasn't bent there with the boxes. Careful not to dislodge any of the plaster, he touched it with two fingers. Brittle and frail. A flake of white paint came away in his hand and he half expected to see a bird's beak break through.

'The things you start to notice,' he said.

'What's that?'

'All the things you start to notice.'

And again the sensation of pressure against his folded legs, the damp lumps of bark. He tried to gather the memory, recall where he might've snuck into a tree, whether it was in the park not far from his parents' home, whether it was a school trip, but he could not place it, only the idea of his body squeezed into that tight space and the smell of earth around him. He had the feeling that it was after his father died, of which he had no real memories besides the bus trip to the hospital, sitting beside his mother as they climbed a particular hill fringed with tall hedges, and even then he was uncertain if it was a real memory of that moment or whether it was something his mind had mislabelled from an earlier time, because he could also remember his father sitting beside him on the bus, as if his ghost was going to see his own body in the hospital bed. He would have taken that bus trip many times so most likely it wasn't a moment at all but a series of moments that he had condensed into one, and perhaps his father hadn't been sitting beside him in any of those moments, and maybe it was only the longing for him to be there, so strong that he remembered it as something real, or perhaps he had been on the same bus route to the hospital with his father for something else entirely, the ear trouble he'd had as a toddler, and maybe there were years between those times but he remembered them as one.

Eggshell
alabaster sheets.

'The kids are confident,' said Liz from the sofa; she was framed by the pane, backlit, so he couldn't quite make out the expression on her face.

'It's important, particularly in children,' he said, and it was as if someone else was talking through him. He sat beside her. A silver ripple passed behind his wife's eyes, cold and pale. Something was still wrong and he did not know how to fix it.

He raised her bare feet, put them across his lap.

'They're a little spoiled but confident,' she said, wiggling the toes of one foot. 'Not to sound mean but if she's not careful they're going to get bratty, the way they expect things.'

He squeezed the soft arch, massaging the muscle. 'I think we'll set more rules.'

They fell into silence as he rubbed her foot, drawing circles with his thumbs. Somewhere in the house a clock struck the hour. She could feel herself getting faintly turned on.

'Do you remember the reptile house?' he asked.

She hummed.

In London Zoo they'd stayed for a long time watching the tigers. She'd always been fascinated by animals, their way of being that felt to her ineffable. The tigers had been barely visible, two of them in different parts of the enclosure, shrouded by dense vegetation. A long tail lolling. She had confessed to him that she'd wanted a pet tiger when she was a girl, even though her family lived in a flat with no garden. The magpie that visited her and the tiger could've been friends. It would've been cruel but zoos weren't much better, were they, keeping these animals in cages, even if they were big cages. What is to be done? They watched the tigers for a long time and she asked him about Hannah. What is to be done? And they kissed for the first time in the reptile house, dim and warm, and they stopped when a family came to look at the crocodile beneath the heat lamp. It was with the giraffes when she'd asked him if he believed in God, carefully, and she'd only asked it because of the way he spoke about the animals, as if he thought they were created by some divine hand, and she'd wanted to say that she felt the opposite; that when she watched something like a giraffe she found the whole idea of God stupid and sorry had she offended him? Not at all. She'd taken in the animal, its strange head looming, and she'd said she had a strong feeling about these things, that there was no soul, no spirit or anything like that. It was probably because when she was a girl there had been a fire in her local zoo that had set alight to the giraffe enclosure and all the giraffes had died, and she remembered in school they had to write letters about the dead giraffes to be sent to the mourning zookeepers and she'd been so sad about it, she'd told him; so broken up about it, and she used to have nightmares about giraffes on fire running around like mad and it got so bad that one day her mum had to sit her down and tell her that giraffes have no souls, which was meant as a comfort and in a way it was.

In the garden they worked together to move the piled offcuts around the back of the house and across to where John had designated the bonfire to be built beside the lake. Soon they found a rhythm, Liz collecting the weeds, dropping them into the wheelbarrow for John to take and push and then back again for another load. They could do this forever and be happy, or at least content, with just the right amount of effort needed to make each trip between the garden and the shore an endeavour, and he found himself concentrating on nothing but the balance of the load, the speed of the wheelbarrow, the care of manoeuvring it around the corner and between a tight gap where tools and old plant pots had been stored. The landscape became less present as John focused on his hands, which were gripping the worn wooden handles, the strain on his arms as he guided the wheelbarrow down an incline, the sound of his boots and the wheel on the shingle, his body occupied. Let this be the peace, let this be the way of things, out here in this home of theirs, let them keep themselves busy with the gradual improvement of their boundaries, the widening of life, the removal of the dead and the dying, the old brambles, the broken cups. Let the world perch watchful at their patient work, done with what else could you call it but love. Let this be in the right direction, little by little, pushed away from death and climbing into new life, into beds of roses. Let them be stubborn in their labour, done in all seasons with the knowledge that it was nudging things forward, forever forward, with each green stem breaking into sunlight, each bee heavy with pollen, and let there be a time when they will look back at the state of things as they were now and barely recognise the paradise they have made.

John tipped the wheelbarrow, the roots and the vines swelling the pile by the edge of the lake, already a formidable size, up to his chest and with more to come. He was pleased at the lightness he felt at the prospect of more loads to carry and when he pushed the empty wheelbarrow back to the garden he neither rushed nor lilted but walked with the steady pace of someone who had found their rhythm. But Liz was no longer waiting to shovel another heap. She was standing over one of the newly cleared flower beds, attention on the soil, and John joined just as she knelt to touch something half-buried. Liz picked up the glove by pinching a seam and held it for him to see. 'Just an endless amount of crap,' she said and handed him the glove, made of white cotton and damp from the ground: a woman's glove, not the kind for gardening, more fitting for a formal occasion. He looked for its match in the soil but couldn't see one. He thought of the fingers that once would have slipped inside. He handed it back to Liz, who patted it down, dislodged a few blackish clumps and draped it flat over her own right hand. Had it been missed? Had it been searched for? She let it lie on top of her, as if she were guiding a phantom.

'This would've been nice once,' she said before stuffing it into her pocket. Then she was straight onto the plans she had for planting perennials, to be harvested through the year, and they would look wild and pretty, or so she'd read, and Good King Henry was a little like asparagus, often called a weed but not a weed at all.

'I like the name,' he said and she looked past him to the rest of the garden as if she could already see it growing.

When he had told her about Harrie's fainting Liz had thought about her sister, how scared she must have been.

Scratching against the floor.
Black dog in the hall.

Inside, she watched him lift the stopper from the glass decanter and pour some scotch over sugar and bitters. She'd read about curses. In Japan there was a curse cast in the dead of night, a straw effigy nailed to a sacred tree. When she'd come across that she'd had to put her phone face down and force herself not to think about how things had played out.

Later that evening Liz asked him outright if he was okay to have sex. She wasn't one hundred per cent but if her calculations were correct then they needed to, really. 'And it might be fun,' she said with such obvious disbelief that he couldn't help but laugh. She did too, both of them cracking up on the sofa. She put a hand on his crotch, clumsy, still laughing although it had simmered. They went upstairs and undressed and soon they were entangled and it worked for a while, was perfect for a while, until he felt a weight of pressure and he lost hold, kept trying in spite of it, hoped the movement would put him back on track, smother the thoughts, but he was badly stuffing a pillow into a pillowcase and Liz pulled back, saw the problem, breathed deeply, touched his cheek, asked if he just wanted to lie there, side by side, but he knew it needed to happen, that it was the bottom line and he was failing, the shame of it a hot coal on his forehead, but he did as she said, lying there with her hands on him, and he touched her between her legs and the wetness put the blood back in him, there we go, and she was going to suck him but he wanted to get back to it, show that he could, and she helped him inside but almost immediately lost hold again, could feel it slipping, and he had failed and when he turned over on the mattress she lay there for a while still, both of them still.

Eventually she turned to him, her eyes searching. It's her, he saw, still her. How could he have doubted? Permanent Elizabeth, the name unchanging and so too the person. Trust in that. Go to sleep and wake to find her there, still there, the core remaining, her humour, her warmth, as when they jumped the barriers beneath Blackfriars Bridge and were careful down the steps, alone at night, drunk and kissing as they stalked in front of the river, all of London teetering above its waters, and they too close to slipping, she held his hand and he felt himself anchored, knowing to let go would be to fall. This is a person he knows, who knows him in return. There is no hard thing, no great destruction.

*

The water rocked us beneath a clutch of stars that came in and out of light, so quickly the clouds moved over our heads. We were sheltered by the standing cover of the boat's wheel and instruments, so we moved in a strange calm despite the wind. I didn't mind the sound of it and I was only faintly aware of the fear of drowning.

93

My love, against all reason, broke away from our embrace just as I was settling into his heartbeat. My first thought was that he was still stung about the failed sex. I have all the time in the world for his feelings but the wounded pride is uniquely frustrating, it has to be said. I was about to tell him not to get wound up; that getting wound up will help nothing, when he suddenly bent over the side of the gunwale. I thought it may be to vomit and for a moment felt guilty that I'd been unaware of his nausea. But there was no retching, only something seen and pulled out of the water.

At first I had no idea what it was, only that it was long, made of two lines that started separate but joined at the end. Two other lines, small lines, joined them at the top and midway. The top line was curved and the middle straight. Taken together it looked like the letter A, if that letter's strokes were bound together at the bottom, the fulcrum in the middle stretching the top. He held it up like an exclamation. It was only when he handed it to me that I understood it was a crutch, made of light aluminium, its curved top lined with leather padding. I would've had an easier time recognising it if it wasn't on its own. I always think of crutches as coming in pairs. There was no sign of another in the water as far as we could see. I tapped the bottom against the hull and it made a satisfying knock that seemed to quiet the wind. I wedged the top into my armpit and, careful not to fall overboard, leant my weight into its shape.

In a green parlour I felt as delicate as clouded glass. I snapped my fingers at the wax leaves waiting for music to begin, my organs held together with a lick of Sellotape. Walk and they will break out of place, so I chose not to move, to keep my bounds. The mind goes where it wants. I imagined a fireplace roaring, certainly more comfortable than the cold air hitting my face as I moved too far from the awning above the boat's wheel. I pictured a baby naked and sleeping on a sheepskin rug, the rain constant and hard against the windows. The end of the crutch made a clack clack on the boards but I stopped moving before I was unbalanced. I did not fancy being fished out of the water.

Sitting opposite one another I passed my love the crutch. In his hands it looked as severe as the hammer, as if that object had grown to become another, its handle extending, its head softening but losing none of its threat. I had something to say. It was on the tip of my tongue. He tapped the rubber end of the crutch against the boards. Tap, tap, tap.

FIVE

H ARRIE EMERGED FROM THE treeline with Ciara on his back, her small arms folded over the top of his head. All of a sudden he broke into a run, the girl howling as she rattled about his shoulders, and when they came to a stop by the veranda she did not want to let her father go. Finn followed behind, trying his hardest to be part of the fun, pulling at Harrie's shirt as soon as Ciara had been placed on the boards, begging to be lifted like his sister but they were done with that, he was told. A shame, thought John, to see the boy so spurned, but he didn't feel like giving his nephew a piggyback either, didn't have the energy, so stayed where he was on the antique chair and watched them come.

'Wave to the king.'

In response, John wafted a hand like a monarch. The furniture had still not arrived. It would be a few more days until the delivery got there, they'd been told. There was an issue at the warehouse, delays in the supply chains, so they were left with their old sofa and too few seats, not enough things to fill the rooms. With some effort he'd carried the antique outside along with the stool and the four cheap chairs. They would have to take them all back inside if the weather turned.

The students were there too. It had been Monica's suggestion to invite them, apparently. Over the last couple of days they'd been a regular presence in the campsite, Harrie said. They'd joined for meals, played with the children. Tariq in particular had a good way with them, patient with their whims, unembarrassed to act the monster, roaring and stomping when they wanted him to chase them. He was quiet with the others, a little introverted, but with Ciara and Finn he was an engine of laughter, always moving them towards shrieks of joy, mad runnings. Alma had been endlessly inquisitive about their lives, open about her own, and Richard was a charming young man. Sharp. You could tell he was paying attention to what people were saying.

Despite this generous assessment, it was difficult to know whether Harrie actually wanted the students there. He smirked when John commented that he must have enough of students at work. 'They wanted to see the house,' he said. 'I think Alma in particular was curious, this English house in the country, very pretty.'

The visitors had, at least, brought a sense of surety. Here was the feeling that everything would be okay, thought John. Here was some normality. He found he could speak then of a future in a way he used to, as when he would say: we have plans for dinner, we have places to be; dates in the calendar, appointments set. There was something in that, the future a horizon close enough to see. He looked at the woods and the hills beyond, willing himself to see them as defined, contained, nothing more than one tree beside the next, on and on and up the slope. But it was difficult against the expanse, a line wavering, his own borders pinpricked and running. There was a terrible tightness in his chest, a black dog prowling between the trees, four paws pressing heavy against the dirt. He felt a dig of shame, a scratch of fear, the dog's eye fixed on him and he had to move from the spot, stand from the antique chair and stretch his legs.

'No way in hell you'll win, have you seen the size of me? *Hello there John.* I'm already at the water and where are you, not even out the door?'

Richard stood with arms folded, looking back at Alma who was running half-heartedly towards the shore. 'Hi hi hi hi,' she said to John as she passed.

The guests had brought their swimming costumes despite the overcast weather. 'Will you be the judge?' asked Richard. 'First to the end of the jetty, there you go, a fair arbiter with a fine pair of eyes.'

'Will you shut up,' said Alma.

'I'll never be silent about your eyes, John. No matter what she says.' Richard grinned.

John blinked. 'No, it's alright, I'll watch.'

'I'll be the one in the distance,' said Richard.

They ran into the water and John was left with a sharp little memory. Already they were slipping further from the shore, already harder to see amongst the splashing. They were carried off and so was he, his mind turning above Liverpool Street to bad words said too late, a sudden chill and the end of it clear, which should

99

have come as a relief but he had felt only guilt as they'd rumbled in stops and starts, red lights blotched from condensation through the bus window. Poor Hannah. She hadn't deserved any of it. When they'd got back to the flat she had said she wanted to go for a walk. At one in the morning he'd left a desperate voice note and who else to call then but Liz. She'd told him that everything would be fine; that Hannah had probably gone to stay with a friend. Birdsong, never before so loud. Until then he'd seen himself as incapable of hurting someone he loved. (Alma had reached the end of the jetty, Richard close behind.) She'd been hit by a car. An accident, a little drunk. He'd gone to the hospital but she didn't want him there. The orderlies made him leave. He waited in the flat for news. Eventually her parents called and told him she was being kept there. Broken ribs, an arm and a leg. He needed to be gone by the time they arrived. They didn't want to see a single trace of him.

John walked across the shore, following the boards to the jetty. His heart was racing and he did his best to calm it, breathe and settle. Why all this now? The dog on the treeline. Liz used to ask after Hannah as if she were an old friend. What was the latest? Still on crutches? From the jetty he could look down at the water, disturbed by the swimmers. His reflection was scattered. What more could they have done? Mercy, mercy. His mind dispersed. That tightness again in his chest. He tried to remember, if there was a door, a cavern, through which he could pass and there to know, in that place to know the moment, his time in the hollow of the tree with his knees to his chest, wrapped in bark, no doubt hiding, perhaps a game, as part of a game, there in the hollow, and it was important to know because never before, never since, had he been so close to that beating, that ceaseless beating.

There now was Harrie walking from the house in blue swimming trunks, belly spilled. He was happy to have himself covered, it seemed, from the way he rushed beneath the waterline. Harrie swam then alongside the jetty, John's reflection disturbed again by the motion. He listened to the splashing, the sounds of birds, and for a moment was spread out amongst them as a thousand figments. Whose voice is that in my throat? It cannot be mine. Harrie swam level to where John stood on the jetty, trod water and smiled. 'It's not too cold,' he said. 'Why don't you come in?'

In the end John compromised by taking off his shoes and socks, walking out a little until the water lapped close to his rolled-up trousers. By then Harrie had vanished somewhere beyond the jetty. Alma and Richard were returning. He gave her the thumbs-up as she went back towards the house. He tried to enjoy the sensation of his bare toes on the silt, the faint pressure of the lake on his shins. It could start spitting at any moment. I shall pay less attention to myself, he thought. I shall not concern myself with this ceaseless rotation around the same old things, always turning to catch a reflection but seeing only pieces. I carry on and I shall do so quietly, no need for a stir, no need to raise my eyes. I shall let it be as others do, running on their own steam. Trust in that: a path pressed by a hundred thousand feet and if I should stray I shall trust in myself to resume, somewhere or another, further down the line.

Liz was coming from the house. Now she saw him, he thought. Now she stood on the shore with a glass in hand, watching the swimmers. *Let me in.* Already the spin of his mind slowed. They were together and they had made a home, that was what mattered. This place was theirs and it would be their child's too. I am not one thing ageing but forever renewed, he thought, the green and the light, the shoots forever reaching, my knees against my chest in the hollow of a tree, ready at a moment's notice to burst forth. He wiggled his toes against the silt.

She drank and felt the coolness against the roof of her mouth. Here he was with his feet in the water, looking silly in his shirt and trousers, golden strands running between them through the air. She longed to close the distance that she could feel widening, she longed to draw it to nothing.

She'd worn the white glove when nobody was around, soil still under her nails despite a brush under a running tap. It suited her. If she could find the other then she might keep the pair. There would be occasions, no doubt. It was a nice thought, the potential of things, two elegant gloves and a dress. They could be childless and have parties, be hosts to friends. Only a matter of time, once they were settled, get Ali and Neena, Mark and Chris and Emma and Lee, get them and their kids up here for a long weekend. No doubt Monica and Harrie would be back. They could make it a regular thing, the kids, somewhere to get away when they grew older. Her sister would come and see. Her sister was laughing at her, snickering, making fun of her sad little attempt at things. The ice knocked against her teeth. *They want to get a wriggle on*, Monica would say. *They're not getting any younger.* She watched John wade back to the shore. She would make it a mission to find the other glove, show her sister how well they fit. At that moment a heron flew low across the lake, coming to land in a patch of reeds. There was a knot inside her. Surrender my body, she thought. Take me up. Come and drink from my bones, grow from my blood. The clouds had darkened. The day was passing. Soon Monica was smoking, Richard too, still in his swimming trunks despite the coldness in the air. Alma had run back from the house and was speaking to John, a blue towel around her shoulders. With some urgency he went away from her towards the kitchen door.

'Your brother was looking for him,' said Alma, soon beside her.

'Brother-in-law.'

Alma squinted, as if to see her better. 'He cut his foot, I think.'

They stood there watching Monica talk to Richard on the jetty, the children splashing nearby in the shallows with Tariq.

'Look, look!' shouted Finn, and when Tariq was looking he jumped up and down.

'Wow!'

Richard's arms were folded across his chest. Monica slowly brought the cigarette to her lips. She was looking up at him as he spoke.

Liz didn't particularly want to talk to Alma, would rather they didn't have to play out an exchange that cast her as the lady of the house. But they were standing there without saying anything, so: 'Nice summer?'

'Fun. Endless.'

'Where will you go next?'

'Richard wants to spend a couple of days just the two of us in Newcastle.'

'That'll be nice.'

'Tariq doesn't know about it yet.'

Liz had no real idea about the relationship between the three students, whether Tariq should or shouldn't know, although she could make a guess that he should, inevitably would. 'I'm not really sure what to do.' Alma said it with a flatness that felt misleading.

'Right,' said Liz. There was a pressure to say more. 'Right,' she said again.

'He won't be happy about it.'

Liz felt compelled to meet her eye and there she found an expression that was intense enough to take her aback for a moment. Why was she telling her this? She hardly knew her. When Liz didn't immediately respond, Alma repositioned the towel on her shoulders. Liz searched for words that would help, wanted to help, but only managed to make a concerned hum.

They looked back to the others. Under their gaze Monica finished her cigarette and searched around her feet for the best place to be rid of it, deciding in the end to drop it right where she was and swivel the toe of her trainers on its embers. The way Alma sighed then through her teeth, looking over the pair to the hills in the distance; she was teetering on the edge of something, could see it coming, and Liz felt a genuine sympathy for her. 'Newcastle is impressive,' she said in the end. 'The bridges.'

'I've heard they're impressive.'

'Oh yes, big bridges. Much bigger than they look in pictures.'

Alma used the towel to ruffle dry her hair. Perhaps she was glad Liz hadn't helped. In either case, the moment had gone. Alma placed the towel back around her shoulders and it was as if she had reset herself. She smiled again. Perhaps she was someone Liz could have been friends with, at one time.

*

Something new was draped on the mantelpiece: the white cotton glove, its slender fingers hanging over the edge so that it seemed a limp hand had emerged from the wall. John assumed his wife would have thrown it away with the rest of the rubbish but there it was, the dirt dusted off, placed above the fireplace with a deliberateness that suggested she had wanted it to be seen. He didn't like the sight of it hanging over, too much as if there might still be a hand within. He studied the length of the fingers, thought of the warmth of the palm, a bannister gripped, a search in a pocket, teaspoons stirred, hot breath blown above three feet of snow. When his father had died, his shirts had remained in his mother's wardrobe. What shape was kept there, waiting to be forgotten? A flame and then darkness, a body in the world, fingers twitching, a voice echoing on the walls as if it would never disappear but it too in time, all in time, my hands in time, he thought, noticing then the fine hairs on his knuckles. Sausage meat squeezed from the grinder, fat and hanging in the window and brought home as a treat, he remembered, his father cooking them in a pan so they'd sizzle and spit. What hand was in the glove, what tenderness remains in its stitching? All there, somewhere. Where else would it be? It cannot be lost, the dark cannot gain forever. There must be some stirring, some groping back to strike a match and in doing so bring those memories onto their feet once more. His father singing above the smell of the sausages. That remains, it must remain, housed there amongst their belongings, their photographs, their furniture, their shoes and socks, within the polished wood. And for the first time he felt close to the previous inhabitants, began to understand why they had wanted to leave their empty bottles and fag ends scattered about.

Harrie was in the bathroom, still in his swimming trunks. One of his feet was wrapped in toilet paper. 'I was looking for plasters,' he said, peeled back the paper and showed John a nasty gash on the bottom of his right foot. The skin was wrinkly from being in the water, blood began to seep in a way that reminded John of lightning. In the centre of the arch, the cut exposed an inch of flesh. Before any more blood could drip onto the tiles, Harrie pressed the toilet paper back into place, raised his leg so that it lay across the side of the bathtub. There was a pink towel on the floor, a darker red patch where Harrie must have wrapped it around his foot. John searched through the cupboards but couldn't find the plasters there. There was still a box of unpacked toiletries so he knelt down and set about looking beneath the tubes of moisturiser and packets of painkillers.

'Are the kids having fun?' asked Harrie.

'I think so.'

At the bottom of the box he found a roll of bandages and a small cardboard container of plasters.

Harrie blew air out of his mouth, relieved. John passed the box of plasters to his brother-in-law who picked the biggest in the pack: a pink square that he peeled from its backing and, lifting the toilet paper, covered the gash in his foot. Even though he could no longer see it, the sliver of exposed flesh remained in John's mind. Next he passed the roll of bandages and Harrie hesitated. Two faints, she'd said. Nothing found.

'Do you think the others saw me limping?'

'Alma said you hurt yourself.'

'Did she?'

'"Harrie has hurt himself."'

His brother-in-law looked dismayed. 'I told her I needed your help with the car.'

John was about to offer to help with the bandage when Harrie grabbed the roll, unspooled the white mesh and wound it fast around his foot, all without a word. He stood tentatively, wincing at too much weight on the cut, eventually finding a way of moving that put the pressure on the inner side of his foot.

'A sharp stone, I think.'

'You want to be careful.'

John thought of Harrie's blood disappearing in the water. As the afternoon tightened it began to drizzle. They put out bowls of crisps and pretzels, brought the chairs inside and set them up in the dining room around the table. The drinks they had stored away were opened. He realised then that Richard had taken the antique, Alma perching on one of its armrests. 'It's very old,' he warned in a small voice to his wife. Alma heard this and stood at once looking sheepish but Monica sucked her teeth.

'Do you expect them to sit on the floor?'

Liz cleared her throat. 'It is very old.'

'Nonsense. I've seen the exact same in John Lewis.'

'It's *fine*,' John said. 'There's a stool somewhere but it's fine.'

The stool, it turned out, had been dragged beneath the window that overlooked the jetty. One of their mugs was on the floor, a few cigarette ends inside. He picked up the stool and brought it to the empty edge of the dinner table. By then Richard and Alma were back on the antique at the head and everyone seemed happy, so he took his place.

'I'm bored,' said Ciara.

Harrie leant forward on his knees to speak to his daughter.

'Why don't you go watch some TV?'

'Can Tariq come?'

'Give the poor man a break.'

'It's alright. I don't mind.'

'No. Baby, let the grown-ups talk.'

'Get yourself an ice lolly,' said Monica.

'Can I have a Fab?'

'Did we get Fabs?'

'We did,' said Liz.

'Yes, get a Fab. One for your brother too. Off you go.'

With the children gone, Harrie cracked his knuckles and launched into an article he'd read about a landlord in Birmingham who'd been held captive by her own tenants. This landlord had planned to raise the rent because the tenants, a family, had four more people living in the property than was allowed according to their agreement. In response they'd barricaded the landlord inside a linen cupboard. Harrie found it amusing. Tariq had seen the same story and when Harrie told him it was mad, completely mad, Tariq smiled faintly. Salt had been spilt on the table and John dabbed it with a finger, pushed it into a heap with the side of his hand.

'She's pressing charges, of course.'

'How'd she get out?'

'Called the police, I'd imagine.'

'So they let her keep her phone?'

'Yes, Monica. I don't know.' He looked to the head of the table for another kind of response. 'This is where we are,' he said. 'The state of things. You must have some renting stories, some nightmares between you.'

Instead of responding to this, Richard turned his attention downwards, to the free armrest of the chair, a groove there in the wood that he caressed with the tip of a finger.

'Things shouldn't be allowed to come to this,' said Harrie.

'No, no,' agreed Liz. She was only half listening, thinking of a small, eager mouth in the dark. She repositioned her weight on the chair, her body felt so unlike her own. Why was this coming on so strongly?

'Better rent control,' said Harrie. 'I suspect that's something you'd like to see, yes?' Brow raised, encouraging nod. He seemed intent on pleasing the students but Richard still did not look up.

'They tried something like that in Berlin,' said John, although he wasn't sure if it was actually Barcelona, or Brussels, whether it had worked out or failed, whether he really knew what rent control meant, if he was forced to describe it. The topic was making him feel awkward. He didn't want to get onto the neighbour's inheritance. Mrs Walsh and her apple tree. Mrs Walsh on a ventilator. They would say he was part of the problem. He pinched the top of his small heap of collected salt between his thumb and forefinger, felt the hard grains, imagined a stone pyramid. Alma was whispering something in Richard's ear.

Tariq coughed. 'It's a shame but I don't think these things work a lot of the time,' he said. 'In a lot of cities, if you put a limit on rent, older landlords will simply sell up.'

'Yes,' said Harrie. 'But if you build more properties, if you have a government-backed approach...' He opened his hands.

'London is ridiculous now,' said Monica. 'Fucking silly.'

'There are ways to make it work. What's the alternative?' A sharpness had entered Harrie's voice. Was this the voice he used when he delivered his lectures, Liz wondered. 'There have to be protections. I'm sure you agree on that, yes?'

'Yeah, all right,' said Tariq.

Liz tried to think of something to say, but she found herself fixed on the small mound of salt John had made.

She felt a swell of fondness at the sight of it. Come to me, my love. Come and we can try again.

'If you ask me, they should've gone further than locking her in the cupboard,' said Richard, finally saying something. He gave a leonine smile. 'Landlords will always find ways to wriggle free. The biggest sack couldn't hold them.'

'Haha, yes, right,' said Harrie.

Richard mimed shooting a gun.

Harrie smirked. 'I forgot I was speaking to students.'

'You can't expect a parasite to stop sucking blood,' said Richard. His eyes were playful, warm and light. 'It's too late, these things you're suggesting. They just won't do.'

'Well,' said Harrie. 'I know where you're coming from.'

'No, you don't.'

Harrie went a little red then. What made it worse is that he focused his eyes on Alma, looking at her with pleading entreaty. She seemed uncomfortable with his attention. 'I think it isn't enough at this point in history to make compromises that nobody wants,' she said. Her voice was confident, the sentence rolling off her tongue.

John left his salt and impatiently went to the window, dug his fingers to the painted wood beneath the pane, stiff, but with a little effort it opened, the cool evening air quick on his face, the world given an entrance, and there was the lake, spread before him, reflecting nothing but the clouds. The drizzle had stopped but the light was nearly gone. The children were outside, he realised. He could just about see them playing on the shore.

'Shit, shit,' said Monica when he told the room. She rushed up and out.

John looked beyond the lake to the woods and the hills. To grow, to spread, to wake one morning and know the bounds are pushed a little further, even an inch, small steps each day that make up a future, the possibility of a future, that much had to be true, he wanted it to be true, despite the dying light, the cool air, the hills beyond the woods; an impenetrable ridge, or so it seemed then from the window, their furthest reaches impossible to trace and if he tried to scale them he would only tumble backwards. To grow, to push, only to fall back, to plummet thwarted into the water.

Monica reached the children and pointed aggressively back to the house. Harrie fell into a grump. He paid attention to the topics of conversation, even chuckled when Liz told a story about a colleague who'd forgotten to mute a work call when going to the toilet, but he didn't venture a new topic of conversation, didn't crack his knees or knuckles, not even once.

The students seemed to be waiting for one of them to offer more food. Monica, maybe sensing this, mentioned she was getting hungry and instead of that being a signal for them to leave Harrie grunted and sipped his drink. He was not listening, he seemed elsewhere in his head. Liz brought in more crisps, the last of what they had, and as soon as the bowls were full, they were empty again. John volunteered to collect some of the empty glasses. He circled the table, passing Tariq just as the student patted his palms flat to underline a point about Kabul airport. *Here is someone clear in their thoughts.* John disliked it, recognised a time he himself used to talk and talk on the Old Kent Road, the glow in the night and no doubt in his mind about the ideas he was having, brought back to a flat shared with friends, to drink and sit and talk some more, always talking, happy to spend with no care for the currency. A gabbling prat. He cringed at the thought, the belief of knowing enough, so certain and confident, the ownership of it, the connections easily drawn, and all so mistaken. What an embarrassment. They will see this, one day closer than they know. He thought of crumbling stone. The Library of Alexandria. He used to pick paint from the walls and speak about God knows what like he'd cracked the code. The arrogance of it. 'Do you need help?' asked Tariq. His brow was raised, lips pursed into an expression of performed consideration. He'd started to move from his chair, just enough to show willing although not enough to commit to standing.

'No need, no need.'

A smile and then Tariq went back to talking, but not before a glance in the direction of Alma, still on the armrest of the antique, a hand in Richard's as he stroked the small of her back with the other.

Liz also noticed the way Tariq stared at the pair. There was a flare from a crack in the earth. She remembered Alma's indecision and could see then the danger, the poor boy's heart in the maw. Careful steps were needed otherwise it would end in tears, she could promise that. Ah! The drama. Delicious. Not to be cruel, she thought, but it's a fun thing to get your teeth stuck into a ripe bit of emotional peril. Her lips curled and she was aware of it, careful that Tariq didn't catch her amusement, poor Tariq, lovestruck Tariq, mindful Alma, although not that mindful if she's fondling the back of Richard's hair, twirling a strand of his long hair around a finger.

Was she already past that? Everything falls through, she supposed. Everything falls and there's the hope of another ground beneath, new considerations, the mortgage, the house, the work needed, the baby. Was the longing she felt not a longing at all? Was it something told to her, some expectation she had hoisted upon herself and could, with enough concentration, push off? Who had told her to put it there? Who could've been so thoughtless? Her mother, her father, John, Monica. She can feel the weight but with enough concentration she could shift it.

Better besides for the planet not to have one.

In the hallway John found Harrie staring down at an open book with one hand covering his left eye as if he were at the optician's. When his brother-in-law saw him, he stopped immediately, looked sheepish.

'How's the foot?'

Harrie lifted his right foot a little off the floor, rotated his ankle.

'Yes, good. Hurts a bit.'

John expected his brother-in-law to take the opportunity to launch into a rant about the students being naive or idealistic, fringed with the anticipation that John would agree. To be honest he was ready to do so. But Harrie only smiled and fiddled awkwardly with the book in his hand, a copy of *Mansfield Park* that Liz had kept from her degree, had only put on the bookshelf because it was a hardback. Harrie flicked the front cover open and closed with his thumb, making a buk buk sound. He looks pale, thought John. But there must be a source of strength he tapped into because all of a sudden his posture changed, his height regained. 'We'll need to get the boat out on the lake before the holiday is over,' he said.

There was a loud crack followed by a shriek.

John rushed back into the room in time to see Alma picking herself off the floor, Tariq there to help her onto her feet. Richard was still sitting in the antique chair, brow frozen in an expression of surprise. With horror John realised the left armrest had given way, the wood bent backwards like a broken bone.

'Oh dear,' said Monica.

Harrie hobbled in, book still in his hands. He surveyed the scene and immediately turned on the ceiling light. Everyone squinted at the sudden brightness.

'Are you hurt?' shouted Harrie. He moved about the room like a bomb had gone off, and in the face of his sudden, violent force the others took on a strange quiet. Alma began to apologise to John but he shook his head and waved his hand. It was an accident. Richard too looked flustered and wouldn't meet John's eye. Tariq asked Liz if they could give her some money.

'Yes,' said Alma, searching her bag and pulling out her wallet. John spotted a wad of twenties.

'No need,' said Liz. 'It's *fine.*'

Monica went to get the children from the TV. She hadn't realised how late it was. Harrie inspected the damage. Carefully he pulled the armrest upright but it was clear that there was nothing to be done. The wood had splintered and the ornate supports were broken into pieces.

*

Later John thought of walking into the woods, away from the light of the house, around the lake to the other side and further still, towards the hills, weaving between the trees and their many branches. There was nothing seen, a thousand murmurs and only one way to go, further from the lake as the ground curved upwards, the trees thinning as he felt the strain in his muscles, the murmurs behind. They could scream themselves blue for all he cared, they could whistle and shout for all the good it would do them. He pressed on, not looking back for Liz, shamefully, not even for her, because there was only a little more to go and nothing would stop him this time, pushing up, forcing up, foot by foot, the summit in reach, in sight, there to grasp, and again the knowledge dawning, remembered, that this will not occur, will not be allowed. It has defeated me before, better than me before. Still, the climb, in spite, because, falling back, plummeting through the trees, into the lake.

A window thrown open, dark beyond but the promise of light.

A mattress beneath his clammy skin, a duvet up to his neck. John rose, then, moved to the curtains, parted enough to see beyond, into the gloom. He put his forehead to the glass, felt its coolness, stayed there for a moment and could hear Liz behind him, her light snoring.

Out on the lake, its surface barely seen, John looked for movement, looked for something to hook his eyes around. What time is it? How long until the sun rises? He opened the window and the air felt fresh on his skin. He stuck his head out and tried to get a better look at the view, at the woods and the hills beyond. In time his eyes adjusted. He searched for a shape on the water, a mark on the pale and glassy sprawl.

Something moved close to the treeline. At first he took it for a person, but as it walked onto the shore he could see it for what it was. A deer. It dipped its head to the water, drank, then looked towards the house.

*

Together we set out, the hooked pole in my love's hands, and it was not long before we came across the head of an animal. Its black eyes watched us as we brought it in, the neck followed by a single unbreaking line, followed by an axle and a pair of wheels.

Back on the shore, I watched as she rode the hobby horse. It was too small for her, so she ended up carrying the head between her legs and letting the stick-body dangle. I was reminded of when she'd played with the children in the campsite, throwing the Frisbee back and forth and rolling on the grass. In their absence, she walked up and down without enthusiasm, the faintest of smiles on her lips when she passed it to me, and I did the same, more from a sense of obligation than any actual desire to play. What else would you do with a hobby horse? I held onto the wooden handlebars that jutted out of each side of the horse's neck, crouched low enough for the wheels at the end of the pole to touch the shingle, decided that it would be too much effort to move in that position, so walked upright for a few paces, turned and walked the few paces back.

After that we let it lie on the ground between us as we sat on our stones. She seemed to be studying it and, not wanting to stare at her and with nowhere else to look, I fixed my eyes on it too. One of the wheels was slowly turning, pushed by the wind. The brown hair of the horse's mane also moved, tousled unevenly. I compared it in my mind to the crutch, its length and thinness, but also to the mirror, the two stubs that stuck out on either side of its wooden frame and, here, the two wooden handlebars that were made for a child to hold. I imagined its wheels on a lush carpet, two small legs tottering forward. Outside the green parlour, the rain was unceasing, no landscape to see outside of the room, nothing but water on the glass.

To one side of us was the house, to the other the lake. Finding it difficult to look at the hobby horse, difficult to look at my love, I turned to the unlit windows reflecting the shore and imagined our lives going on within.

SIX

JOHN HAD IT IN his mind that he would fix the chair, so as soon as he was up, he was downstairs. He'd half forgotten that Tariq had passed out on the sofa the night before and jolted at the sight of him at the dining table, his head cradled in one hand, staring down at his phone. He made them both a coffee and soon Tariq began to talk about Richard. 'He was at the Labour society and there was this other history student, Martin Badeau. French. This Martin used to always say that things were fishy. *So and so's fishy. There's something fishy about this and that.* Just one of those things. An English phrase he liked. Nothing wrong with it.'

Tariq sipped his coffee. For being drunk the night before, he seemed buoyant.

'There's something fishy about the anarcho-syndicalists. There's something fishy about the opera.'

John wanted to begin fixing the chair.

'One time we're having drinks and out of nowhere there's a horrible screech. And you know what it was? Richard has a finger hooked into Martin Badeau's mouth and he's leading him around the room.'

Tariq mimed it with his own mouth, sticking a finger into the corner of his lips and pulling his head like a fish that had been caught with a fisherman's hook.

'I mean, Richard apologised, said he wasn't feeling well. But it got him kicked out of the club for a term. Literally all anyone could talk about. *What the hell was Richard Bartlett thinking?*'

Tariq massaged his cheek where he'd hooked himself, too hard, it seemed. He had lit up speaking about his friend, John noticed, although he didn't care to fan any flame. Soon Liz came down and he took it as an opportunity to get up from the table.

'A few weeks after that and Richard's being talked about again for sleeping with a tutor, a postdoc, who was engaged, by the way.'

'Wow,' said Liz.

Tariq nodded enthusiastically.

'Before you know it, he's getting a bit of a reputation and I was brought up to avoid people with a reputation, you know. But we got talking at a literary reading and he was by far the most interesting person there. He had a lot of thoughts about the way things are going, what's needed.'

'The way things are going,' she echoed.

'Richard's on the right side of things,' Tariq said, knowingly, angling his head as if he were letting them into his confidence.

John focused on the splintered side of the antique. A few new slats, he hoped. If only it had been a clean break and not this twisting tear, the panel damaged, but thankfully the figure was untouched, the figure in the woods, there with one ear to the sound of distant bleating, the wind at night and what can he do but listen.

'We're at the stage where the current social order is in its death throes,' said Tariq. 'That can't be denied. It has totally failed to combat the impending climate breakdown and the only correct response is a total reaction against social norms.'

'Like what?' asked Liz, open and direct, and John loved her for that.

'Work, pleasure, the day-to-day. It's all designed around a paradigm that doesn't hold up. These things might have had meaning, once upon a time, but they don't have any now. They're hollow. And we've all been pretending, you know?'

Liz glanced at John, knelt on the floor with his broken chair. He'll mope about it for a few weeks, she thought. She'll hold him tightly on the sofa and ask him what's on his mind, something has clearly been on his mind, and he won't say it's the chair but he'll say he wished they'd been clearer about where people could sit and it will sound like he's blaming her, she'll say. And when she tells him it wasn't her fault he'll say he never said it was, that it was just a shame that their new furniture hadn't come in time.

'I think you're right about the failure, at least,' she said. 'There's a lack of imagination and it's deadly, these days, when you can't muster the political will to properly face the realities people are dealing with.'

Tariq screwed up his face. 'People act like it's a choice,' he said. 'There is no choice. Things are going to come apart one way or another.'

She had wanted him to agree with her sentiment. It was said for him to agree with. She could have rolled her eyes at the generalisations he was putting out there, but she had chosen to help him along.

'It all sounds very dramatic,' she said flatly.

He had a smug expression on his lips. It would have been quite easy to dislike him, she thought, if not for the brightness in his eyes. He was ridiculous and young so why then did she care what he thought of her? She rocked John's near-empty cup of coffee backwards and forwards. Tariq no doubt saw her as culpable and in truth she did feel complicit. She was at least guilty of becoming lax in her cares about the world. Guilty of political inarticulation, of wanting a child.

'Richard's not a nihilist,' said Tariq, quite suddenly. 'He says he's a realist.'

'And are you a realist?'

'Not in the way he means it.'

He appeared then to be taken up by some sadness. Liz found it difficult to look at him, perhaps out of pity, although she was also aware that an unease was being established in the room; an agitation that was causing Tariq to pluck the fingers of one hand with the other.

'Richard wants us to meet this guy in Newcastle. An engineer.'

One of his shoes was tapping the air.

'An engineer?'

'Do you have any more coffee?'

She didn't do anything for a moment. She didn't like the way he'd asked, as if she were a waitress.

John turned from his work on the chair. 'What does Richard want to meet an engineer for?'

'Richard has this way of slowly closing and opening his eyes when he's listening carefully, did you notice that? Like a cat. I've always thought of it like something cats do. It's funny.' Tariq rearranged his legs, unfolding and folding in the other direction. Why bring these things up and then act like they were foisted on him? Liz could see he'd rather talk about something else but she resented his hold on their attention.

'Like a civil engineer?' she asked.

'I really don't know.'

'Is it for work?'

'I think so. I don't know. More of a mechanic.'

'A car mechanic?'

'Maybe.' Tariq screwed up his face again. 'He's going to help with a thing or two. Apparently he's a nice guy.'

She imagined a pyramid of transparent triangular cells. The social order. Glass panels bordered by steel beams, stacked one on top of the other in the middle of a desert, the interior empty but the deeper you attempted to look, the more obscure it became. When she got back to the dining room with a fresh cafetière, Tariq was reading from a book. John was nowhere to be seen. The book, Liz noticed, was a literary magazine that she had been published in years ago. He must have taken it from the shelf.

'I saw your name,' he said, a little coy. His way of holding himself was different to how it had been a few minutes before. He seemed nervous, thought Liz. Less sure of himself.

He showed her the front cover, as if to prove the fact that her name was there. It was joined by others who had contributed, overlaid on a painting. The painting contained a blue smear surrounded by loops and coils of brown and black and a darker blue. All this against white. It was by a Chinese artist, she remembered, although she couldn't recall the name. He turned the page. She watched his eyes move backwards and forwards and she remembered what the story was. Now she understood the reason for his coyness. She could do him a mercy and leave the room, she considered, but he could also stop reading; he could decide to put the literary magazine down and he had chosen not to. Was he reading the section she was thinking about? From his expression she thought it was likely, his brow fixed in performative concentration, trying his hardest to look serious and unaffected, an intellectual distance. He swallowed some saliva in his mouth, it gave him away, but still his eyes did not leave the page. She was enjoying this, she realised. Now she stood with a sense of power. Her gaze was fixed on his face, daring his eyes to meet her. They did not. His eyes moved back and forth. Was he taking it in, she wondered, or was he too distracted by her presence? Look up from the page, see me watching, see the judgement on my face. He had not turned a page for a while. She stood with her arms by her side, even though she wanted to cross them. Look up from the page, see me watching.

In the kitchen, John searched a plastic bag for the tape measure. He honestly had no idea how to fix the chair but it seemed within his powers to take measurements. The talk of upending social conventions had made him cringe. Why? It wouldn't have, even a few years ago. Now he felt uncomfortable. He feared some expectation to understand things more than he did. Where was the tape measure? They would need a proper toolbox. He'd order one that week. He would be someone with a toolbox. A man with a toolbox. He pulled out a hard case of screws and put them on the floorboards. 'Have you seen the tape measure?' he shouted down the corridor. It was only recently that he'd begun to identify what control meant to him. He'd always thought of himself as someone who enjoyed a little uncertainty. It was a not unsizeable part of his charm, he had thought, an unpredictability that pulled conversations in unexpected and interesting directions. But over the past few months he had felt a genuine discomfort at the idea that he had made a mistake in his work. A mistranslation. Somewhere in those pages was a sentence out of his control, he thought. There was some sense freewheeling out of his control. He had been misunderstood. Where was the tape measure? There again was the feeling that he was unable when he should have been able. Able in the eyes of men like Harrie de Groot, who was good with his hands; had replaced all the floorboards in their flat after woodworm was found. John pulled out a flat-head screwdriver and laid it on the case of screws. Where was the tape measure? He had not read anything in Hungarian for at least a fortnight. Liz did not speak it. Whenever he thought of the language he thought of a glass cabinet filled with miniature objects. But he had been wrong. He had been mistaken.

'Have you seen the tape measure?'

His head was around the doorway. Tariq was alone, reading at the table. At the sight of John he raised his eyebrows and opened his palms to the ceiling.

'Try the plastic bag by the sink.' Liz's voice came from upstairs.

'I did.'

'Well then I don't know.'

*

John drove Tariq back to the campsite. 'Your wife is nice,' the student said. He had decided to sit in the back and was staring at a field of yellow flowers.

'Are the other two waiting for you?'

'Alma's probably asleep.'

Why sit in the back? John wondered. It made him feel like a taxi driver.

'She loves her sleep,' said Tariq. 'Creative minds. Your wife as well?'

'Sometimes.'

'She reminds me of Alma. They have the same energy.'

John realised Tariq was looking at him in the rear-view mirror. He lowered the sunscreen. 'I don't know if they do.'

'Don't you think that people can echo each other?'

'I just don't think they're that similar.'

Tariq fell silent. The yellow flowers gave way to a bank of trees, the sunlight coming in and out of their canopies. One thing is certain, that the day is only so many hours, the trees themselves content in the knowledge, John liked to think; to stand and soak, knowing they will be rooted in the dark as much as the light. He'd once read that trees talk to each other underground. The strange ways of plants. Done with fungus. They would send each other warnings. Would they talk with trepidation about the sunset? Would they share, all times and tenses at once, all voices, all tones and lilts and slights of tongue, their concerns about the light no longer flowing across their leaves? If you asked him to put his ear to the dirt he would, gladly, provided you could promise he would hear some juicy bit of gossip. Do the trees mumble about the dying light, or about the promise of more light to come?

'They both have an openness,' said the student as they crossed an empty junction. 'I think so. It's striking. There are open and closed people, don't you think? More people are closed than open. Alma and Liz are open. Open to ideas. It's a great quality.'

'Sure.'

In truth, it was something John had for a long time thought of as a part of his wife's character, beautiful in its resilience and its volatility. He had seen it emerge at times that had caught him by surprise, over a plate of mussels, under the stained glass of a cathedral. He didn't appreciate the way Tariq was attempting to articulate it.

'Are you open?' John asked.

'Not as open as Alma. I have fixed ideas.'

The whole thing had a strong whiff of misogyny, this openness.

'Yeah, I'm closed,' said Tariq. 'Or at least closing. I should be open. I act open, at least to certain people.' He was staring out of the car window again. 'But Alma is really open. When she hears a piece of music, it fills her. I think your wife has that too. I got a sense of it. The way she talks.'

'Maybe.'

They bordered a farmhouse and a horse in a field, wearing what looked like a bright blue raincoat. Endless lines of fungus beneath us, John thought. Surges in the dirt, ceaseless and coming from every direction, even the hole he'd dug for that poor fawn, patted down the soil, sent not into nothing, he realised, but into some subterranean conversation.

'Did your wife talk much to Richard yesterday?'

'A bit, I think.'

'Do you know what she made of him?'

'No. Sorry.'

John glanced in the mirror at Tariq. The student stared back through the glass at the horse in the field, its face covered in a hood.

*

Soon after they had parked in the campsite, Tariq disappeared inside his tent. Before John got back into the driver's seat, he called to see if any of the family were around. Their blue Toyota was parked. A bottle of sunscreen had been left on the fold-out camping table. He caught sight of a figure some distance away, through the trees. It was a man of Harrie's size and he was bent forward as if he was catching his breath. John closed the car door and started to walk in his direction. He wanted to be sure it was Harrie before he called his name.

The man moved into a crouching position. There was no one else that John could see.

'Harrie,' he called, fear rising.

The man remained crouching.

'Harrie.'

John walked quicker.

Harrie must have heard him, because he slowly raised himself to stand upright, one hand on a tree for support. When John got close he could see that the colour of his face was not right. His brother-in-law's eyes, defiant, met John's and quivered with realisation; but then, his hand sweeping his face as if pulling a spider's web from his brow, he blinked at the ground with a drop of shame.

'I'm just having a walk.'

'Do you need to sit down?'

Harrie shook his head and looked off into the woods.

'Have the others gone out?'

'What's that?'

'Monica and the kids.'

'They're riding their bikes.'

John thought for a moment of taking Harrie by the arm and guiding him back to the tent.

'Are we meant to be meeting today?' asked his brother-in-law.

'I was just dropping one of your neighbours back.'

'Ah, one of the revellers!' Harrie made an effort to stand without support, taking his hand off the tree. 'It was a fun night, wasn't it? Good to talk.'

They had begun to walk back towards the tent, Harrie once more himself although limping slightly on his injured foot. Neither Tariq nor anyone else had emerged from their part of the campsite. Harrie had already picked up a notepad that had been tucked into the tent's entrance and was laying it out on the camping table. 'A fun night,' he said, starting to work. 'A good time.'

*

There on the wall were two shapes, just about visible. Two outlines, although the lines were vague enough to be abstract. Liz touched part of the line on the bigger of the two shapes; where the shoulders ran into the neck. The line was light. Had the children drawn around their mother and father? Liz felt a throb of anger. Making marks on their walls, not even bothering to clean it up. She imagined the scene, Harrie playing along with their game, standing up straight as Monica helped Ciara to get the pencil over his head and shoulders. Might as well have taken a wee on the walls. Alright, not as bad as that. Still though, the cheek.

She traced the line where it looped into a head of sorts. If she didn't have children she would regret it. For the rest of her life she would regret it. She stood back and observed the shapes, side by side. Where was the want for children? Where did it live in her body? She thought of it as solid matter, a plum stone. Was this the truth of things, the fact of things, the spirit waiting beneath the toil, the day-to-day, the prolonging, the continuance? Was this the reason for the pressure in the back of her head? The weather had come in, the clouds, the rain, because her body knows, better than her it knows, that the continuance is utmost, sacred, matters more than little fears, little oscillations from day to day, and who can argue with the core truth to life, that it only matters to keep on, no point beyond, make your own meaning, all of that, might as well, nothing else to do except make your own and let yourself be carried by the current that yearns between the banks of the river. I am prolonging, she thought, and that is that, not as if this is news, given all the books on the subject she'd read at university, the crises, standing on the New Cross Road with a dirty tote on her shoulder, the library books, and she could've told you then that there wasn't much to it beyond the continuance of life. Not that she felt it, not really, not in her stomach the way she felt it that morning, seized by the hands of uncaring forces. Oh where were their new things? Take comfort in furniture. See a pleasingly upholstered armchair as an anchor, the form of an invisible body, come to think of it as a stable point. Take pleasure in an oak dining table and think not of the tree but only the potential for those to sit around, to share and laugh, bang a fist. Fuck on the table. How many more days would it be before the furniture arrived?

I will take it into my own hands. I am a benefactor of fire, she thought. I am on Mount Olympus, trickling life to the plains below. That's power for you, real power, and who gives a fly's fart if it's in the name of continuance, as if that should stop her from enjoying the knowledge that it's in her to make a brain and bones and kidneys and kings and queens, the soul given form, if you go in for that. Giraffes don't have souls. We are gods of a lesser order, she thought. I will make the hair on a soft little head. One day, not far from now, as we sit in a darkened room and you sleep on my chest, I will feel powerful in the knowledge that I have made you what you are.

On the TV was a report about an explosion at Kabul airport. She heard the front door close. She thought about calling Neena to see how she was getting on. It would be nice to hear about Mia who was, what, two? Genuinely nice. She got as far as picking up her phone. Neena would go on about her nice holidays and she didn't have time for that. When you're at university you think you're the same, but when the time comes for homes and children, that's when you see who gets a leg-up. The muscles of familial wealth stand out and you realise they have always been there for them, hidden from view, ready if ever needed beneath the gas bills. The money is one thing but it's a realisation that they are not just themselves, you are not just yourself. And what do you do? Grow bitter, grow apart? Do you pretend not to notice? Convince yourself that you do not care? There, the bitterness, when she was the one with a house and so keen to make her sister jealous. Hypocrite. She was part of it, the cares that took all of them sooner or later.

Liz had seen the rich. She had served them dessert wine. Much easier, when she was twenty-one, to think of them as something monstrous and ridiculous and other, the people she encountered on catering jobs. She didn't think then that they could be her friends, not until a friend's wedding in an old country house. The shock wasn't the house, plenty of people played make-believe for their wedding, but the comfort of the bride with the act of being served, the expectation, in fact, and then you saw her father and her mother and her brother and her brother's wife and children and the whole thing made sense. Liz had felt an immense and sudden shame, for reasons she could not fully place.

Get the guillotine, she'd whispered to John as they'd smoked beneath the bunting. *Chop off their heads.*

She thought it would be Richard, if any of the students, who had rich parents. He spoke like someone with rich parents, the way he held himself, his height. They're always tall or making themselves taller, the sons of privilege.

She would steel herself against them.

Maybe it was her work or maybe it was Ionesco but she'd this idea that being pregnant would turn her into a rhinoceros. More specifically, she imagined she would feel like the rhinoceros in Dürer's woodcut, which he made without having seen a rhinoceros. She could still picture the sheets of strange armour on its lined belly and its grotesque bumpy face. She thought about this with a combination of dread and anticipation. Her body as she knew it would be taken from her, and that terrified her, but at the same time she would be a rhinoceros. All the worry about SCRUM workflows would be splinters beneath her feet. So sustained had this feeling been that lately when she had seen pictures of the black rhinos in Kenya she'd had a sensation she would describe as empathy, as if she too would soon be in their situation. Then, as she saw the rhino on her desktop, she opened a browser to hide it from sight.

On the table was the literary magazine that Tariq had taken from the shelf, face down. It was still open on her story.

'His penis was soft. I was careful not to touch it with my fingers.'

Almost immediately she felt a dislocation, as if she was encountering something written by a different person. 'Instead of kissing him,' she continued, saying the words out loud, barely. 'Instead of kissing him, I lowered my face to his testicles, which I cradled in my hand. The lights had long been switched off and the curtain drawn around the bed. He had been washed only a few hours before, so the odour of soap had not yet faded, but if I dug my nose into the nook of his groin I could taste his scent. I imagined the roots of a potato growing in a dark cupboard. He let out the smallest of moans. Opening my mouth, I covered one of his testicles with my lips.'

She looked up from the page. John was sitting motionless on his broken chair, staring into space. How long had he been there?

'I began to suck on a testicle, softly. It was enjoyable. I knew that my lips, even my lips, were at that moment capable of causing him great pain.'

Her voice had become louder, now that she was reading for an audience. 'I did not touch his penis with my hands, even though it was by then pointing upwards to his belly button. I'll admit I was surprised that he did not attempt to stroke himself, only hold the bed sheet on either side of his hips. He moaned again, a small helpless sound. Patiently, I moved onto the other testicle, doing the same as before, opening my mouth, taking it in, slowly sucking while moving my tongue against the tender skin.'

She looked up again. John was still staring into space.

'Would you like me to keep going?' she asked.

'Yes.'

'His testicles were wet with my saliva. The hair beneath them was slick with drool. I was a little surprised at how much spit had come out of my mouth. I wiped my lips and listened for another moan, urging me to continue, but I could only hear the laboured breathing of those in the beds around us. I moved up and touched the side of my face against his penis. It was surprisingly hot, as if it too had a fever. I felt once more that I was capable of causing him pain, that it was in me to move beyond the threshold of my responsibility and to hurt him. It was in me to damage him in a way from which he could not easily recover, if recover at all.'

She felt a wave of desire inside her, almost sickly, at what she was reading.

'With care I pushed his penis down against his body, using my cheek, then my neck. I could feel his blood pumping against the alcove of my jaw. I thought again about roots searching for soil. I let him move his hips against me. I could tell he enjoyed being there, becoming more confident in his thrusting against my neck. I guided him with my hand away from my collar. I didn't want my uniform to be stained with his precum. His tip was then against the corner of my lips, then the corner of my eye.'

When she had written this, it had been John's body she had imagined. Strange that now it was a body to itself, not John's at all. It was as if by leaving this piece of writing alone, it had grown outwards. She thought of Tariq's hands, Harrie's neck. There were the bodies of men she'd seen on TV. The man in the story flitted between them.

'Against my eye, he didn't dare to move. I could feel a drop of liquid roll down my cheek. I cupped his testicles and gently pulled. It was in me to hurt him. I moved my face away, studied his reaction as I squeezed, as I ran a finger against his tip. I touched myself just to know how wet I was, stroked my clitoris, but the pleasure wasn't coming from there. It was in me to destroy him, as much as to heal him. He shuddered. I watched his face as he came. His penis quivered as the final drops of semen fell onto his stomach and then I left him there.'

She looked at John for a reaction.

'This is the part in the bombed-out city?' he asked.

'Yes.'

'I wonder if you'd write like that now.'

She let the book fall in one hand by her side.

'Do you have an erection?'

When he didn't answer she lifted up the book, looked at the passage again, running through the words.

'I don't think I'd write like this now,' she said.

They had sex on the upstairs landing.

*

My love was already waiting in the boat, impatient to get away, or was it only the moon reflecting on the glass cabin screen, perfectly aligned with his face, one imposed on the other, so that I misread the expression, took his eyes for a trick of light? As we set off from the jetty I believe both of us were quiet because of the moon, which shone with a particular radiance, like a singer dressed in blue standing in front of a red curtain, the threat palpable that she could at any moment step back, or perhaps be pulled back, and disappear into the dark.

There in the water was a cup. I used the hooked pole to snag its handle and hold it aloft. My love was careful in the way he guided it towards him, lowered the hooked end and freed the cup without it crashing onto the boards. He could have been handling a living thing and I wanted to say something about that to him, something that would make him realise it showed him for who I knew him to be, but I could not think of the words.

The cup was ceramic, blue-grey, bulbous and crooked. The glaze was thin around the rim so that it appeared a darker shade. I considered whether I should in fact call it a mug but cup suited it best. It was attractive, handmade and unchipped, but at the same time haunted as if by some part that had been essential to its design but was now absent. I tried to imagine a saucer, how it might look. For whatever reason, I had the strong feeling, I'll call it certainty, that the saucer was broken. Do you understand these things? As untouched as the cup was, I believed its saucer had been shattered into a hundred pieces. It would have been the same colour, blue-grey, round but uneven with an indentation in its centre where the cup would sit, moon-like. Unlike the glass decanter, which had been complete with its stopper, it was difficult to consider the cup holding anything for long. I tipped it out, as if pouring cold tea down the drain. Only a few drops of lake water fell as I shook it dry. I could have been convinced that I'd had a similar cup, a long time ago, when we'd lived with others and our crockery was mixed together. If so, it would have been one of the cups that stayed at the back of the cupboard beside the oven, only the outline of a cup, filling space, over the years accruing a layer of dust-caked grease from the evaporated fluids that we cooked on the stove. A shame, because the cup was misleading in its simplicity, its blue-grey glaze filled with shades and faint spots that I could have contemplated for a long time if it had sat on my writing desk.

My love did not ask to hold it but I handed it to him all the same, and when he cradled it between his two hands I thought again that he could have been holding a living thing, a baby bird, as if the cup was more delicate than I had realised and he wanted to do everything possible to preserve whatever it was he saw as he stared into its interior. I was reminded of the lake on which we were floating. The water was still and the boat was all but motionless, but I felt for some reason more precarious than I had been when the waters were rough, as if even a foot out of place would disrupt the balance of weight and I would stumble into the water. My mind drifted again to a dark green parlour, the rain outside never stopping, the cup filled almost to the brim with tea and a delicate coil of steam rising, a finger hooking around the handle to bring its rim to a pair of red lips, the hot tea touching the mouth before the cup is lowered onto its saucer with a clink.

SEVEN

'I JUST THINK IT's silly,' said Monica. 'We can call 111 now and they can get you an appointment.'

Harrie waved out his hand as if he were batting a fly. 'You know what they'll say. "Recommended to see a medical professional in 48 hours." We might get a call back from an out-of-hours GP, *if we're lucky.*'

'They might say you should go to A&E.'

'Then we'll wait hours and hours to talk to a doctor who'll tell me to follow up with my GP and we'll have wasted the day.'

Monica was breathing hard through her nostrils, Liz saw, feeling suddenly aware of herself. She was close enough to be part of the conversation, but stood there dumb. If only Monica had decided to have this argument somewhere more private, less demanding of her involvement. She nudged a tent peg with the tip of her shoe. And now this silence, which she was no doubt expected to fill. Why couldn't she bring herself to say something? A better sister would've offered something in support, would have added her weight to the push against Harrie's obstinacy.

'Everything is being sent to A&E because the GPs can't cope,' said Harrie. 'And A&E can't cope! I don't want to make things worse.

'I'm absolutely fine,' he said.

'John and Liz are here,' he said, pointing at her.

Monica strode away from the tent.

Harrie stared at the ground, then traipsed after his wife. He caught up not far down the track where they stopped and spoke. Liz was left with John and the children, who were throwing small red berries at the trunk of a nearby tree. Monica's voice was momentarily loud enough to be made out. '… that fucking tent,' she said. Harrie put a hand on her arm. Liz tried not to be seen looking as John knelt beside the children and feigned an interest in their choice of berry.

In time they came back together. Harrie wanted to spend 'only an hour' on his research, but he seemed to realise that his argument for not going to see a doctor was predicated on making the most of the day, so he dropped it quickly. Liz suggested they drive to a swimming pool on one of the leaflets the children had collected from the campsite reception. It was only twenty minutes away and the weather was getting hot, and privately she had a fondness for water slides, enjoyed being flung around their bends. But as they were packing the towels Monica closed herself into the tent and refused to come out, saying only that she didn't want to go anywhere. This time Liz spoke to her through the blue polyester sheet. Not being able to see her, somehow it made it easier to talk. They did not speak about Harrie, only Monica's sudden lethargy, which Liz said was to be expected after days spent outdoors. The fresh air. She offered to take her for something to eat, just the two of them.

In a cafe a short drive away they opted to sit outside, on the back patio where there were flowers in pots and a string of lightbulbs running beneath a large green canvas awning for shade. 'Very cool,' said Monica and she sounded like she meant it. There was the noise of a grass strimmer nearby and the strong smell of food being prepared in the kitchen. Peppers, cumin.

'The university needs to start treating its academics with a little more dignity,' said Monica. 'They have absolutely no conception of how much he does for them.'

Liz disliked that their talk was quickly shackled to Harrie and John and the children. On a cobbled lane leading to the sea they'd once made songs about mint chocolate chip ice cream. Her sister was going to great lengths to speak with utmost certainty, which she always did when she was feeling insecure.

'I'm sure Harrie's fine,' Liz said, dismissively, hearing herself become the younger sister.

'He's under a lot of pressure.'

'I'm not saying he isn't.' She knew it sounded defensive and in response Monica turned her attention up, disconnecting. Liz looked up too. The canvas awning dipped significantly right above their heads. She hadn't noticed it when she'd chosen where to sit.

The sunlight shone through the fabric and she could make out the shapes of many maple seeds floating in a pool of rainwater. The bulge of water and seeds was so great that the rope the cafe had used to tether that particular section of canvas to a brick wall had torn near its edges. There was a good chance, sooner or later, that the rip would spread and the water would break over the heads of whoever was sitting at the table.

'We're considering homeschooling,' said Monica.

'Oh, wow, really? Why?' She'd reacted too much, she realised.

Monica stiffened. 'Well, there's a lot that's antiquated about the school system. We've been to some home ed meetings. We haven't decided yet.'

'You'd give up work?'

'There are some places that do hybrid teaching now. I'd go down a day or two. Maybe Harrie as well.' Her sister shuffled her hands awkwardly on the table. 'Finn was getting into a few fights. You don't know what other children are like.'

There was contempt in the last sentence and even though she knew it wasn't directed at her, Liz felt a blow. They fell again into a pause. Restless, Liz raised an arm and touched the bottom of the bulge in the green canvas. Monica watched her with interest. The tips of Liz's fingers pressed slowly upwards and she could feel the weight of the collected rainwater. As she touched the canvas, some displaced water ran through the tear near its binding, spilling loudly onto an empty patio chair. Monica looked horrified, to Liz's delight.

'Do you know enough to teach them?' Liz asked, lowering her arm. 'I'm not suggesting you're stupid or anything,' she added, even though this had in fact been her intention. 'But with the maths, you know.'

'I work in a bank.'

'That's more customer service.'

'No.'

'Didn't you get a C at GCSE?'

'You remember that, do you? You don't remember to book the bikes, but you remember my maths GCSE.'

Liz gasped. 'I *did* remember the bikes.'

'You were meant to book them for the whole two weeks.'

'It wasn't cost-effective, not if we're only using them for a few days.'

Monica was about to respond when the waitress emerged from the doorway with their coffees on a tray. She smiled and they smiled back. She told them their fajita wraps would be out in a minute. A robin flew down and hopped on the floor, pecked at a dried maple seed then a cigarette end.

'Anyway, I got a B in maths,' said Monica. 'Almost an A.'

She was looking off at something on the brick wall. Liz took in her sister's profile, the lines under her eyes. 'There must be a lot of parents thinking the same, about what to do with schools,' she offered.

'It's different now.'

In response to this, Liz blew the air out of her mouth.

'What?'

'Nothing,' Liz sighed. 'Look, I'm sure Finn and Ciara will be fine with whatever. They're confident kids.'

She hoped it would satisfy her. Monica often praised her children's confidence, loved to talk about them leading other kids at school, taking control of games. It was the same as Liz's manager, who loved to call his son a ringleader, the same as Neena, who would talk about little Mia and her love of art, her control of the paintbrush. Parents see what they want to see, she supposed. Here's what I hold dear, there it is in you. Here is what I fear I do not have, not enough. Where did it leave the child if every parent was pulling out themselves? What qualities in her child would she tell others were in abundance? *You should see the way she cracks a joke, her farts are sublime.*

She pictured a top hat upended on a round glass table, a magician's sleeve plunging into the interior, rooting around.

'I don't know,' Monica said. She was looking away again from the table, now towards the kitchen window clouded with steam. 'They don't tell you how hard it is. Just wait until they start nursery and school and you're dealing with bug after bug after bug. Non-stop! They don't tell you that, not the full extent. I'm surprised more people don't go mad.'

'Yeah.'

'You're sick all the fucking time. You're doing everything with a head cold or a horrible cough or chills. It's not as bad as it was when they were smaller but, fuck… Nobody tells you.'

Monica was by then leaning back in the patio chair, but her eyes were still on the kitchen window. Liz watched as her sister closed them for a few seconds, as if she were a cat resting in the sunlight.

The robin flew down and pecked around the same spot as before. Was it expecting something else? *Nobody tells you.* There again the shut door, her body square behind. Oh no, not me, I've never been preggers. Then again, that wasn't entirely true, was it? She justified it to herself with the fuzziness of the memory, like something she'd read rather than experienced, so too the slightness of the event, which did not strike her as major, certainly not traumatic, just one of those things that went un-recalled. Kieran Crouch, who had got her pregnant, she supposed, if you called two days a pregnancy, a month late and a positive test she'd bought from Boots on her lunch break, but still then only two days when she was twenty-two, in which she did not quiver and shake and lie awake at night, but it was two days like any other, perhaps a bit more to drink, but she had made plans to go out and she was not one for early nights. She did not tell her friends, she did not tell anyone, and when on Sunday she bled she certainly did not tell Kieran Crouch, who was a friend from university and even though they had been sleeping with each other she had known at the time they were growing apart. The nights when he would ask if she was *up* felt a part of that knowledge, not at all an attempt to reverse or transcend into some new way of being in each other's lives. The sex was without exception rough. A split condom wouldn't have been a surprise but if it had happened he hadn't told her. For her part, she hadn't noticed. John would naturally want to know why she'd kept it from him. The honest truth is that it had not been important to her. Only now did it strike her. Only now would she think of it.

She turned back on her chair, looked at the kitchen window and wished the food would come.

*

John pictured lines from parent to child, not like those on a family tree, not as ordered, more as lines running and joining and shaping the features of the face, the almond shape of Finn's eyes, the angle of his nose, the lines in fact being all there was and the bodies a knot, a nodule on their path. Here was Harrie and there was Finn and they were buds on a line just as he was a tight little tangle on his own, converging beneath his own mother and father, stemming onwards with a mind of its own, if you looked at things that way, took a step back and took the whole vast tangle for what it was, forever reaching for no discernible reason beyond competition, the passing on. The boundaries between

150

Harrie and Finn were at that moment insignificant, while simultaneously John felt a grand separation, the only member of their party with a line unwoven.

They walked because John couldn't get a rental bike for the day. Harrie seemed to know where he was going and walking was no problem, he'd said, slapping his plump thigh as if it were the bonnet of a car. He set a pace, despite the slight limp on his injured foot, that they soon had to slow when Ciara complained she'd lost a shoe, which they found at a fork in the road and Harrie said something about second opportunities and led them in a different direction, seemingly arbitrarily, which John did not appreciate, even though one way was as good as the other. 'Weren't we going that way?' he said, attempting to come across as unbothered but aware also that he had slowed and was looking back at the fork.

'Don't worry, I have a cognitive map,' Harrie replied, tapping his head. Why was he always saying things like that? John did not want to contend with his brother-in-law's cheerful domination but going back to the fork and insisting on their original path felt like the pettiest thing imaginable. As they walked on, the light shone staccato through the trees and John remembered a story about soldiers in the First World War who, marching in the woods, grew intoxicated by the rhythm of light through branches. He read that it could put you into a trance, the sunlight flashing.

'The girls worry,' said Harrie.

The girls, thought John.

'It's not an emergency.'

'Yes, no,' said John, and then: 'when I had a stomach ache Liz made me see a doctor.' In truth, Liz had not made him see a doctor, even if she had insisted, even if he had felt at the time that she'd only wanted him to get help so that he would stop his moaning. Harrie rolled his eyes and clucked his tongue. He would be assured, John thought, now that he had established some sympathy against his wife.

'We cut through here,' said Harrie.

'Monica only wants to make sure,' said John, thinking there was more to come but tripping over himself so that the final words hung awkwardly over the chatter of Ciara and Finn.

'My own father sometimes needed to lie down,' said Harrie, adamant. 'I remember one time we laid him on the dining table.'

'Right so.' John thought of his father fallen against the back door, the impossibility of it, yes, the wrongness.

'We didn't give it a second thought,' said Harrie. He clambered up, clumsy on a bank of dirt. 'It's not an emergency.'

As they continued down a narrow bridle path Finn began to say 'emergency' over and over. Ciara joined in.

'Emergency,' said Ciara.

'Emergency,' said Finn.

They were now saying it to each other. Every time they repeated the word, it was held differently, now it bumped in the middle, now it rose at the end. Finn was saying it quickly now, the end and the beginning deformed so that the word was all but killed completely.

'MERgecyMERgecy.'

Ciara had gone back to walking in silence and Finn also seemed to be losing interest in what he was doing but he kept repeating himself nevertheless, despite the fact he had stopped to pick up a branch, snapped off the twigs to make it smooth. His voice took on a life of its own, the word no longer running into itself but spoken in whispered bursts.

'Emergency... emergency.'

John said 'emergency' to himself, quietly inside his mouth. He said it again, conscious this time of his desire to flatten it out like pockets of air in wallpaper. The separation between the words now felt artificial. Regency, emerge, Gen Z, immerse, just see. He couldn't imagine it on a sign in a hospital. Accident and emergency. How has the word ever contained a sense of importance? What had given it power when the sound it was making felt so arbitrary? 'Emergency,' he said in his mouth, and perhaps Harrie saw him do this because he turned to Finn and spoke firmly.

'Can you please *stop it*.'

Harrie blew the air out of his nostrils and focused on the path ahead. Finn swished his stick at the broad leaves that hung low, bringing one to the ground. He kept his gaze down as he swished and swished at the leaves.

John thought about his mistake, the black dog crossing the river. The longer he went without practising Hungarian, the less sense he'd be able to make, the language would sour in his head. Already he was uncertain, like a tightrope walker suddenly awake to the distance below. He had made mistakes before. To learn a language is to make mistakes. Why was he so knocked? Told off. There were blotches on the broad flat leaves. He wished he knew the name of this tree. Light brown blotches in many places, visible through the sunlit undersides. Diseased or part of the natural course of things? He wished he could say the name of the tree. The woods so calm. A light breeze. Was this the turning point? A change in temperament. If only he could know the name of the tree.

All of a sudden, a dizzying sense that he was not unseen by the woods around him. He, who used to give little thought to the cycles of plants and who cringed at the personification of wild things on TV.

He cringed too at the thought of an epiphany, so privileged.

You spend so long not getting someone pregnant, he thought. Not that there's a worry. It's not an emergency. *Emergency.* He looked at the sunlight through the leaves, coming in and out. How will things change between us? The edges of the light, the limit. What possessed you to ask a question like that? I'll give you the answer. No, I won't. I'll struggle around it. Remember, I'm an honest soul, despite it all. I just can't go on if you won't see me for what I am. The line of the light on the floorboards, only clear at hours like this. He wanted a cigarette, even though he had not smoked in months. We are together in life, for the purposes of life. Whose voice is this, he thought, coming out of me now? You stopped me on the bridge over the A-road and I promised you it was what I wanted. I was on my way to the train station.

In the hallway of the optician's, where a trio of fold-out chairs had been set up, blue and black, there had been the smell of freshly settled rain. So unmistakable was the scent that, after scanning the green walls for signs of damp, he'd twisted each ankle in turn to inspect the undersides of his shoes. The optician had been a woman his age and she'd stood very straight in a white coat with her hands neatly folded, in a way that made her seem totally in control of her environment. She'd gestured to the stool where he was to sit. No room to refuse. He'd done as he was told, resting his chin on a small plastic stand as instructed. Only when she'd asked if he was comfortable did he recognise her as a woman he had earlier that same morning made repeated eye contact with on the train. She'd flicked the switch. His right eye had been suspended in a beam of white light. She'd asked him to look to the left then the right. He'd been able to hear her breathing and had been mindful of his own. She'd asked him to keep looking at the light. He'd done so, and as she'd once again refocused the machine, he'd caught a glimpse of the reflection of his eye, what she must've been seeing. He'd exhaled slowly through his nostrils. The eye had been unlike his own, totally unlike his impression of his eye. She'd asked him to look up and then she'd told him that if God lived anywhere, it would be in our eyes.

Finn pulled on his father's sleeve. He could spy a man, he said. They did not stop walking. Harrie looked in the direction his son was pointing, told him in a cheery voice that it was probably another person enjoying a stroll in the woods. John could not see anyone at first. Then, a flash of light a little further and, there, a person standing between the trees, all but invisible if not for the glint of sun on the lenses of their binoculars. John saw it was Sweet, aiming interest square in their direction. He was wearing the same drooping black sun hat as before, the rest of him clad now in camo, and he must've noticed their awareness, it seemed, because he lowered his binoculars, turned slightly to one side and raised them again at something else. They would likely have left him if it weren't for Ciara, who strode away from the bridle path.

'Ciara!' shouted Harrie, mouth cupped with both hands.

'Sorry!' he shouted to Sweet when she reached him. 'Ciara! Let's leave him alone!'

'She's fine!' shouted Sweet in return.

'He just saw a blackbird!' shouted Ciara.

Next Finn, then Harrie, then John left the path and walked to where Jim Sweet was standing. He smiled as they neared but soon appeared sheepish to have them surround him. The children were fascinated with the binoculars, both of them studiously following the clunky black object in his hand.

Beyond the initial hellos and how are yous, there was a strained pause as they waited for him to tell them what he was doing. With the slightly put-upon air of someone not prepared to give a presentation to the general public, he explained he was surveying the local bird population.

'Sorry to bother you at work,' said Harrie.

'No, no.'

'It must have been a surprise to see us through your binoculars,' said John.

'It was certainly a surprise to see this one,' Sweet gestured to Ciara, 'walking towards me when I was so taken up with the branches.'

'But you saw us on the path too.'

He shook his head. 'Had no idea you were here until you come up to me. A nice surprise though.'

He kept John's gaze.

'You must've been looking just over our heads then.'

Sweet did have a clipboard with him and who was John to fall into fearful tropes when he had done nothing but his work, which he had no grounds to begin judging. It was narcissism to think this man did not have things to be getting on with, that he had been for whatever reason watching them.

'Fewer swifts each year,' Sweet said with a stoic flatness. 'More buzzards,' he added, an upward inflection, helping them to understand that this was not all bad, there are winners as well as losers. John had some faint thought about the risk of imbalance, more buzzards, more pressure on prey, but he had no real certainty about what buzzards ate on a day-to-day basis and he did not want to ask a question that even the children could answer.

'How often do you have to do this?' he asked and it sounded patronising when he had meant it to be friendly, the 'have', which he regretted and felt again that he was losing control over language, not only Hungarian but English, as if the movement of his limbs had become loose and flailing, as in a dream when you need to land a punch but cannot draw the power. The 'have' took Sweet's agency away and in that moment he could see the effect, as the warden cast an agitated glance to the binoculars and the clipboard in turn.

'There's about twelve spots I'm to go, and I go to them all every two weeks.'

'Nice to be outside in this weather,' said Harrie.

John thought of fewer swifts. An empty sky where a swift should be. It was odd to consider life as only having one chance in all instances. If a body was smashed to bits, obliterated, then it made sense for life to have no home, but a body that for only a moment had pushed life out. Why could it not come back? Last night he'd watched on his phone a video of a woman freeing a baby stingray that had become stuck in its egg sac. The little thing was unmoving until it was pulled free, unalive until it had been unfurled and only then had it rippled strangely out of sight. It had been alive the whole time, of course, but nobody would have noticed if it had stopped living, clutch down, before the necessity of surging back into existence. Why shouldn't life come back, especially when it had barely started, a false start, another try? Only fair, you'd think. If all the parts were still there, the soul could surely be coaxed, surely tempted, if it wasn't such a flighty thing. Mermaid's purses, they call them, those dark alien-looking sacs that incubate rays, sharks. No pockets when you have a fish tail, he guessed. He imagined a mermaid rooting around for her keys.

*

We sat for a good while with the boat still tied to the jetty, wordlessly enjoying the motion of the lake knocking us against the side. The tyre that was tied to the hull made a satisfying squelch and sigh and I lost for a few moments my grasp of time, so that I could not recall if we had agreed to take the boat out onto the lake; whether this was something either of us wanted, or whether it was enough to sit opposite one another in view of the house, in easy reach of land.

I noticed then that my love was looking beyond me, out onto the waters, with a look of determined concentration, as if she were watching a film on a cinema screen. When I followed her gaze I could see nothing but the water stretching off into the distance, not even the opposite shore, the trees, the hills that rose up as a ridge on the horizon. But what is a horizon if you cannot see it? My love was unwavering in her focus and I wanted to know what she could see playing out in front of her, what was making her clench her jaw and stare so fixedly, as if in looking away she would fail. I stood to untie the rope from the jetty and only then did she turn to me, fearful, knowing that we would soon move close to what she had seen from a distance.

We moved slowly until we were to my estimation in the centre of the lake, the opposite shore unseen, and there she gasped, reaching for my arm and making me stop the engine. She pointed to something in the water. At first I could barely make it out, the body was face down and its legs were submerged. The pole was just about long enough. With two hands I could grasp one end and let the other fall on top, which pushed the body for a moment beneath the surface before it rose again. There were no clothes to catch hold of, but if I was careful I could position the hook so that it found purchase on some cavity of the back. It would have been impossible to hook the body enough to lift it out of the water onto the jetty. It was too heavy and the hook was small, only meant for catching a latch on the window. But if I was gentle and if the boat was slow I could drag it beside us as we returned to the shore. Although I knew my love was beside me I did not want to meet her eye. She took the wheel and I held the pole.

When we reached the jetty I left the boat for the boards, step by step until the body was brought closer to the shore, until it touched the ground. I did not want to tear anything by forcing it further but I urged it a few inches more, just enough so that it was unlikely to be taken back up by the water. The smell was rank, sickly-sweet, like a drop of perfume on rotting meat. It lay there face down, a man in form, but a form swollen to the point of breaking, as if its bounds could crack and leak, an expanding puddle, pink and skittish before shrinking, evaporating in the night air. With my hand on my nose I approached and knelt, observing the face turned away from the shore, bloated beyond recognition and cast in shadow.

T HEY GOT TO THE pool just as it was opening, the car park nearly empty but already a small trail of cars filtering in from the main road. Inside the complex there was a long row of segmented stalls to undress and change before passing through another door that had the word POOL on a yellow plastic sign, the two 'O's made to look like striped rubber rings. It was a clever little system, thought John, as he folded down the wooden bench that doubled as a lock for both of the inward-turning doors. How many people have had sex here, he wondered, the sound from other stalls clear in the echoey space, Harrie's voice clearest of all. 'Put your shoes here. Wait. Don't lift that yet, dear. Daddy's still getting changed.' Liz was turned away from him, pulling up her swimsuit.

'You look great,' he said.

She looked over her shoulder then carried on.

'What's wrong?'

'What?' she whispered.

'Is something wrong?'

'No.'

He hadn't worn his trunks for at least two years and they felt tight, no mirror in the stall but he could tell his sides would look squeezed and the shame of it pulled at his posture so that he walked unnaturally as they gathered their bags, now stuffed with their clothes, and crossed the threshold into a large room of lockers. The real world was left behind. He caught a glimpse of himself in a mirror, perhaps not as bad as he'd feared, if he held himself straight, led with his chest. His upper arms looked strong, at least not weak, and besides he would soon be hidden in the water. The rest of the family spilled from a stall further down the row. 'Holdonholdon,' called Harrie. Monica rolled her eyes at John.

The interior was sprawling and elaborate, with nooks and openings that led to different avenues for water to flow. It was also, John saw, Japanese themed, with a statue of a sumo wrestler near a sauna area and a small, red arched bridge across a section of the pool that wouldn't have looked out of place in a lush Japanese garden, at least how he imagined a Japanese garden might look. Standing there, he could see a large central area where a wave machine was roiling the pool in great swellings that rippled down to the shallows, close to the mouth of a slide where water poured from a large tube shaped like a dragon's jaw. The kids ran straight to the steps that would take them to its summit, Liz close behind. Elsewhere there was a sauna and steam room and John could see a section of the pool appeared to pass below some sort of plastic curtain, daylight visible beyond, and presumably some further reaches were out in the open. He was filled with a sense of wonder, he realised, at the level of care and thought that had been taken in the design of this place. Above him red beams arched into a central domed ceiling, much more elaborate than was needed for a family-friendly swimming pool, and this gave the many-sided space a sense of unity that bordered on the ecclesiastical, an engineered dream of collective bathing held within a grand pagoda.

Places like this hadn't been reopened for long. How many people would feel comfortable enough to come? He eyed up the plastic curtain that led outside, fiddled with the blue rubber band around his wrist that held his locker key and crossed the bridge to Harrie and Monica.

*

Finn threw himself into the dark when the light turned to green. His scream was comical in the way it echoed back up to Liz, who was then alone in the white-tiled space, no one else queuing for the slide and no lifeguard to stop her, only a set of automated lights. As his screaming came to an end, she stepped forward into the rushing water, both hands on an overhanging bar. She eyed the red light, suddenly tense. She could hear the wet slap of bare feet below her, someone climbing the stairs. They would soon reach her. The light was still red. She wanted to go before they reached her. She tightened her grip on the bar, playing in her head the way she would

swing herself forwards. The footsteps were close, someone else was behind her. She did not turn around. The
light was red. The light was green.

Could it have taken, she thought, at this very moment,
deep within, some obscure chemistry enacting its plan
with little care for the rest of her, getting on in silence
as she sloshed down the tube? Done in the dark with
a mind of its own, part and not part of her, part of her
still, she'd say, one cell turning to two, to four, to eight
and on and on as she'd seen in videos, a shorthand for
new life, its exponential spread but all within her, a body
directed by a body. Follow the instructions to the letter
and you can't go wrong. I am at the moment only myself,
she thought, only with myself, even if I am without my
knowledge playing host to cells that are unfolding like
pieces of paper, neat and square, unfurling until they
push against my sides. His semen dripped down my
leg. I wiped it with a tissue. I am myself alone in the
dark, she thought and wished there was a way to know
already, one hand touching her navel. This time, maybe.
My God! You're glowing, they'll coo on a crisp autumn
morning, a winter baby, a golden host, no matter the
blood diverted, the calcium sucked from her bones. I
am myself, only with myself, in all likeliness, because it
might well be nothing, most probably nothing. There's
the voice of reason. Nothing to know and in any case
it is nothing more than what she'd wanted for herself,
all these months of wanting. Could it really have taken?
Not impossible. She'll need to tighten the reins if she's

to grow, get as good a grip before being pulled in every which way, lungs and liver squished in ungodly positions. She will need to collect herself, neaten the chairs and dust the shelves and there's time for that still, in spite of fatty folds above her knees, in spite of gravity, which will no doubt spit her out in the end, after she's been stretched and sucked, her breasts like old socks. Why this fear coming over her now? It is only what she'd wanted, flung to the side of the tube as the slide curled outside of the building and for a moment the red plastic alight with sun and a giddy thought that she was not alone and she would soon surrender herself to forces that were beyond her, that would take her and bend her into shapes that she could not have imagined, and so the fear was mingled with excitement at the prospect of transformation. I will be cut in half, she thought, both pieces me, always me, at least until it has a name but even then, she thought, even then it is made of me. At this moment in time, God willing, it is without doubt a part of me, my voice speaking for it as much as my toenails, which have something of a life of their own, the way they grow without command, following the instruction that has been passed on and passed on from Christ knows where. I am myself alone in the dark, she thought. If there is another unfolding then it does so under my jurisdiction, the cloak of my keeping, and it is my voice alone that breaks the silence. I am not smudged by my body, not even in the moments I am most humbled by my instincts, as when I make a resigned lurch to the toilet bowl and accept that I will throw up, mouth wet, warm saliva, or when I am bent over from a period, my voice remaining, uneroded, a house atop a sheer cliff. I will not be annihilated, she told herself as she was propelled downwards and knocked an elbow, the pain fleeting. I will not be annihilated by what will press my kidneys and entrails, which is what I have asked for, which I have taken to be inevitable, like the coming of winter, not winter, spring, of course spring, naturally, spring.

She was shot out into the light, her head underwater and a moment of sheer panic at the plunge before standing and treading from the mouth of the dragon. Finn and Ciara were ecstatic above a silver ladder.

'Your face was so funny it went glub glub glub,' shouted Finn, contorting his lips.

Liz felt self-conscious as she climbed out of the pool, her swimming costume overspilling with water in a way that made her feel like a dredged bicycle. She scanned for the others. A gong sounded and a group of swimmers began to rise and fall with the motion of the wave machine. Finn ran back to the stairs that led to the top of the water slide.

'I need a wee,' said Ciara.

Liz took her by the hand. She searched again for Harrie or Monica. They walked back to the locker room, over the red bridge, Liz looking all the while for the parents, but they were soon by the women's toilets and so they went in. There she ushered Ciara towards a cubicle but her niece did not close the door and she realised she was expected to join, so she went in too, feeling unprepared but also trusted. She helped Ciara with her swimsuit and then let her do her business, which was done in song, as the girl launched into a rendition of 'He's got the whole world in his hands' that was surprisingly loud and abrasive. Ciara kicked her legs as she sang and looked Liz square in the eye. In return Liz smiled and nodded her head, and when Ciara was finished she quietly clapped.

When they washed Ciara's hands in the sink another woman was there, wearing a bright blue swim cap. '*Very* good singing,' she told them. This compelled Ciara to begin again, although the words had slipped, replaced by throaty sounds that carried only a faint memory of the original tune.

'How old is she?'

'Eight.'

The woman waited for her to say more. Liz was aware of the assumption. Not the first time. In the past she'd laughed and shaken her head, *no, no, no.*

'She has a lot of energy,' the woman ventured.

'She's at that age.'

There was a bright spin of transgression. Liz put more soap on her niece's hands.

'I honestly don't know where they get it all,' the woman said, her posture becoming more relaxed. 'I look after my grandson and the things that come out of his mouth.' There was the loud sound of the dryer as the woman lowered and raised her hands in hot air. Ciara turned on a tap and gave herself a cursory splash but was then away from Liz, running out of the ladies' toilet towards the pool. The woman had finished drying her hands although she did not immediately move away.

'You don't want them to change,' said Liz.

'No.'

The woman in the blue swim cap gave a smile and looked then as if she might turn to leave.

'She had a difficult birth,' said Liz.

The woman's brow narrowed into an expression of concern. She leant slightly towards Liz, at the same time her eyes glancing at the door. 'Oh?'

Liz could feel her heart beating. She was getting away from herself. Never before had she done this. A hint of panic had come across the woman's face and Liz wondered if it was because she took her for someone who was unpredictable, perhaps unstable. She had blurted the words, hardly a calm admission.

'So it always makes me happy to hear her sing,' Liz said, and this went some way to assure the woman that she was not in distress. The worry shifted into a look of understanding. The woman's expression grew kindly and it reminded Liz of her mother.

'She's a beautiful little girl,' said the woman, adamant. 'You should be proud.' Some stem of emotion appeared then to rise in the older woman, her eyes moistening and the kindness on her face deepening into another shade, one that froze Liz to the spot as if the woman in the blue swim cap had decided at that moment to take her by the hands and grasp them tightly. From where had this come, she wondered, imagining her mother singing along to the radio one Easter Sunday morning, when she had walked into the kitchen unheard and her mother had turned with a lingering intensity that Liz had never witnessed on her before or since, as if she had been caught naked but also on fire and from the look on her face it had been clear she did not want to be extinguished.

*

Harrie was immersed, up to his eyes in water that was cooler for being in the open, even though the sun was already hot and John could feel himself burning. Both he and Monica were perched on a submerged ledge with the waterline around their collarbones, but Harrie had crouched lower, a few feet apart from them, his hair slicked back and his eyes closed to the light so that he appeared reptilian. Nearby some children had passed through the plastic curtain and were exploring the outside section of the pool but they gave the trio of adults a wide berth and John thought it must be because of the way Harrie was crouched, which even he would have felt scared of disturbing.

'A bit of peace,' said Monica, directed at her husband. Harrie opened his eyes a fraction to squint at her, raised himself just enough for his lips to breach the water.

'Is Prune with them?'

He glanced at John, then closed his eyes once more, lowering his lips back beneath the surface.

'She can manage with them for a few minutes,' said Monica.

The parents of the children had joined them outside, as well as a younger man and woman, who walked through the water to an isolated nook in the outdoor pool, built and styled to look like some kind of lagoon. The daylight made it harder for the illusion to stand up, with the tiling clear and the sight of the complex with its broad concrete walls and the red coil of the water-slide passing in and out of the building above them. The couple sat together, her on his lap, both facing in the direction of Harrie and sharing some words that were too quiet for John to make out. The woman arched her head to kiss the man, the boy, he could have been a teenager. John noticed that Monica was also watch-ing but she must have become aware of staring because she turned her attention upwards, to the red slide that was translucent enough to make out the vague shape of a body as it passed through that particular section of the tube. John thought of the small intestine, as far as he understood it; the toasted muffin he'd eaten that morning.

'Give her a taste of things to come,' said Monica.

'What's that?'

'Put her through her paces.'

He made a face of grim understanding, which she seemed to enjoy. Her attention was for a brief moment on his lips. 'See how she does,' she said, and he was aware of a cruel edge to her voice that he decided to hear as playful.

The sun had by then moved directly behind the winding water slide and all three of them were cast in red. Soon Ciara crossed the threshold to the outdoor pool. Liz was close behind, directing her to where the adults were sitting. Monica waved enthusiastically at the sight of her daughter, who splashed over and launched into a narrative about the slide, how fast it had been and how she'd almost hit the person in front of her who was going too slow and sitting up like a *sillyman* instead of lying on his back.

Harrie stood up in the water and looked beyond Liz to the plastic curtain.

'I can't stand the bumps,' said Monica. 'Those little ridges all the way down bump bump bump on your spine.'

'Is Finn not with you?'

With the water glistening on his skin and the damp dark hair of his not insubstantial stomach lit by the red shadow of the water slide, Harrie looked even more like a creature of another time. He held an intensity which for the first time made John uneasy, as if Harrie might turn to him there, sitting beside Monica, with real anger. Liz told Harrie she thought Finn was on the slide. Wordlessly, he waded away from them, disappearing behind the plastic curtain.

Liz's face fell.

'It's okay,' said Monica with surprising calmness, and John thought it was because she was happy her sister had failed. 'It's not easy keeping on top of them,' Monica said, shuffling closer on the underwater ledge to John and beckoning Liz to sit on her other side. Her hip was touching his. There they watched Ciara put on her goggles and hold her head below the waterline for a few seconds before resurfacing in a gasp of air.

After a little while, Harrie came back through the plastic curtain. He was alone. 'Can I have your help?' His voice was composed, directed at Monica.

Instead of wading, she pulled herself out of the pool and walked quickly to a glass door that led to the interior. John and Liz met each other's eyes. Ciara swam towards the young couple in the nook. The man was kissing the woman's shoulder but she pulled away when the interloper approached. They said hello to Ciara, who sank down below the surface and at this the woman moved with some urgency from the man's lap.

'Should we go in?' asked John. He didn't want to make Liz feel worse but he was struggling to sit still, feeling an event looming that would crash on top of them if he didn't try to fix it.

'What about Ciara?' Her lips were pursed. She shot an accusatory look at her niece and lowered her voice. 'I only left him because she needed the toilet.'

He leant back on the ledge in an effort to look relaxed. The couple had surrendered their nook and were wading to another section of the pool. Ciara was face down in the water.

'He'll be fine,' he said.

They went inside and Liz made Ciara hold her hand as they searched for her parents. It was not immediately obvious where they were and John tried to be calm as he scanned the groups of bathers for a recognisable face. It was as if they had drifted into a no man's land, where he was the lost child and his parents had long departed. The splendour of the swimming pool became mocking and he wished it was a daydream from which he could stir himself.

It transpired that Finn had wedged himself into a sheltered bend on the rapids, where water was pushed through a winding corridor by submerged jets, and he had been kicking out at anyone who was taken up by the current. Harrie had been forced to grab him as the water carried him past, and John saw the father scolding the son on the side of the pool, holding one of his wrists, bent close to his face as he spoke. He wasn't close enough to hear what was being said, Harrie wasn't shouting, but there was a look of shame on Finn's face that gave John a sudden and terrible feeling of empathy. He thought of his own father, how scary he could be.

Soon, in the wave pool, they rose together, the children in their parents' arms, pushing off from the floor tiles to keep their heads above water. The group had tightened ranks. John's body became thoughtless, un-articulated except for the instinct to jump when the waves surged, his limits drawn tight to a core and at the same time enmeshed with those around, the family structured like diamonds as they laughed with a manic fervour. There in front of him were Liz's hands and there was Harrie's wide and wild eyes and Monica's open mouth and they were all reliant on each other. Harrie flung Ciara into the air with the next wave and time froze as she hung suspended, her teeth bared.

Later in the shallows John thought of his neighbour and her kindness to him. Mrs Walsh and her apple tree. When he would help her gather the fallen fruit in the late summer she would tell him jokes that he did not understand but was always so happy in the telling of them that he'd laugh all the same. She gave his mother an apple pie with his father's name written in pastry the year he died. But he hadn't spoken to her for more than a decade. He'd only been told by his mother that she'd died on a ventilator and it had been sad to hear but she'd been old and he didn't know her very well. A few days later he found out that she wanted her savings to go to him. He, who had helped to pick up her fallen apples, who had done nothing for her since leaving home many years before and who had given her no thought amongst his strivings.

He overheard Monica asking Harrie if a sauna was the best thing for him. His response was whispered but whatever was said made her raise her hands in surrender.

There was a weight in her eyes that might have been too much to bear, but she took a deep breath as if drawing herself together and she turned, resolute, to her sister. 'They do cocktails.'

*

It was only midday when they sat, the two of them, in the bar, their towels around their shoulders and a clear view of the crowded pool. Monica angled the straw of her piña colada in Liz's direction. She declined with a headshake. She would have, if not for the feeling that she was pregnant, which was probably nothing but she had it in her head. Monica's eyes lingered, a slight rise of the eyebrow but nothing said. There was space given for Liz to protest or deny or correct but she did not want to cross the line into language, not if it would set her up to be knocked back. She was worried Monica would push the matter further but her sister only sucked her straw and stared out at the men who were carrying one child each on their shoulders and letting them fight to unseat the other.

'Will you get a piano?' asked Monica.

Liz blew the air out of her cheeks.

'No?'

'Meh.'

Maybe she will write something instead, she thought. Why not string some sentences together, see where it takes her? The more time away from work, the more she felt the possibility of breaking once again into that space. She could feel the movement within her, like burrowing creatures, and it was possible to press her hands to the sand, dig them out. The thought excited her. She did not know yet what to write but there was movement and that was a start, and if the movement was still there by the time she got home she would take a pen and paper from the kitchen drawer, no excuse.

Finn gripped his sister's wrists and cackled as he bent one way in an attempt to unbalance her from Harrie's shoulders. There were words within reach, very close to the surface, as if she could already say them but did not know what they meant. If she dived into the pool, if she got away from the others. Monica sucked the last of her drink from the ice. Liz spotted then the woman with the blue swim cap, sitting in the water with a younger woman and a boy. She turned in her direction and Liz immediately looked away, back to Monica, who was still watching the others but with a faraway expression on her face, as if she was not looking at all. Ciara fell into the water with a splash. 'This is the life,' said Liz, wanting her sister to agree. Monica did not seem to hear her. She looked out at the pool and sucked again the ice at the bottom of her glass.

'This is the life,' Liz repeated, cringing at the platitude, which she'd only said in the first place to raise her sister out of whatever foul mood she was dipping her toe into. Was she pretending not to hear her on purpose?

Was this about the piano? She wouldn't say it again, she decided, and sipped her pineapple juice. Liz realised then that the woman in the blue swim cap was coming towards them. The little boy was in tow, holding onto his grandmother's hand as they went to find something to drink. As she passed, Liz put down her glass and smiled warmly but the woman made an active effort to avoid meeting her gaze.

'Yeah,' said Monica, leaning back in her chair and looking up to the high, domed ceiling. 'This is life.'

*

The sauna was a squeeze. Harrie and John took the second row, a bald stranger sat slumped below them on the first. The light was dim and amber and it burnished their sweat-soaked bellies. Harrie breathed deeply. It seemed he wanted to be free of some tension. He pushed the hot air out of his mouth, cracked his knuckles and slapped his hands on his wet thighs loud enough for the stranger to momentarily raise his head. John felt conscious again of his sides. He would join Liz on her next run, he would start again on the dumb-bells. The stranger coughed into his hand and their silence took a sharper angle.

'When do you want to go fishing?' asked John, pushing out his chest and feeling a bead of sweat drip down his back. Harrie blew the air from his nostrils and smiled slightly without looking up. He knew what was being attempted, John thought. He could see his paltry effort to bridge a space between them.

'I don't know but I'm glad you're keen.'

He turned to John with a look that was inscrutable. Was he angry? What reason could he have, when he'd done nothing to insult him. It would be ridiculous to apologise. He wouldn't even know what he was apologising for.

'Let's see if Monica allows me,' Harrie added, rolling his shoulders in a way that made him take up more space. After this he exhaled and settled, closing his eyes, and John did not want to push on with the conversation if it would mean picking at the frays. He uttered an ambiguous but sympathetic hum that was taken no further and for several minutes they sat without speaking as the hot air passed in and out of them. At one point the stranger raised his head and let out a quiet, tuneful sigh, but then slumped and was silent once more. When Monica opened the glass door there was a relief of coolness. She asked if Harrie could keep an eye on the children, give her a break. Liz was no longer enough, it seemed. John stood up too but Harrie urged him to sit and so he remained in the sauna as Monica climbed beside him.

'Was he okay?' she asked after the door was closed behind her husband.

'Fine.'

She breathed deeply. He thought then of a heavy red curtain pulled open along a brass rail. The stranger

ran a hand over his bald head and seemed to somehow slump even further forward. Harrie was fine, he
repeated to himself. He felt Monica's hand on his. Her
fingers were searching for his palm. Without hesitation
he moved his thumb around her knuckles. They held
hands then without saying anything and he did not
know what to make of it. He looked at the glass door.
Their hands were low enough on the bench that he
could slip free if it opened without being seen. Their
skin was wet. He did not move an inch and neither
did she. He thought of Harrie, leant against a tree in
the woods. Was Monica thinking of him too? She
squeezed his hand and let go.

In the men's showers he stood naked with Harrie
and Finn, the father rubbing shampoo into his son's
hair and Finn resisting, crying out as the foam touched
his eyes. There were other men around them and nearly
all were turned to face the wall. John did the same,
wanting to hide his nudity even if part of him wanted
it to be seen. It would put him back into his skin, he
thought. He had felt unreal since Monica held his hand,
as if it was only something he had imagined. On reflection it was childlike, or at least that's how he chose to
think of it and how he would describe it if anyone were
to ask him. She had been anxious about Harrie and she
had needed someone to hold onto, and he had wanted
to show her that he was a point of stability, an iron
hoop nailed into the rocks. They had known each other
a long time.

John noticed then a redness to the water running off Harrie and Finn. He pointed it out and Harrie raised his right foot. The gash was bleeding slightly, the plaster fallen away.

*

My love and I brought the boat out a while from the shore, the night sky covered with a lid of clouds. We could barely make each other out, the motion of the water gently rocking us back and forth. The day had been tiring but fun and after hours of swimming it was strange to be close to water without sinking within it. I thought to suggest that we dip our toes, our feet dangling above the limestone depths with their miles of caves that wound in every direction, or so we'd been told. I was about to say something but noticed that he had turned away from me, looking towards the front of the boat and the direction of the opposite shore, and the dislocation of his attention, the simple act of turning away from my face, sent across me a terrible loneliness.

Perhaps this was as much my fault as his. Wasn't I also tumbling elsewhere in my thoughts, away from him? There was the possibility of telling him about my suspicion, even if it was nothing more than a feeling. I could tell him and there would be a joining of sorts. Sometimes it helps to put things into words. But I did not want him to tell me it was only a feeling.

I wanted to sit with the possibility that I was pregnant without the certainty of being pregnant, not yet. With certainty there would come conversations, family matters, appointments. There would be tests and results, so there was no harm in keeping it unsaid, with only myself to disappoint.

Something knocked against the side of the boat. Had he seen it coming? I realised then that this was what he had been so intensely watching. He struggled to pull it up to the deck while keeping balance and so I went to help, grabbing hold of a corner and together heaving the object. It was a heavy wooden chair. The design was familiar, an intricate carving on the backrest, although I couldn't make out the detail in the dark. I ran my fingers across it, handsome and delicate.

In the green parlour there is a scholarly air and the heavy wooden chair sits well there, I thought, with its deep brown lacquer and intricately carved back. It sits quite comfortably by a writing desk, the same colour wood, and an invitation of paper beside a silver fountain pen; a handsome scene, that is what I imagined. I sit there at the desk and put together piece by piece a story that runs on and on through the weeks and months until it is complete and I am satisfied it is a true expression of myself, and even though the windows of the parlour are leaking, making big puddles on the carpet, I do not think of the murky water that is pressing against the glass, nor of the caverns that run beyond, dark and drowned, forever branching.

Despite the dampness of the seat, I perched lightly, happy with the pose, with the feeling I had completed the chair by fulfilling its purpose. My love considered me there on the deck of the boat. I was hoping he would say something but he showed no amusement. He was so still that, in the dark, I thought for a moment his face had disappeared.

NINE

H E FOUND HIMSELF FOLLOWING the line, not conscious of a choice to do so. He pressed the soft side of the kitchen sponge to the wall, just above the skirting board, rubbed it with what he judged to be enough pressure to take the pencil mark but not the paint. With some relief he could see it working, a portion of the light pencilling gone after a few strokes, only the very corner of the yellow sponge pinched between his forefinger and thumb. Still he did not rush and found some pleasure in the rhythm of wiping, small zigzags that followed the outline piece by piece, every so often stooping to dip the sponge in a cream enamelled saucepan. Hot soapy water. The paint could withstand a broader brushing but he'd started like this and there was no reason not to carry on, this way of clearing away the two figures felt more dignified, respectful, and it was with a sense of satisfaction that John grew aware of his own rougher line of water in the sponge's wake, which was a ghost of the drawing, which would soon evaporate but for the moment allowed the shape of the stranger's body to linger. It was the least he could do. After all, it was difficult to imagine a reason for the outlines to exist without some joy being involved in their making and although he would snuff it out, as surely the previous inhabitants knew someone eventually would, he could do it in the same spirit, enjoyably.

Harrie had fainted again. This time paramedics had been called. His vitals were normal but they'd taken him to the nearest hospital as a precaution, where in the early morning the family were informed about slight irregularities in his ECG results but nothing that was an emergency and the best thing would be for them to follow it up with their doctor in London who could refer them for further tests.

John had got as far as the first outline's elbow when Liz explained the situation to him. As far as Monica was concerned, the holiday was over, but Harrie was adamant that they still enjoy themselves. He was fine, he'd insisted, and besides, they'd travelled all this way and the children would only climb the walls in Tottenham. Liz kindly suggested that they at least leave the campsite and come to stay in the house. John wondered if Monica had intended for the conversation to travel in that direction. When Liz told him about the offer she stood with her feet rooted to the floor and a tension in her arms, as if she were expecting a fight.

'She didn't sound herself.'

Squatting, he squeezed the sponge above the pan. 'It must be hard on her.'

Liz nodded.

'She held my hand,' he said. 'In the swimming pool, in the sauna.'

He wished he'd made the admission with a little more grace.

Liz looked at his face, not his eyes. 'Okay,' she said.

It didn't leave him anywhere to turn. He dropped the sponge into the pan, stood, wiped his wet hands on his jeans. He thought of giving a reassurance but didn't want to make an assumption about where her mind was running. In the end, he stood there until she exhaled and granted him a look that was not unhappy.

'How much time do you need?' she asked, turning her attention to what was left of the outlines, as if this was some personal project of his. What to make of it, she thought. He'd spoken like he'd known he'd done wrong, but also nothing, nothing wrong, a little comfort. Why tell her at all, then? She took it as a gloat. He wanted someone to know. *I am desired.* She hadn't the energy. No doubt she would hold it against her sister in some form but it was too early in the morning and she felt out of sorts at the thought that they had been in the hospital all night while she and John had slept.

'It'll take half an hour, I don't know.'

'Half an hour?'

'I don't want to damage the paint.'

What was that man doing with himself, falling over all the time? She had awoken with the feeling of pregnancy, although it had taken on a different character since the pool, both more and less; another layer on the idea, easier to stand, but also aware that it was built on nothing, at least nothing she could talk about. She was less sure but at the same time she felt more keenly its potential to be real. She imagined her sister taking John's hand in the sauna, holding it between two of her own, squeezing it onto her lap. On the phone her voice had been quiet, as if she was talking somewhere she shouldn't. She'd spoken with gaps between the words that threatened to spill and Liz had to catch them, she had to, or else they would be left listening to each other breathe. *Come to the house and we can keep an eye on him.* She pictured John slipping his fingers between hers, pressing his hand on hers as she leant back on the wooden sauna ledge. Liz walked downstairs. Has she been betrayed? She did not know how she was expected to feel.

Before they were married she'd shared a bed with a well-known author. They'd not had sex. The author had been teaching a week-long course in Totleigh Barton. He had been charming and had said her prose was beautiful. She was not naive but his praise was specific enough that she enjoyed it, and when they shared a joint in his bedroom he had encouraged her to send her work out to agents. Even though he did not suggest his own agent she felt taken seriously and he only tried to kiss her once.

She rearranged the white glove on the mantelpiece.

Waiting for them to come, she found herself in useless minutes. A good time to write, feeling spiteful and picking up one of her old notebooks, small and black, that she must have brought with her to interview people for articles when she did that kind of thing because the first few pages were full of scrawled words and snippets of speech, the word 'implication' circled, and 'real time' and 'symphony orchestra'. She used to write in her notebook for the show of it, the action of circling words more important than whatever was being circled. It made the actor, or the author, or the politician, or the academic take you seriously, when you circled something. She rarely wore her glasses but she used to wear them to interviews for the same reason. She would sometimes wait until the other person had said something, lean back in her chair, take off her glasses, pause, then ask a question. If you really wanted to sell it you could wipe the lens as you spoke. She was never a proper journalist though. Only a dabbler. Freelance. Maybe she could pitch something. It would be a pain to travel anywhere but she could talk to people on the phone. A fee and a deadline, nothing wrong with that. She flicked the corner of a page. No, it was not what she wanted. If she was going to write it would be on her own terms.

She wanted to be saved from her agony, she wrote. *She reached for his hand and held it in her own.*

It was with a sense of relief that John continued to wipe away the outlines on the wall. There was nothing remotely inappropriate in the sauna, he was sure of that now, but the way it could sound if you were to describe it... He thought of his wife's face and wished he had said more to reassure her. When the others arrived he would make it his objective to be kind, loving, to demonstrate his love, which he had in high supply. He would kiss her hand and tell her she meant the world to him.

Only when one figure was gone did he think of taking a picture. He had stopped posting, an unconscious decision that was becoming conscious, in part because he could feel the pull, had felt it stronger over the past few days than ever before, the pull to snap, a way of seeing that turned the world into the potential for social capital. He did not like the stranglehold. He'd read articles on the matter. There, the light from the window, cast askew over the outline and the ghost in water, beginning to fade. The pull to post, absent when he'd been absorbed with the sponge, but now, with a moment to think. Is he so programmed? When Liz wrote stories she would post pictures of books, proofs, paragraphs that were the right size and shape. She'd deleted her account on her birthday, two weeks after Neena had given birth. He should do the same. Silicon Valley. What to do but resist their cuntish ways, a tickling of vanity passed off as expression? The water was fading. Ali would like it, he always liked John's pictures, even though they hadn't seen each other for at least a year, all but stopped messaging, still in each other's lives but not at all. When someone asked him how Ali was doing John would say I saw he was doing this and doing that, their baby getting bigger. Did you see that they took her to the Isle of Wight? So many pictures of babies. Friends only. Inner circle. He took the phone out of his trouser pocket. Resist the urge. No one would comment.

He took a picture of the outline. He would not post it, he told himself. It was for his own memory.

Later, when the children had dropped off their bags in the room, he showed the picture to Harrie but you could barely see anything on the screen on his phone. His brother-in-law told him he'd once found a set of names written in pencil behind their oven when they'd had it replaced, nothing else but a short column of first names and he'd assumed it was a family that had lived in the flat once upon a time. People like to leave traces of themselves. They were all written so neatly and in the same style of handwriting and he'd been struck by that. 'I didn't see any reason to wipe them away,' he said, and John couldn't help but feel judged. 'I think of them sometimes when I'm making dinner.'

Liz had made an excuse to Monica about going to the toilet, to lie in her bed and stare at the ceiling. She had her notebook on her stomach, one hand on its cover, and could feel it rising and falling with her breath. Pieces of sentences were coming to her but she did not write them. They came and they went and she let them. *We can't cut the chair in half.* John slipped into the room. He gave her a lingering kiss and put his hand on her waist. She appreciated that he was initiating but her mind was not in the right place. She hummed and patted his arm.

'If it isn't working,' he said, trailed off. There were fast footsteps coming down the corridor. Ciara called her brother's name. 'We meet the NHS criteria,' he said.

This surprised her. 'You've looked?'

He nodded.

She clicked her tongue. 'The waiting lists, they can't be good.'

The footsteps went down the corridor, down the stairs. Ciara called for Finn again.

'Doing it private costs a lot.'

She didn't like the way he said it, as if a decision had already been made. 'I could pay a bit more,' she said and watched him for a reaction.

'We meet the NHS criteria.'

'In case we don't.'

'We do.'

There was the sound of laughter from downstairs.

'I have a good feeling,' she said. It came without any real calculation. His face softened. 'I think the other night,' she said. 'I don't know... I think. Who knows?' He smiled and she was happy they had retraced their steps. They did not need to go down that path, not yet. She brought him towards her, to kiss him the same way he had done to her.

A good feeling could be anything, thought John. She would say it all the time when they used to force themselves. The fun part of making babies. Wink, wink. Not fun when one window shuts after another, lamplight dimming, faces clouded with another pane of glass. In the kitchen Harrie looked tired but he said as much, laughed loudly when Liz commented on the heaviness of his eyes. 'I'm used to sleepless nights,' he said, rolling his eyes at the children on the kitchen floor playing with origami paper, red and orange, folded into swans.

Monica moved through the room as if in a trance, passing outdoors, and from where he was standing John could see her walk beyond the veranda, towards the lake and out of view. Nobody else paid her the least bit of attention. He walked to the doorway and saw her pass beyond the treeline.

'She's going for a walk,' narrated Liz from the counter, a look that was pointedly blank.

Would her good feeling be something? Would all the worry be for nothing, little more than a blip? Would they rejoin their friends, would his mother say *yippee*? Would they take pictures and fill albums decorated with hand-marbled paper, write captions, begin to emerge from their floating days, roots underfoot, leaves mixed with hair and the promise of spreading beyond the ridge of hills? John wandered through the rooms. The new furniture would soon arrive. There was no point clinging to half-finished and broken things and so he made a decision, standing in the dining room with the view of the lake and the trees, the sound of Liz's voice carrying down the hall.

Harrie helped him with the damaged chair as he brought it through the kitchen, no need, he'd said, but they were already walking together and he thought maybe his brother-in-law wanted to show Liz he had strength still in him. Harrie expected them to put it there, it seemed, from his slight reluctance towards the outside door, but John guided it to the threshold and Harrie was forced to step backwards into the open.

'We'll have to find time for fishing,' Harrie said as they carried the broken chair beyond the veranda on the bare ground. John faced forward and Harrie tried to keep up with his pace whilst walking backwards.

'We don't even have rods, Harrie.'

His brother-in-law smiled thinly, then fell silent. The further they moved from the house the more anxious he appeared. Only when they approached the bonfire heap by the side of the lake did he seem to understand. 'You just need a bit of glue,' he muttered, unbelieving. He put his side of the chair down and the sudden movement made it fall out of John's hands. The broken armrest toppled a few feet away from the body. Harrie snatched it up from the ground.

'It's a fine chair,' he said, forcefully.

John for a moment wondered if Harrie would stop him from picking it back up. The chair had fallen in such a way that its carved panel faced up towards the clouded sky, the shepherd with his cloak, his face wrapped in leaves, an ear a window. He was right that it was a fine thing. John thought about whether a mistake was being made. Surely it was salvageable.

'I'd rather not have to deal with it,' John said, adamant, and stood the chair upright at the base of the heap. It made for a striking scene, like something from a story. Harrie shook his head then stared as if John had wronged him, as if he were no longer certain of whether to put faith in him.

'I can't believe he's getting rid of that lovely old chair,' Harrie said with mock-outrage to Liz when they returned to the kitchen. She had her thumb in her closed notebook and was making circles with her forefinger. *She reached for his hand and held it in her own.*

'He is?'

Harrie threw his hands up, rolled his eyes, bigger than life. He wagged a finger clown-like at John as he came back in. 'A hasty man, your husband.'

John looked boyish in his obstinacy.

'What will we sit on now?' she asked.

'One of us can stand.'

At some point in the afternoon Monica returned from her walk and when she did Liz found herself noticing things about her sister's appearance, the oval shape of her head, the size of her canines, things that had not changed but things she was seeing anew, as if they were meeting for the first time. She had the same teeth as her sister, she thought. If she were to describe Monica in writing, where would she start? Not with her hairline, not with her neck, certainly not with her teeth.

There was a knock and Sweet was on the doorstep, wearing a big hiking backpack and carrying a box of tools. Liz had forgotten all about their arrangement and it must have shown on her face because the warden's smile faded. She invited him in, explaining that her sister's family were also staying but they would find room. Equally, if he wanted to stay somewhere else she wouldn't be offended. With a forced cheeriness he said a sofa was fine, that he appreciated the hospitality, and at this she grew resentful. Couldn't he read the room? It was arrogant to insist on her charity. Another day. Any other day. It can't save all that much time being there. Clearly they already had enough on their hands, clearly it didn't need to be said and there he stood like an awkward lump still in his work boots.

'Would you like to take your shoes off?' she asked.

He'd been waiting to be prompted, it seemed, from the speed he undid his laces. Without a word he carried them to a specific spot in the hallway, even though it was not where they put their shoes. He was smiling then as he took in the living room. Was he happy? Relieved? He eased himself onto the sofa, black socks now on the floor. The children were a little uncertain at his presence. Ciara curled into her mother's leg, looking sideways at the warden. 'What are you doing here?' she asked. Monica let the question stand.

Sweet seemed unsure of who to respond to. In the end he directed himself to Monica. 'Bat habitats,' he explained.

'Bad habitats?'

'Bat. Bats.' He flapped his arms. 'I have an early start.'

'Oh, right.'

The delight that Monica had come away with from their previous meeting was absent. No longer was she charmed by his presence, and it was clear she had little patience for conversation. Liz leant against the wall. Her sister's hands were slender, she noticed.

'The old Palmers were very nice to me,' Sweet said to the room. He put his hands down on his thighs and looked so stiff and awkward, Liz thought, so aware of himself. It was the kind of pose you might see from a king but it was brought down by the strained look on his face. Clearly he was not used to being so close to children and their presence was a source of anxiety. He looked at his own feet. He was disappointed, she thought. The company was meant to be a treat for him. She saw that now. In the years before they moved there he must have looked forward to evenings spent in this house, a cooked dinner with friends, for he saw them as friends, the previous inhabitants, that was clear. Perhaps he realised how much he missed them, that time had moved on. She resented the comparison. She and John were nice people, weren't they? They were just as hospitable.

'Working on a bank holiday,' she said, puffing the air out of her cheeks.

'No bank holiday for bats.'

There was silence then, until Monica excused herself. Liz put on the TV. Sweet had no opinion on what they watched, he was happy with everything. Likely he saw things for how they were, she thought. The house and the lake and the surroundings. He saw them in a way they did not, could not yet. She thought about him sitting in the exact same spot before they had even thought to search for a new place to live. Had he discussed their coming with the previous inhabitants? Now that they had arrived, did they match his expectation? He watched the TV with his hands neatly folded in his lap, the children on the floor nearby. She was hovering, did not want to sit. He would know how things were, the trees and the paths that ran between them, the roads and the routes, all oblique, she was never one for directions, but no doubt he could find them on a map, pin their house in a blotch of green. She had no idea where he lived, hadn't the faintest where he called home.

John met Monica on the way to the kitchen. She asked him about Sweet staying, he continued to walk, explaining it was something they'd agreed to a while ago, a bit of a pain. She'd stopped where she was. He eventually came to a standstill, a too-long distance between them.

'He does all this work on his own?' she asked.

'I suppose.' He angled himself to suggest they keep on their way, better to talk in the kitchen, where there was reason for being.

'Who does he work for?'

Hadn't Sweet said something about the Forestry Commission? He couldn't recall. In the end he shrugged and blew the air out of his lips, making a sound like a horse. Monica gave him a look of faint disdain. *If it was me, I'd want to know.* In truth he did begin to wonder. He doubted anything would come up if he searched for Jim Sweet online. He pictured the carved shepherd; a candle lit, the sheep in the paddock, hot steam rising from a dozen animal mouths but one missing, bleating in the dark of the woods.

Harrie came back with expensive cuts of steak, button mushrooms, new potatoes and runner beans. He insisted on cooking. It was a thank you for hosting them when it hadn't been expected, he said, with serious weight. Sweet's presence came as a surprise and he wished someone had told him, eyes to Monica, but it turned out he'd bought full-sized cuts for the children and they wouldn't eat all that, his wife said, so there were ways around it. When John offered to help chop the mushrooms Harrie shooed him out of the kitchen. 'Relax,' he said. 'I have it under control.'

He came to them only once, to ask where their steak knives were, which they didn't have, John explained. A look of confusion flashed on Harrie's face and John came close to telling him to sit down while he took it from there, but he stayed where he was, tapping his foot and half watching the news, assurances from the Taliban, safe departure. There were definitely not enough chairs around the dining table, Harrie noted with an edge to his voice, so they brought the seats into the living room and set them opposite the knackered sofa.

The food was delicious. John's cut was perfect medium rare. For a few seconds, everyone was quiet with their plates balanced on their knees. The mushrooms had been pan-fried in butter and it matched the succulence of the meat in a way that reminded John of something he could not quite grasp, but it reminded him of it strongly, and as he chewed he searched for the memory, as if settling on a picture of the scene would let him claim this happiness for his own. 'This is a real success,' he blurted after he swallowed and he meant it, wanted Harrie to know that he had meant it, so when his brother-in-law only glanced at him he plunged immediately into an anger that surprised him with its depth. 'You've actually managed something,' he said, and could hear how it sounded: bare and mean-spirited. Once more he had fumbled. Even the children looked at him. 'Something,' he echoed, looking for the next word. 'Something easy to understand,' he added, hoping that the meanness could soften to mockery. Harrie and his impenetrable books, Harrie and his cleverness. Liz was wide-eyed. Harrie gave a sad smile.

'It's very nice,' said Sweet, from his place on the sofa. He pierced a new potato with his fork and ran it along the plate, soaking up the juices from the meat before eating it in one.

He knows the house better than we do, Liz thought. He has seen it in all seasons, knows the way the winter light will look on the frosted tiles, the first buds of colour coming in around the shore. Her small notebook was under her thigh, sandwiched between her leg and the cushioned seat. Within it was a uni-ball pen, her preference, and the bump it made in the notebook felt good.

'Did you go to church today?' she asked.

The others went quiet, waiting for his answer. She didn't mean to make him a curiosity but at the same time she wanted a better sense of what Sweet did with himself.

'I go to the morning service,' he said.

'That must be nice,' said Monica, taking a sip of water.

'They've been good to me over the past few years.'

Sweet didn't take it any further and neither did anyone else, and it wasn't long before Harrie swept in with talk about how well stocked the nearest shop was. Liz imagined Sweet on a wooden pew, praying for those that were dear to him. She thought about him basked in the light of a stained-glass window, motionless and mute.

'Half an hour,' said Harrie, later, standing in the doorway to the kitchen. With the dirty plates piled he had excused himself to do a little work, in his words. Just a little. Monica said no, not for the first time, and it was sharp enough to stop the conversation.

There was a storm brewing in Harrie's eyes, Liz noticed. Let him do his work, she thought. She slipped out her notebook, wrote 'she', scribbled it out. It'll give him somewhere to put his mind. Who can begrudge him that? Let him believe in a pristine glass. Let him think that others would love to drink from it. He held himself straight, recalcitrant, and to her surprise she thought him noble. Still ridiculous. He was unsuited to the world, would be crushed by it in time. He was too proud to give himself up, too forgone. Still, she wanted them to see him working, as when he had brought out his books and spread them across the dining-room table but hadn't read from a single one, only stared at his paper. Allow him that. What harm is there? Monica followed him upstairs. She would not let him get his books.

Liz followed after a while. She lay in bed and listened to them argue through the wall, at first quiet, hardly heard. *Leading her down an overgrown path*, she wrote in her notebook. *At any time she could loosen her grip, slip free.* Allow him his pointless work. He plans it as a gift for all mankind. Allow him that much, it will keep him occupied.

*

John was in the bad habit of pissing with the seat down and this had done for him in the dimness of the evening, his attention away on the bath tiles and a splash on the rim, cystitis, the final few drops and the nasty sensation of more to come. Had he picked it up from the pool? He tried not to focus on the soreness as he dabbed the urine with toilet tissue. Tomorrow, cranberry juice. There was the sound of Harrie's raised voice. John listened for more, opened the bathroom door an inch and heard Monica speaking back to her husband, a word like 'priorities', and John suspected matters had spun out since the dinner table. There was a pang and he winced at the pain, closed the door because the last thing he wanted was for them to come out into the corridor and see him spying. He heard his own name, definitely his name but it was like a face in a crowd swept up and he could not place it in the low rumble of their voices, now indistinct through the door.

He shouldn't have told Liz about the sauna, it was only a friendly gesture, nothing to be made of it, nothing to read beyond the care Monica needed, a sign of support when Christ knows her mind must be full, her husband and his faints, enough for anyone to look for comfort in loved ones. He thought of fingers in marble, Greek heroes, horses carved from stone with pieces missing, chipped or blasted in the British Museum. She was family. He cared for her. Stone figures in a vaulted room, cavernous and cut with wide pools of water, the Palace of the Gods, nude figures reflected, their poses doubled, hands held or pointing. He would feel such a shameful knock searching in the bathroom mirror, as if he were to be found in the particulars of his jaw, as in a white shirt hung at the back of a grand oak wardrobe in a room at the top of a marble tower, where he would climb the spiralling steps two at a time, cross the arched bridge and search there with the knowledge that nothing would be found. He'd try to catch a glimpse of his father staring back at him in the mirror but he couldn't remember how he'd looked, only the clothes that his mother had kept, and it was shameful because John felt like he should be able to recall his father's face. You'd be forgiven, others would say. You were only small when Jack was lost to us.

Were the new lines in the corners of his eyes those his father had also noticed? He'd been his age once, John could still say that, at least for a few more years. Had he found the same lines and thought of time like a billowing sheet that had blown through the window? Standing in the bathroom his father would've heard a child in the hall. John's voice, only small. What would he do when he passed him? There were years to go, so much to do.

How had his father seen himself in photographs? Picked up in an envelope from Boots. John remembered going together, must've been together, in particular the escalator, for reasons beyond him, holding his father's hand on the escalator to the second floor of Boots, or at least the idea of his hand, a phantom, his presence there in those memories but never really a body, more a certainty of a body, a certainty in the kitchen sizzling sausages, a certainty when John was placed naked and small into the bathwater, a bowl of warm soapy water poured over his head and his father's hand on his shoulder in case he should startle. In one of their boxes from the move were photographs that his mother had given him and amongst those albums his father held him close, a ruined church behind them. Whitby, maybe. Had his father looked at that photo, looked at his own face smiling and felt the same strangeness at the lines in the corners of his eyes? *Is that what other people see of me?*

John heard Sweet's voice from the living room. He was telling the children a story, it seemed. 'The mother deer asked the snake, have you seen my baby?'

Instead of entering the room and disrupting him, John stayed near the threshold to listen to the warden speak. His voice was alive, totally committed. It was amusing to hear Sweet sound like this, so unlike the way he'd spoken for the rest of the evening.

'The snake slithered and shook his head. No!'

'No!' the children joined in. Clearly a pattern had been established. From his laughter, Sweet seemed delighted at the response.

'I have not s-s-seen your baby,' he hissed like a snake. 'Well in that case I am very sorry to bother you, said the mother deer. She moved deeper into the forest. She heard an owl hooting high in a tree.'

'Hoo hoo,' said Finn.

'The mother deer asked the owl, have you seen my baby? The owl ruffled her feathers and—'

'No!' the children chimed.

'No!' said Sweet. 'I have not seen your baby.'

Did Sweet know John was standing there, just out of view? From his perspective of the room, only the warden's outstretched legs could be seen, two large feet in black socks. He was sitting on the floor, his back against the front of the sofa. John shifted his weight, careful not to make a creak. It allowed him to see up to Sweet's torso. The warden's hands were neatly folded on his belly. He was not reading from any book. Neither Ciara nor Finn were in view, John supposed they were curled up on the sofa. Eventually Sweet led the mother deer to a cave.

'What should she do?' he asked the children.

'Look in,' said Finn. His voice had lost some of its earlier energy.

'In the cave there was no light. The mother deer walked deeper and deeper. She walked until she could walk no further. She asked the dark, have you seen my baby?'

There was a pause as the children waited for a response.

'The dark said yes, I have seen your baby, his little white spots.'

There was another pause, a sound of movement. When Sweet next spoke, he did so softly.

'I wonder, said the dark. Have you spoken to God? I doubt you have. And why not, I wonder. Wouldn't he know more than any snake or owl? Are you a coward, I wonder. Is it because you will feel foolish, unanswered?'

The children remained silent.

'You used to think that change was impossible. For your whole life you lived as if change was an idea, nothing more. But now you see that change has taken place.'

John thought to step forward into the room but found himself unable. He wanted to put a hand on the door but it seemed an impossible distance.

'You have come to me but not to God,' continued Sweet. 'You accept things for the way they will be but you do not understand them. No, you accept but you do not understand.'

Sweet had reached the end of his story, it seemed. Slowly the warden raised himself from the floor and as he did so John quietly backed away from the doorway, towards the dining room which he quickly entered and took the chair by the table. If Sweet came in he would tell him he was working. He waited like that for a little while, listening for footsteps that didn't come.

When he eventually worked up the courage to go back into the living room, he was prepared to meet Sweet but the warden was no longer there. The children were asleep on either end of the sofa.

*

Liz noticed movement through the clouded glass, a dot of fire that burned and eased as Sweet drew on his cigarette. He had stood on their doorstep many times before them, she thought. He would stand on it again. He knew more than any of them, he saw the woods for what they were, saw them without the romance she and John forced on them, saw the trees on their own terms. If she hadn't left her notebook upstairs she would've taken it out and written on the counter, carried her thought to its next place. She poured herself a glass of water. The dot of fire burned and eased. Soon he would come back inside and she didn't particularly want to meet him there, where they would have to talk to each other. She would much rather they stayed in silence, like this, with a pane of glass between them.

*

My love leant over the side of the boat, by now expecting a discovery. Even though the waves were rocking us, I did not pull her back. I like to think I am not someone who worries unnecessarily. She was close enough that if she stumbled I could catch her in time. It was drizzling. My face was wet. Without the engine there was only the sound of the wind and how long could we stay there, I wondered, without becoming miserable. If not for the light of the house, I could've taken one way for another.

The opposite shore was uniformly dark, or so I thought, but as I studied the gloom I spotted a dot of light swell and fade.

My love raised her head in disbelief as I turned us around. Only when we reached the shore did she let go of the side of the boat. Whatever she wanted to say, she bit her tongue. Following her lead, we did not go inside but sat instead with our feet dangling from the edge of the jetty. I thought I could still make out a pinprick of light on the opposite shore but my love seemed in no mood to talk about my suspicions. Perhaps I lingered because I felt a discovery was inevitable. There was a pressure in my ribs. A growing part of me wanted to take my love by the hand and lead us away from the water before she could see whatever had surfaced. Still, I did not leave. The waves lapped against the wooden posts that reached down into the ground. My love had the hooked pole in her hand, resting it across her thighs. The moments were burdened then with the reading of shapes. I searched for an object, perhaps thinking that if I made it out first I could decide its qualities.

She held aloft what I took at first for a fish, its body broken, dangling from her hand. When she brought it closer I could see she was not gripping a fin but rather the strap of a concertina. It was waterlogged and her first attempt at making a sound was a wet blurt of dissonance. She persisted and in time the sound became more solid, a random note held as she squeezed the instrument closed and another as she drew it wide. My love opened and closed its folded middle, each time with a random assortment of notes that rarely came together to create anything approaching harmony. I thought of the family inside. What would the children make of our mewling?

Of all the things we could have found, the concertina had a lightness about it. Like the hobby horse, it was an invitation to play. Even in the mess of sound, there was the possibility for something beautiful to break through.

After a little while my love offered it to me, showing where to put my hands so that my fingers were positioned above rows of small white buttons. I pressed some at random as I slowly drew the instrument open, careful to be quieter than she had been although I was no more successful in making a harmony. The right panel consisted of low notes, the left panel the high notes. The object was handsome, the panelling a deep red, fringed by small metallic pieces that protected the edges of its hexagon. As I played, I imagined another set of hands held within its leather straps, those who knew how to shape a chord, who had the muscle memory to snap from one manoeuvre to the next. In the green parlour these hands were parting and coming together, the music covering the creak of the dripping windows in their panes.

I settled on a low note, kept the key resolute as I slowly opened and closed the concertina so that it sounded like a monster breathing. I wanted to be systematic in my approach. Tentative, I joined the deep note with another, a success. I glanced at my love to see what she made of my attempt and was encouraged by her attention. The sound was warm and deep and there was something in its slight vibrato that gave it an impression of genuine feeling, as if a voice was cracking and the cracking was the truth of the matter. But the third note was a misstep. Too high, too small. It had no reason to be there and brought the whole thing back to earth.

Frustrated at my inability, I unstrapped my hands from the concertina and tossed it behind me on the wooden boards. Neither of us touched it again. I wished my love would. I wanted her to pick it up. Keep going. I would have listened. She swayed her legs back and forth above the water. I looked for the spot of light on the opposite shore.

TEN

RICHARD HAD ABOUT HIM an electricity. John wondered if he had been drinking. It was not yet eleven. The students had arrived unannounced, uninvited, it transpired, although for a good hour John assumed someone had asked them to come. 'Well, *I* didn't invite them,' whispered Monica, a little too loud as Richard helped himself to the coffee in their cupboard.

'Would you like us to go?' Richard scooped the ground coffee into a filter.

'No no no, of course not,' said Monica.

Liz widened her eyes at her sister. It was the bank holiday. Sweet had departed in the early hours, leaving only a bowl and spoon in the sink and a fleck of mud in the hallway where his boots had been placed. He was not mentioned, not once, and this made his visit feel unreal to John, as if more than one night had passed since his staying, as if it were something that had happened months ago. He thought about Sweet at work, checking the habitats of bats, a clearing at dawn, a notebook in his hand and his eyes focused on the quick, curved lines of flight. To whom would he submit this information?

With a concern bordering on aggression Richard asked if John had fixed the old chair they'd broken during their last visit.

'Don't listen to him,' said Alma. 'He's already seen it outside.'

'I could've fixed it for you,' said Richard, pouring out the kettle.

'It was a nice chair,' said Tariq, by the doorway, engrossed in his phone. He'd been with the children, watching TV.

'I could've helped,' said Richard, his eyes alight. For a moment John could see his appeal, could imagine the way he spoke to Tariq and Alma about the future of the country, the mistakes of their parents, the things that no longer worked, no longer carried meaning. Did he have it in him to change things, truly change things, John wondered.

At some point Liz realised she was left alone in the kitchen with Alma, who had a sly little face on her like a newt. Liz wanted to give her bad advice. 'From the way you talk about him…' She left it there, raised her eyebrows, gave a grim smile. Alma was evasive, taking in the sentiment with a tight expression, her eyes just beyond Liz, over her shoulder to the doorway. She's sharp, Liz thought. Sharper than her friends.

'Richard wants me to meet someone in Newcastle.'

'That's right, the engineer.'

Alma's brow furrowed.

'Tariq said something to us about an engineer,' Liz explained, enjoying the fact she knew more about things.

'Tariq said something?' The poor girl seemed genuinely confused at the mention of his name.

'An engineer or a mechanic. He was a bit vague about the whole thing.'

Whatever reason Alma had for bringing up Newcastle was being wrongfooted and this brought Liz no small amount of pleasure to witness, the way the student had stopped whispering. Still she had the urge to give her bad advice, to push her in the wrong direction.

'Richard told me he's a teacher,' Alma said. 'I think they've only ever spoken online. Richard says he's a nihilist and that's a good thing, apparently. You should hear him talk about this man. Richard isn't easily impressed. He never talks about anyone like this.'

Liz patted her arm. 'He'll show you the sights, I'm sure. Oh! He can tell you about the bridges.'

'They've talked about me, apparently. This teacher, Richard says he's called Mandeau, is impressed with me. Why do I care if he's impressed?' She looked at Liz like she wanted an answer but then kept talking. 'I mean, really, who calls themselves a nihilist?'

'It is a bit silly.'

'You should hear Richard go on about him. And this is Richard. So I am intrigued. He says Mandeau wants to reclaim it, nihilism I guess, but that's not important, what's important is he's connected and if we want to make things happen we should know people like him.'

'Sounds like he's worth meeting, at least.'

With this encouragement, Alma became more animated in her speech. 'Well, something needs to happen. We can't pretend otherwise.' Her cheeks seemed to glow. 'We can't afford not to be sceptical. The new generation can't make the same mistakes yours did.'

'I mean, we're the same generation.'

'Yeah. Yes.' Alma studied her face.

Liz hadn't been on a march since the rise in student fees. Protesters had climbed on the balcony at Fortnum & Mason, someone had thrown a Molotov. It had been like something from a movie. 'We're living in a different world to our parents' generation,' Liz said. 'We need new ideas.'

'Right,' said Alma. She was still studying her face. Liz felt herself going red. She didn't fully know what she was saying but she felt a desire to express herself.

'Britain can't imagine an alternative.' It sounded cliché. 'We as a nation are unable, literally unable.' Push through, she thought. In Piccadilly she'd run away with a group up Air Street to avoid being kettled and they'd talked giddily about it in a pub on Brewer Street. What had it achieved? What had her thrill achieved for the state of the world? 'We have to imagine, but we can't bring ourselves to do it.'

There was the smallest of smiles on Alma's lips. 'Yeah,' she said. 'Yeah,' she said again. There were footsteps beyond them, through the open window. Alma seemed content to study her face without speaking. Liz glanced outside. No one was there.

'I'm sure you'll have a nice time with the boys,' Liz said as she got herself a glass of water.

Alma seemed to deflate. 'Are you sure Tariq is coming to Newcastle?'

'That's my understanding. You'll have a lovely time,' and she thought of bathtubs full of fertiliser. 'What will you do, the three of you?' she asked.

Alma shrugged. Liz patted her arm. 'Honestly, the bridges,' she said. 'Immense.' She meant to do more, she cared about things, cared deeply about the state of the country, of course she did, how could you not, and she believed that crowds on the streets were necessary, for pressure, for optics. She supported it, the right ones, she'd meant to go on more, she should've gone, she knew it was hypocritical, worse, and she'd lied when people had asked, more than once she'd lied and said she'd been on a march when she hadn't. Something convinced her that it wouldn't matter, that she could take action elsewhere in her life, in her mind, in small things, that it was in fact maturity to realise this. Had she been wrong?

In the living room Ciara wanted Tariq to play with her. He sat her on his knees and sang. 'I went to the shop to buy a lollipop.' He bounced her up and down. 'I sat on a chair and the chair went pop.' With the final word he opened his legs and she yelped as she fell, his hands under her armpits to stop her hitting the carpet.

Later Liz saw Alma confront Richard on the shore and imagined she was asking why Tariq knew about their secret trip to Newcastle. Was he always meant to be coming? John was then sitting beside her and he too looked out at the lovers, far away enough for their movements to be unclear – but when Richard held Alma's wrists and pulled her towards him, wrapping his arms around her, holding her like that for a long time, Liz was left with no doubt in her mind that there would be nothing good for her in Newcastle.

'We were like that,' John teased.

She made a sing-song hum. She would buy a pregnancy test later that day. Her period was due, it had not come. She felt different, still different, and that was a thing to take seriously. Her body knew, soon she would too, then the real task would begin. What look would be on John's face when she told him? She would tell him first, before her sister, who would jump up and down and call out to Harrie that she *knew* it. Better maybe for the three months to be out of the way, that would be John's approach, the way things normally go, the first scan, the reassurance, only then the family let in. What would be on his face, she wondered. Would his jaw drop? Tears? She hadn't seen him cry since he'd almost lost her. His eyes would get watery at sad songs but that didn't count. She would like a little cry, a convulsive sob, signs of fire. He'd shed tears when she'd searched for her coat, couldn't find her coat for the life of her and she'd thought at the time that it was undermining, ruining in a big way her attempt at storming off into the night. For some reason it made him cry in a way their fight hadn't, her stomping from room to room in search of her coat, him standing in the hallway in his briefs, the outline of his cock showing, tears running down his cheeks. That was all she wanted.

Perhaps it would kick her off, almost two years of trying brought to a happy conclusion. Then they would know where they stood, their roles firm, the oldest roles of all. Already she could feel the name, its weight. She had been or was still a daughter, a sister, a girlfriend, a fiancée, a wife. Not long until the biggest of the lot took her, gobbled her up.

'Aw,' John went, he was still watching Richard and Alma as they hugged on the shore. 'We're *still* like that.'

More and more he felt dislodged from the words he put out in the world. *We're still like that.* It wasn't what he meant to say. He had meant to assure her. He was fumbling. He thought of the dog in the hallway, the black dog, its laboured breath. So many people dead, he thought. The dead and the dying. The light was bright on Richard's shoulders. The summer would soon be over, Liz would go back to work and his unemployment would be all the more obvious. He would get back in touch with Total Translations. He would try another firm. He couldn't contend with it. Even English was becoming a problem. More and more he was fumbling. The dog in the hallway. *The dog in the hallway.* It was becoming harder to hold, one restless inside the other.

He watched Richard reach the end of the jetty, showing no sign of stopping. The sun came out from behind the clouds and it made the surface of the water shine. Time has not passed, he thought. The days have stayed where they are.

He scrolled and, for whatever reason, the powers above showed him videos of animals being eaten alive. A baby antelope was pressed between the paws of a cheetah, the antelope calm, or so it appeared. Most likely in shock. Another cheetah was sniffing around its hind. He watched the bowels of the antelope pulled out like a magician's handkerchief. The scroll went on to show him teenagers making jokes, actually pretty funny. Then a group of ducklings beneath a horse. The horse, very large, lowered its head, sniffed at the tiny yellow animals, gobbled one up. Mother duck quacked frantically in a way that sounded human, the worst thing about it, that sound. How did these clips get past the moderators? Why were they being served to him? Later, when they went back inside, he thought of the horse, its stillness when it had crunched up the duckling. Most unpleasant. What did the horse feel at that moment? Nothing. A slight hunger.

She thought about strangling her newborn with its own umbilical cord. As soon as it was out, the doctors would hand it to her, she would cradle it close, then wrap, loop, an awful thought, some relish, though, in the thinking of it. The terrible act would take them by surprise. Labour done, stitches needed, the moment of respite, the great meeting. She felt shameful at her own sickly lingering. John would stop her, or the midwife if he was too frozen by horror. That's him, to hesitate. She made an effort to stop dwelling on intrusive thoughts, why were they coming to her? Was it to have control over matters outside of her grip? She thought hard about holding a baby to her breast, tried to feel its warmth, its breath on her skin. She thought then of the dog breathing in the hallway, the dog they had found, its pink belly where the fur was thinnest. What a poor omen it had been.

Richard was gleefully talking about the hopelessness of the current political situation.

'With the right leader,' insisted Tariq. There was desperation to his words. He wanted his friend to agree with him but he did not look at Richard when he spoke, as if he already knew he would disagree, worse, castigate him for the suggestion. Time had passed, the students had joined them in the kitchen. Alma and Richard were wrapped in towels. Tariq hadn't gone swimming but when the others had returned he'd rolled up the already-short sleeves of his T-shirt.

'We had the right leader and look where it got us,' said Alma. 'I don't think—'

'It's too long to wait,' interrupted Richard.

'There'll be a general election sooner rather than later,' said Tariq.

'As I was saying.'

'Sorry, Alma,' said Tariq.

'I don't think we can—'

'Yes, we can't, I'm agreeing with you,' said Richard, defensive.

'We're agreeing,' said Tariq.

Alma tightened the towel around her chest. Her hands were unhurried, thought Liz. 'I don't think we can rely on Labour as it currently stands.'

'That goes without saying,' said Richard.

Her hands were calm, thought Liz, even as her thumbnail flicked against the skin of her forefinger.

'I've also been disappointed in Starmer,' said Liz.

'We don't have the time,' said Richard. 'We need radical action now.'

'There's everything at stake and you're caught up in role-play,' mumbled Harrie. Neither Richard nor Tariq paid this much attention. Liz met Harrie's eye and he looked away, down to his hands, which rested on his belly, the two forefingers tapping to a rhythm only he could hear.

'We have the worst people in charge at the worst possible time,' said John, putting on a serious face that was too much, thought Liz, for platitudes.

'We don't have the time for any of this,' urged Richard.

Tariq reached out to hold Richard's hand, to calm him. It was an intimacy Liz had not before witnessed. Richard immediately withdrew his hand from Tariq's, held it stiff by his side.

'There is such violence in the government today, such cruelty and violence,' said Alma. Her voice was strong. Liz could imagine her on the radio, the *Today* programme.

'But Richard is right,' Alma went on. 'It's too late to wait for a system to turn that is no longer fit for purpose. I wish it wasn't the case. I really do. I wish I could trust the professional politicians in this country but they are playing games that no longer make sense.'

'Fuck!' said Richard, but to whom, Liz wondered. He glowered above their heads, through the open door. Then Tariq did something strange, gently hooked the corner of Richard's lip with the tip of his forefinger. It was a surprising, intimate gesture. Richard froze, stared at Tariq. The finger stayed where it was, as if Tariq was waiting for Richard to respond. Only when Richard put on a grudging smile did Tariq remove his finger. It must be something between them, Liz thought. An inside joke.

They were all fucking each other, thought John. Good for them. He tried not to stare at Richard but couldn't help noticing the expression on his face, as if he had been told off, privately fuming. Liz had been mimicking Alma's body language. When the student crossed her arms, Liz did the same. He would tell her that later, make a joke out of it, sure to do it in a way that helped things, made it light. In fact he would swap it around, that's right, tell her Alma was copying her movements. Yes. You can see she pays attention, he'd say. Liz would like to hear that. He must remember. If he could keep it in his head without fumbling. They'd have a good laugh at the students, enough drama to pick at for weeks. Richard had disappeared into the house and Tariq was glancing at the way he'd gone. John could swear they weren't like this with each other the last time. Was it something new? They would talk about it, might even get Harrie and Monica on board. God, what a gift. He must remember to talk about it. Why had the horse eaten the duckling? It was the start of a good joke. He would talk about that as well, about the ways of animals.

Let me get on with the days, he thought as he looked for his heavy boots at the top of the basement steps. He had a strong desire to busy his hands. Those that know me know I am capable, he thought. I take after my father. It won't be long until we've found a rhythm. I will put this behind me, get to the task, between the walls and the garden, *what we grew up knowing*, no point quaking, this panic and talk, what does it mean, talk about action, there are dents in the walls, dents that need filling. I will move that glove on the mantelpiece, he thought to himself. If she wants to keep it she can keep it in her drawers. The mess has had its hour. Who is our MP? He will find it out, he decided. Sweet would know. His father would've known. He will write to their MP. They were homeowners, they had a stake in things. *Action now.*

He stopped in his tracks. The antique was back in the dining room. He could see it from the doorway. Someone had dragged the broken chair from the bonfire heap, it seemed, and returned it to the house. Was this

Harrie? John approached it carefully, as if it were a trap, half expecting his brother-in-law to jump out from behind the door. The chair looked much as it had done before he'd decided to be rid of it, one armrest broken, placed on the seat. The shepherd wreathed in leaves had his ear to the window. A silence of distant sounds, empty words, white moths, a faint hope in the end of dreams, the ending of a dream that had for the longest time seemed impossible, the sound of wind amongst the ruins, the wind that will pick up, flatten the shacks, a silence that he listens to in the hope of bleating.

*

Out on the veranda Finn was moving small stones. 'Ciara lost interest but he's persevering,' explained Monica as they stood together and for a while they observed him in silence, back and forth, picking up stones from the shore and walking to the house to deposit them, going back for more. Liz faintly recalled this being done before.

'He has his own mind,' said Monica, as if it were a mild concern.

Her attention was fixed on her son in a way that made Liz feel it was fine to remain quiet. The stones were pretty, the way they had been arranged, not so much in rows as in small piles that were nevertheless connected, close enough to overlap, some of the stones still wet so that their configuration glistened in places.

How long had he been at it? When she asked this her sister shrugged.

'At this age he's only just starting to grasp the concept of time.'

Liz made a sound of feigned interest, although in truth she was at least a little interested in what had been said.

'How long have you been picking up stones, Finn?' asked Monica.

'All day,' the boy shouted, halfway to the waterline.

'He hasn't,' said Monica.

Liz picked up one of the stones, grey and smooth. It felt nice to rub her finger against it. She hadn't considered that her nephew saw time differently to her. Babies might have a strange idea of time with all the sleeping, but children could walk and talk, they went to bed and got up for breakfast.

'Ciara knows how to read a clock,' said Monica. 'She's good at it. If you asked her to draw you time, what do you think she would draw?'

'A clock,' Liz said with some reluctance. She resented being quizzed but right then Monica's face lit up, as if they had together reached a point of bewilderment.

'But who knows what Finn would draw?' she said, hands thrown, and Liz was becoming intrigued by the glint in her sister's eye, the suggestion that this was a subject of real interest to her, the way her son saw the world, and not only because of his age, she felt. No, it was because of the way he went about himself, which was different from his sister, different from them.

Finn returned from the shore with an armful of stones. He dumped them on the veranda, some bounced over the side, he knelt and picked at those that remained, putting one beside another for some opaque reason until they were arranged and then he went happily back out for more. If he had been doing this all day, if that's what he thought, then what did he think he was doing it for? Liz imagined time as a sheet kept in place by stones hastily arranged on its corners. She thought about moments pressed down by a weight that had been worn into smooth, grey pieces. Together they watched him walk to the waterline.

Monica took a deep breath as if she had only just remembered to do so. 'You watch them and you watch yourself getting older,' she said and there was not the usual you-don't-understand-this-yet to her words, no closed door. Liz was let in, despite her childlessness, despite the gulf that her sister had taken pains to dig during the past few years. What part of her sister was this? When Liz was a teenager Monica had for a while been interested in science. It was encouraged by their mother. There had been work experience done in a local pharmacy and it had been so funny to go after school and see her sister there behind the counter. She'd brought a lab coat even though nobody else in the pharmacy wore one. One time Liz went in with some friends and asked Monica's advice on a pain she'd made up, listing a stabbing pain in her cervix, toxic gas erupting from her bowels. The actual pharmacist had eavesdropped and in all seriousness advised she see a doctor as soon as she could get an appointment. Monica had let it wash over her. At dinner she would talk excitedly about the responsibilities she was given, how medicines would be diluted, mixed, measured.

Liz herself had at that time wanted to be an actor, was under the impression she was pretty good at it but drama school wasn't ever going to happen, it wouldn't stand a chance with her parents and she understood why, the money, so she hadn't pushed, even if it would've been nice, all that walking around an empty space pretending to be an animal. It wasn't the same for Monica, both parents had loved the idea of her being into science and, now Liz thought about it, there'd been a good year or two when Monica was for all intents and purposes a scientist-in-waiting. Strange to remember, so distant that person. What had happened when she wasn't paying attention? Monica had done business management at City University, Liz could tell you that, and it hadn't struck her at the time as a missed direction, not in the slightest.

Where had the desire gone? What had changed in the years between the pharmacy and leaving home? A wash of shame went over Liz at the thought she had been looking elsewhere, too wrapped up in herself when her sister had wavered from her true purpose. Had she let her down? They were in the kitchen now and Richard was smoking at the threshold. Liz disliked the smell and she wished he would move further away but he was talking to Monica about some Russian artist and she didn't have the energy to tell him what to do.

*

Most of the dead plants had already been moved, carried to the heap by the shore. There were still weeds in places but these too were manageable, the garden no longer dominated by their shapes and in fact those that remained were not unappealing, thought John. After all, a weed is only a name. As he knew little about the names of plants, he made his mind up that they could stay until he learnt otherwise, their nature revealed when they were shoulder to shoulder with the fuchsias or foxgloves, names he only knew because he used to pop little fuchsias between his finger and thumb, foxgloves because he imagined little paws wearing pink and purple.

Cleared of life, the garden's architecture could be better appreciated, the straight sections of bare soil demarcated with brick borders, the grey slabs a walkway between the flower beds, not that there were any flowers, only the dirt, which was not the substance John had expected it to be but was made up of clumps and stones, and if he looked closer he could make out tiny fragments of glass.

'You don't want foxgloves,' said Harrie. 'Super toxic.'

'We'll be careful.'

'Mark my words, toddlers eat everything.'

Harrie shot him a meaningful look. He had his hands on his hips as he faced a rectangular plot the size and shape of a double bed. There was a monumentality to the empty garden. John almost missed the tangle, which was at least a job to be doing.

'They use it in heart medicine,' Harrie said. He did not turn from the soil, absorbed by it, by the ground, bare, or so it seemed to John, who thought then that his brother-in-law might see in the dirt a beginning, for better or worse.

'We'll see,' sighed John.

'See what?'

'About children.'

Harrie turned to him, his eyes no longer as firm, open to read what was on John's face, which John did his best to control but at the same time he wanted something to slip out, something to be shown to make his brother-in-law understand there were things undecided. Harrie went *mmm* as if it were a matter of intrigue and looked him in the eye, a confidence that made John feel weak, a withered branch, broken fingers nursed in the folds of a cloak, tentatively opened, shown to a doctor.

'Yes, we'll see,' John repeated, smiling, this time the words were casual, a tease. He had wrapped the cloak back around his fingers, Harrie appeared to realise it too, the way he stiffened, stared beyond him.

'I would've only had one, if I could go back and change things.' Harrie tapped a finger to his lips. 'Finn is great, I couldn't imagine life without him, but one is enough. One does the job.'

When they inspected the flower beds and spoke about growing runner beans John thought about the men's reproductive health tablets he took with his breakfast, big and purple, and how in the pornography he watched there would be cum in great gallons. *One does the job.* Did Harrie go through his days with the comfort of life's continuance?

'Did you bring my chair back in?' he asked.

'What? No.'

'It's back inside.'

Harrie squinted at him. 'Good.'

*

A deer was close enough to the treeline to be made out, a good few yards away, still far enough that it could turn around, Liz thought, far enough that if they stepped into the woods it would run. Alma and Ciara were closer to the trees, right on the edge of the clearing, her niece alternating between looking at the animal and turning her face up to the student, delight across her, as if she wanted to make sure Alma was also looking, *look!* They had been playing together, the two of them, and Liz had been coming over when the pair had frozen and stared at the trees. She'd been coming because Ciara had laughed so loudly that it was heard in the kitchen and she'd wanted to know what had compelled her niece to make such a noise, who was it that had made her laugh, and when she'd seen it was Alma she'd had the urge to intervene, not that she was jealous, but the laugh had been wild, a little crazed, and it wouldn't be Alma's fault if Ciara was doing something she shouldn't but someone needed to keep an eye. Ciara was pushing boundaries, the parents were elsewhere. Really it should be Monica checking. If she hadn't gone off with Richard she'd be down there. Liz had instincts, she knew Ciara, more than Alma she knew her.

The thought came to her that they were playing on the spot John had buried the fawn. She wasn't sure where that was but it was a fear that bloomed as she'd set out from the house, that her niece would be pulling at a hoof in the ground, nasty little maggots. Now they were standing still and facing the woods, the blue Frisbee in Alma's hands as they moved closer to the treeline. She should be relieved but still there was the sensation that Ciara was loose, untethered, and she could not place it. Her niece did not look at her. She moved beyond the first tree. Liz expected the deer to run but it stayed where it was, its ears alert, its face small and thin and fixed on them. Alma slowly followed. Liz stayed where she was. The student glanced back. Ciara was holding out her hand in front of her. 'I have seen your baby,' the girl said. 'I have seen your baby.'

*

Richard must have found an old bottle of pastis in one of their boxes because when he came into the garden he was carrying it under one arm, three glasses in his other hand. John didn't even remember packing it from their shelf above the oven in the flat. Richard set himself up on one of the flower-bed walls and poured for himself. The other two glasses he left stacked, not offering them to John or Harrie, who tried all the same to be courteous, asking Richard something about face-to-face teaching which John didn't entirely follow, his attention on the two sparrows who had flown from the roof of the house to search for signs of life in the dirt.

'Yes, and you should thank me for it,' said Richard when John asked him if it was he who had brought in the broken chair. 'All it needs is someone to fix the armrest, that's all we did to it.'

'I'm not blaming you.'

'I didn't break anything that can't be fixed.' Richard threw his hands up and his eyes were wild.

Harrie cleared his throat. 'Son. Nobody is out to get you.'

'Oh, please shut up.'

After this outburst Richard looked off at an empty flower bed, then started to poke around at the soil, picking up a small piece of glass, flicking it away. John thought to call him out on his rudeness but talked instead about building a bird feeder. Harrie had a dark look on his face. John considered bringing the chair back out to the heap to spite the both of them, although in truth he liked knowing it was in the house. Maybe he was even thankful to Richard for saving it. There again the feeling that the student might be right about things, that they were running out of meaning, that it would be fatal, and that there was little time to do anything about it.

Soon the others came to the empty garden like debris on a riverbank, first Tariq, then Monica and Finn, then Alma, Liz and Ciara, who spoke with barely contained excitement to her brother about a deer they had seen in the woods. Tariq appeared to be genuinely enthusiastic about the prospect of deciding what to do with their garden. If Sweet was here, they would get along, John thought. Perhaps he had misjudged him. The student was not showy with his interest, rather he listened to them talk about their vague plans, the idea for perennials, maybe some vegetables, at least herbs. He listened and then offered some clear, practical advice. They should think carefully about the light, which areas were in the shade, and if they wanted to get any fruit trees they would be better to wait until the spring, Tariq said, after the frosts had gone but when there was still plenty of rainfall.

'You know your stuff,' said Liz.

'My parents grow things on their balcony.'

'You hate your parents,' hissed Richard.

Tariq gave him a look that was more of concern than irritation. 'I'd say beetroot is an easy place to start.'

Ciara was sitting on one of the flower-bed walls and she had her brother on her lap, perched on her knees, even though she squirmed from his weight. 'I went to the shop to buy a lollipop,' she sang, bouncing Finn up and down to the boy's delight. 'I sat on the chair and the chair went pop.' With the final word she dropped Finn to the ground and he gave out a mock scream then immediately asked her to do it again.

It would make a good picture, John thought, the parents would appreciate a picture of their children on holiday, Harrie would like it. 'Can I borrow your phone,' he asked Liz. His phone was charging. She wanted to know why he needed it, unlocked it and handed it over. There were sparrows on the wall behind and he was careful to get them in shot. Tariq and the children hadn't seen him and it was better that way, without posing. What do sparrows eat? He could fill a bird feeder with whatever made them happy. *I went to the shop to buy a lollipop.* He got a few good ones, looking back at them, zoomed into Finn's face, full of joy. He closed the camera, went on the browser and started to type 'sparrow diet' but he only got to 'sp' when it auto-completed to 'sperm donor'.

Below the words were a list of suggested websites. Websites that she had already visited? There was a place called London Sperm Bank, another that looked like an NHS guide to sperm donation. He didn't follow any of the links. He went no further. He blackened the screen and went over to give Liz back her phone.

She put an arm around his waist as Tariq spoke to them of a meal made with beetroot and chickpeas and yoghurt and harissa paste and a few other things. He would send them the recipe when he was home, but it was really easy to make and delicious, he reassured, he'd eaten it since he was a boy. She squeezed John with her arm, bringing him a little closer, and he looked at the children as they swapped roles and Ciara took to her brother's knee. *And the chair went pop.* He could smell his wife's scent and he imagined the deep purple-red of beetroot.

Then, out of the blue, Richard hooked his forefinger into Tariq's cheek. The poke was rough and Tariq seemed taken aback. He shot Richard a glare, smiled, carried on.

'I'd get a little greenhouse, if there isn't room on your windowsill,' he said to Monica.

Richard tried to hook him again in the cheek. Tariq immediately pushed the hand away and covered the corner of his lips with his palm. There was a wicked grin on Richard's lips. He looked drunk. John could feel the tension coming off him but didn't react because Tariq made light of it, letting out a chuckle, rubbing his sore skin. 'Stop talking,' Richard said, and jabbed his finger again into Tariq's face. This time the others stepped in. Alma asked him what he was doing. John and Harrie stood a little more upright, John put out his hand. 'Playing around,' explained Richard. A hard laugh.

Tariq glanced at Alma, who had taken Richard's hand and was holding it firm by her side. He sniffed, stepped to Richard and jabbed him in the same way, a finger thrust, but either Richard moved or Tariq misjudged because the tip of his finger went deep into Richard's eye.

He made a horrible sound, bent over.

Tariq had his hands on his head. 'Oh fuck oh fuck.'

Richard staggered to push Tariq, John held his hand out again, tried to stop him, grabbed Richard's shirt when he pulled away and a bit of the sleeve ripped off. His left eye was bloodshot and squinting. Tariq for all his apologising took an opportunity and threw a fist at Richard's nose, then the two of them went at each other until Harrie came out of nowhere and wrestled Richard to the ground.

The student screamed at Harrie to get off him and Harrie kept shouting at him to stop moving. He was much larger than Richard and managed to get hold of one of his fingers and he bent it backwards. Richard screamed in pain and fought harder to get free. Harrie bent it further backwards and John told him to stop. Everyone told him to stop, Tariq included. But Richard was still thrashing and Harrie bent the student's forefinger further backwards, and further backwards still until it snapped.

*

'Didn't you want to do science at university?' asked Liz.

'No,' said Monica.

On the TV the news was repeating footage of the final US planes leaving Kabul.

'Yes you did,' said Liz.

'Why does it matter?'

'I remember it.'

Monica turned to her. She looked exhausted. 'If you say so.'

They switched over to *Grand Designs* where there was a house that had an earthen roof, that was the plan at least, but there were questions about whether the reinforced concrete ceiling would support the weight of 500 tonnes of soil or whether it would buckle and collapse and a little daughter was saying she'd thought about putting an umbrella above her bed as she slept. They watched the father urge the builders to spread the concrete from their mixer, even though the foreman warned them it was too runny for the sloping roof. There was movement in the corridor and it sounded like John's footsteps. Liz looked to see if it was him, hoped he would sit beside her.

'They must be seriously over budget,' scoffed Monica.

The father on TV was wearing a hi-vis vest that looked too big for him. The concrete had been set but he seemed stressed. Liz looked at the doorway for her husband but he wasn't there. Was he being distant or was she imagining it?

'They say he needs to be seen by a doctor,' said Harrie as he came into the room.

'John can take him.'

'I think I should do it.'

'Are you serious?' Monica started to say something else to her husband, but instead she got up and went out with Harrie to the corridor where they spoke too quietly for Liz to hear. The turf had been put over the top of the earthen house. She thought of barrows for the dead. Finn and Tariq were playing with a chess set. Ciara was watching something on an iPad. The father in *Grand Designs* was walking through a dark concrete hollow. Filmed in spring 2020, a caption said. Work had paused. After a while Monica returned to her place, tucked her bare feet beside her, but now her body was angled away from Liz, her elbow resting on the armrest of their rubbish sofa. Liz could tell her that she was pregnant, that it might be a possibility. She could say there was a sensation inside her like new life. She wanted her sister back on her side. 'They've put the rooms in,' she said, catching Monica up. What would she tell her but to do a test, they would get one that evening, she would insist, would wait outside the bathroom door while she did it.

'It'll take years to offset all that concrete,' said Tariq from the floor.

There was shuffling in the hallway, a few people moving by. John poked his head in. 'They're going now. Alma's going with them.' He glanced at Tariq but Tariq kept his focus on the chess set. Would he still go to Newcastle, Liz wondered. The student acted as if he hadn't heard anything. He spoke in a quiet voice to Finn about the movement of the bishop and her nephew was trying his best to understand. She felt a cramping. It could be implantation. Did this feel different from the usual cramps? Maybe it did. She thought it did. John lingered at the threshold. She wanted him to come in and sit with them, on her other side, her sister against one arm, him against the other.

There was more activity in the hallway.

'Text me when you get there,' shouted Monica.

The front door slammed shut. John stood on the threshold. Monica looked over at him then back at the TV. Liz would tell her as soon as she knew, she wouldn't wait for the three-month scan. As soon as she knew herself she would let her in, bright and early, it would be a morning, a start to things, the first person she would call as soon as the little pink plus was indisputable, the first person to know, even before John, she decided, maybe even before him, and she would tell her sister that, it would make her feel special, being the first to know. She could feel the possibility inside her, a growing sac that would push her outwards, do things to her bones and her veins that she couldn't yet comprehend, and her sister would tell her things that she'd long kept from her, the fullness of the situation, things that had only been hinted at in their old messages about nausea and sleepless nights. That was when Monica had pulled back from her, Liz thought, talking less to her, or at least differently, a different kind of talking.

She had held John's hand in the sauna. How long had they grasped each other?

Upstairs she checked her knickers and there wasn't anything there, only some wetness. It could well be implantation cramping, she thought. This could be what it feels like.

*

Not long after Harrie had left for the hospital John told the others he wanted to go for a walk. Without conscious thought he took to the path that led around the circumference of the lake. The sight of Richard's bloody eye was something he wanted out of his head and as soon as he had entered the treeline he was struck by the stillness, the windless corridor of the path that took him further from the house and everyone inside it. The sun was close to setting. The sky was copper seen through the trees, long shadows, his body stretched out on the path before him, now here, now taken up by the leaves, the silhouette of an empty chair, his father's lap. The golden hour, time thick and fixed like honey. He thought of the old jars of honey in the back of a cupboard left by the previous inhabitants, cloudy and crystalline. The students will rail for nothing, he thought. They will come up against it.

And the chair went pop.

Jars of white. How long had she been looking at donations? Was he still on the path, he wondered, his shadow raising its long legs, the water just about visible to one side and the endless trees to the other, the pale orange meeting blue. He had not meant to go this far. There you are, you fork in the road. His long shadow leading the way, his father singing above the smell of the sausages, tall in the kitchen with the radio on. They will believe in a golden hour, a pint glass of salt, the gates of parliament blown open wide. I have come this far, about a quarter of the way, nobody is calling me back so why not walk a little further, I will only go so far, can only go so far before I'm brought back. Am I any good to her? A shadow, a chair, his father's voice in the kitchen. He is dripping honey into the pan, runny and soon to sizzle. They will think of change, assuming an eternal, the unchangeable appearance of death. The dog in the hallway. I am at four o'clock, on my way to five. I will come back to you, believe me. It's not in me to leave you behind. A lake of honey. I should take a picture, he thought. I will, he thought, and he stopped and aimed his phone at the view. A spoonful of honey. Whose voice is this speaking? The shadow in front of him, stretched out and cast against the bark of a tree.

He came to the midway point, where days before they had found a heap of cigarette ends, and there he saw someone sitting on a stump by the water. The sun had set but the light was still clear enough to make it out for Sweet. The warden had turned from his view of the house to face him, a cigarette between his lips. He had a look on his face like grim acceptance. He did not stand or turn away but remained there staring at John, who thought then that Sweet must have heard him approaching for some time, so quiet were the woods.

'Stretching your legs,' observed Sweet with calm certainty. John did not speak at first. The surprise of another person was coming on slowly. Some of the lights had already been turned on in the house. The red sky was fading. Sweet drew on his cigarette, bringing a hand to his lips. 'If I'm feeling knotted up I sit very still and I focus on my breathing.'

'Do you, now?'

'It helps, I find.'

Sweet dropped his cigarette. It looked as if he'd barely begun it. He ground it up with the heel of his boot. John thought of continuing on his way, thought about whether it would be quicker pressing forward or going back the way he came, if he had to choose. 'We had a bit of drama,' he said.

Clearing his throat, Sweet stood from his stump, put away his pouch of tobacco and picked up his backpack.

'Did you finish your work with the bats?' John asked.

'I was on my way home, this is on my way.'

There was still light on the lake but it was fading. John attempted to appear collected, calm enough to stare out across the water at his house.

'My dog hasn't come back to me and she always comes back,' said Sweet. 'She's been away before but she always comes back.'

'I didn't know you had a dog.'

'She's a stray and I don't attempt to keep her but maybe I should've. She doesn't have a name, I made up my mind that I wouldn't give her a name.' Sweet raked his fingertips on the blue stubble beneath his chin. 'She sleeps in a pile of old newspapers and I feed her whatever I'm eating. At least I used to. You don't need to listen to me go on. It's not your problem.'

'You were looking for your dog?'

Another light was turned on in the house. John could just about make out the shape of Monica on the veranda.

'Have you seen a dog?' Sweet asked.

'No.'

Sweet gripped his backpack straps.

'She's a lovely girl. Never really barks.'

His expression became strained and heavy, like someone in great pain.

'If I did call her something it would be Lucy, that was my little girl's name.'

The warden looked at the ground. John could ask him to come back to the house, he could offer him a drink. The air was still warm. Sweet wished John a good night and then he walked into the dark of the trees.

*

We got some fresh air and sat on our stones, each with our favourite like a side of the bed, my love to my right but too far to touch, too far for that. There in front of us a crown had washed up on the shore but my love did not leave his stone and neither did I. It could have been metal from the way it carried the moonlight. It could have been part of a costume, plastic, maybe even painted wood. It was a dull golden shade, simple and unadorned.

I wanted to say something to pull him out of himself but I could not think of the right words. I thought back to the hammer and its metal head. I thought of the concertina and its tender ribs. I was still convinced that there was something of value held in the connections between these objects and I sensed a new urgency in my attempts to bring them together. I was finding it harder to hold them all. Was my love feeling the same way? Was he also struggling to understand? I had at one time found it helpful to imagine these things in one room, each in their proper place, but this was becoming laboured as they kept coming, complicating parallels I thought I had squared away.

I tried to envision the green parlour, its drinks cabinet with a hinged panel that doubles as a shelf, a handsome piece of furniture. The lights in the room are dim and cosy, the fireplace lit. There is the smell of wood, I think. The smell of bark. Children's toys have been left on the floor and the light of the fire gives the small objects a life of their own, shadows dancing behind them as if they were each a spirit, the souls of small trains and numbered blocks. In my mind, there are two figures in the room, a man and a woman, and let's say that one of them is me and I am holding a young child who is asleep on my shoulder. The windows are groaning against the weight of water, but the room itself is warm as if it has always been warm.

I did once have an impression of this room, as if it were a distant memory, but I realised then that I had overridden this feeling with something else entirely. I had filled it in, as if it had been a dream that I had tried to articulate and in doing so I had smothered it with a clean white sheet. Where else then to put these things? How else to take them? I had been determined to hold each of the objects we had found, to pay attention to their blemishes and the specific qualities of their materials, but there on the shore of the lake my attempts to unite them felt forced, hollow. The parlour with the dark green walls no longer gave me the sense of relief it once had. I had ruined it by forcing us inside and now we were left with the memory of these things, one thing after the other, and when would it end, I wondered. Would we do this for the rest of our lives?

The night air was not yet cool. The crown was unmoved by the waves that were lapping against it. We stayed on our stones for a while and watched the water come and go.

ELEVEN

T HE FURNITURE ARRIVED DURING breakfast, a
real surprise, when John came back to say the noise
they'd heard was a big white van pulling up beside the
house. What a relief from the quiet they'd fallen into with
their toast and cereal. Harrie had only mumbled that he'd
left Richard and Alma in the waiting room of A&E, nothing more except for the fidgets when Finn had asked if
he'd get to play with Tariq. 'Not today,' said Monica, more
firmly than Liz thought was needed. 'He's gone home.'

They put on their shoes and watched as the men opened
the back of the van and began to carry things through the
front door. First a deep blue three-seater Lawson sofa that
had been on sale, wrapped in protective film, then a set
of sage-green spindle-back chairs that Liz knew would
go well with the light wooden panelling of the dining
room. If the children had seemed out of sorts, it was soon
smoothed away by the palpable excitement of one piece
of furniture being brought in after another. Harrie helped
to stack the flatpack boxes in batches in the hallway and
living room, Ciara and Finn wanting to do the same, but
Monica was worried about crushed little fingers so she
kept them busy with putting the new chairs around the

dining table and moving the old things outside. John carried boxes upstairs and Liz supervised the unloading until it was complete and then she signed the delivery forms, Elizabeth P, and when she came back into the house she was cheered by the activity around her.

'Dry until the afternoon,' Monica called through the kitchen, as if it were an answer to something. She moved her head to look down the corridor but if she was looking for Harrie, he'd already passed into the dining room. From where she was standing, Liz could see him inspecting the label on one of the boxes.

'Monica says it's meant to stay dry until the afternoon.'

'That's alright then,' he said without looking up. 'I wouldn't want your things getting wet.'

'No.'

'I can't be everywhere.'

He was trying, it seemed to Liz, to come across as sensible, knowledgeable. 'Was he okay, then. Richard?' She made it sound innocent, as if Harrie had had no hand in it. He kept his attention on the side of the box.

'Fine, I'm sure. He'd broken it cleanly.'

She recalled that he'd only left them in A&E, not waited for the doctor. Had that been his choice? Had they fought in the waiting room? 'He seemed in a lot of pain,' she said, less innocently. Whatever he had been inspecting on the label passed the test and Harrie, not showing any reaction to what she'd just said, carried the flat box to lean against a different wall, against a different set of boxes. The toast was still on the table and

Harrie picked up a piece, ate it in a few rushed bites, then cracked his knuckles. She felt a cramping.

'Do you like the colour?' she asked, nodding towards the new chairs. The sound of their voices was different around the new furniture, she realised, the acoustics of the dining room softer, less empty. It was only now the change had occurred that she could appreciate how hollow they must have sounded over the past few days.

'Green,' he said. He knelt down to inspect another of the boxes. 'A light green,' he said, and tried to pull at the tape. 'Are the scissors in the kitchen?'

'Don't do it now, Harrie.'

He dusted off his kneecaps. 'I'm just getting the instructions out, Prune.'

Liz didn't want to wait for him to come back, didn't want her good mood to be broken. She had an urge to write something and she did so upstairs in their bedroom, where some more boxes that contained everything needed for a new chest of drawers had been leant against the wall. She checked her knickers and there was no blood. Relieved, she picked up where she'd left off, taking the final few words and stepping out beyond them, not worried about a continuation of the old line but trusting in a new thought that would show through its clouded glass something of her as she was then, with the sound of activity through the open bedroom door, the movement and voices downstairs, the deep blue sofa in the middle of the living room, its protective wrap removed, colour resounding. This was something to capture. The shades she would bring to this place. She would go out later today and buy a pregnancy test, a pack or two, as had been her habit in their first year of trying. She allowed the feeling that was on her to come out in the direction of her sentence. *He was confident these new surroundings would be the key to things.* She pushed forward and was pleased with the pace she was making, tried not to focus on the speed her hand was moving because then she would be self-conscious and the words would cease to come willingly. She would have to force them down in front of her like bricks on a bridge laid on the first crossing, without suspension, and she needed to believe there was suspension otherwise the whole thing would end up in the water.

John appeared, his face bright, and he stood by the bed looking around him, seeing the room anew with fresh potential, she imagined, and he had under his arm a new lampshade, yellow, which he placed by her bare feet, flashed a smile and left without a word. She liked this side of him, the way he had when he was excited about things, infectious, and she continued to put down her words with that in mind. He had a good eye for colour. He was like a bumblebee for colour.

When John came back, it was with the stool, fetched from outside. He was becoming attached to it. He climbed and unscrewed the bare lightbulb. Liz was writing again on the bed. What else had she kept from him, he wondered. He remembered the last time she'd taken it seriously, a disaster, which was a harsh way to put it but how else would you describe a crushed pair of driving glasses? The slow creep of self-doubt that came after the rejections. *I'm just worried it's no good.* He'd reassured her that she was doing well but she went around and around and in the end she'd stepped on her own glasses, the tortoiseshell ones she wore when she worked at the computer. A worrying thing to do. She'd been wiping the lenses and they were still greasy and she'd dropped them on the kitchen floor and crushed them under the heel of her shoe. Still worse, she'd told him about it just as he'd been drifting off, and he'd fallen asleep thinking about tiny shards of glass in the kitchen, the smallest slivers, hard to see but sharp enough to cut your foot.

The lampshade gave the light what it was missing. The bedroom had a glow that should have always been there. He closed the curtains to hide the daylight and their belongings became soft. Liz was watching him. 'It's soft,' he said, but it was not what he meant, not really, more like a ghost of a bedroom imprecise in its memory. Had she already found a donor? In one of her stories there'd been a man who cracked his knees, in another a man had cheated on his partner and he had seen himself there, how could he not? When he'd asked Liz about it she'd said it wasn't him, it wasn't as simple as that, not as neat, she'd said. What else is a person but versions dreamt up by others? Had she already found herself a sperm donor? He felt a pain in his chest, a physical pain, a feeling of pressure. In a tree trunk he'd once been bodiless, no head, no hands, no eyes from which to see the dark. From where was that memory? He needed to place it. When had he ever been inside the trunk of a tree? He remembered clearing away Mrs Walsh's fallen apples. She'd offer him a glass of lemonade, always had a small plate of chocolate digestives ready on the table. Some of the apples were rotten on the grass. He would throw those in a black bucket and the firm ones in a red bucket. He remembered the colours. Mrs Walsh often watched him from the doorway, quiet, not unhappy with his work, just thinking about things. That was the way he liked to imagine she'd put it, if ever he had asked. In Liz's story the man who cheated on his partner had felt great regret. The man would often think of himself like a bruised piece of fruit. He always met a version of himself in her writing, no matter how extrapolated. She would strip him to his bones if she could, take him for parts. Was he really so lacking? Had she already taken everything of use from him?

'How would you describe it?' he asked, looking up at the lampshade.

'It's quite yellow,' she said.

'It's meant to be ochre.'

'I wouldn't say ochre.'

'Hmm.'

'What's ochre?' she asked.

'Browny yellow.'

'I wouldn't say ochre.'

She was back on with her writing. Was she going to put the lampshade in her story, he wondered. He would find it there, he was sure of it. 'We can send it back if you want,' he said.

'Why would you do that?'

'If you don't like it.'

She was writing again, a small frown of concentration. 'We don't have to keep it.'

'I don't hate it,' she said.

What colour will she write it? The apples in Mrs Walsh's garden were red, they weren't red, they weren't any colour he could name, if he were truthful, red and green and brown and yellow, none of those, they didn't fit the picture. Why was this memory on him? He thought of himself contained in the trunk of a tree. Was it something that had actually happened, long ago? He wanted her to lay down her notebook. Her face was strained, for a moment grimacing as if in pain. Whatever she was writing, he did not want it to cause her pain. He wanted her to be happy with things, the furniture here and lots to get on with. If she was upset about him holding her sister's hand, there was nothing to it, nothing at all. 'Shall we go downstairs?' he asked.

'Can you open the curtain?'

She smiled when the daylight was back and returned once more to her notebook. A gorgeous look, he thought, with the day on her skin and the unguarded way she had glanced at him, her cheeks aglow. He wanted to think they knew each other better than anyone else. Please let him think this. Could he trust that she would draw a line around him just as he would draw a line around her?

When he was out of the room she undid her belt and unbuckled her jeans, lifted her knickers. Her period had come after all. She went straight back to writing. *The light from the table lamp struck her differently.* Her heart was dropping and she tried her best not to feel it. There was nothing to be sad about. Her pen kept on. She'd gotten away from herself, that was all. Silly thing to do. She kept on for a little longer and then, as if she had reached a slope and had no strength to climb, she closed her notebook on her lap. There were pads in the bathroom. The blood had been brown, red, little vessels and lining. Nothing new. No harm, no loss. She stared at nothing in particular. Where then was Alma, she wondered. What was she doing at that moment? Liz scraped a fingernail against the ridge of her notebook's closed pages. Scruch, scruch. She imagined a little room with one window, nothing except floorboards, the window open, the sound of traffic and crowds outside. She went downstairs and finished the sentence on the dining-room table, Harrie working quietly on the other side. *There was the noise of crashing water.* She crossed it out, crossed out the page harder than she'd intended and the paper ripped. Harrie looked up from his books at the sound, she expected him to be irritated but his face was serious and fond. *There was the noise of crashing water.* She crossed it out again. Harrie looked away when she met his eye. If he reached his hand across the table she would take it.

'The end of next month,' Harrie said, later, when John asked him when his term would begin. 'Well, as of tomorrow it'll be this month,' said with an air of showy resignation, as if there was a collective understanding that they were teetering on September, the holiday was finishing and they would all of them soon return to routine. She could not right then picture herself at work in the study. The founders, the rhinoceroses, distant and small. Harrie said it would be good to get back to things. He looked washed out, she thought. 'The students really were a breath of fresh air,' he said, even later, the lake beside them as they walked once more its perimeter. His face was a limestone cave, dark, darker still. He did not sound convincing. Liz was holding John's hand. He had reached for her with an urgency and this made her angry, she didn't know why. 'They were so interested in things,' Harrie said to everyone. 'New energy.' Nobody responded. Ciara and Finn were walking beside their mother as they followed the path, this time in the reverse direction to normal, which had been John's idea.

'Deer deer, little deer, where are you little deer deer, little deer, where are you little deer,' Ciara chanted, Finn sometimes joining but losing here and there the rhythm, distracted, it seemed, by looking beyond the trees.

'Stop it,' said Ciara. 'You're not saying it properly.'

'Let him join in, baby,' said Monica.

'He's not saying it properly.'

Liz wanted to go back to the moment before she'd seen the blood in her knickers, as if there were a choice to be made, a different direction she could have travelled, although she knew full well it was impossible and there was only her body and John's body and somewhere between them was a thin but insurmountable pane of glass.

'*I* saw the deer, not him,' said Ciara.

'Deer deer deer,' said Finn. 'The deer hates you and it loves me.'

'No!'

'When can we see Tariq, Mummy?'

'Please shut up,' muttered Harrie. He exhaled loudly. The air became quiet again. Ciara glared at her brother. Monica searched for Finn's hand to hold but the boy pushed her fingers away.

They passed the midway point and John told them he'd seen Sweet out here the night before. 'He was 'aving a fag,' he said, putting on an accent.

It was only when they were back that Liz really thought about it, Sweet at night, sitting on a stump by the edge of the lake. Could he see their house? She would not mind and was surprised by her reaction. She imagined his position, leant forward so that his forearms rested on his knees, a masculine pose, his head wanting to fall downwards and effort needed to raise it up, as he would when he took a drag on his cigarette and for a moment his face would be lit by its fire.

She read a work email from one of the founders saying he was happy with the alpha. It was like reading a script for a play. The founder had a few notes but they seemed inconsequential and she couldn't picture herself taking them into account or for that matter anything else the founders said to her, so remote and unlike herself the whole thing seemed. What was she playing at?

'Who should we talk to about fertility testing?' she asked John when they were alone in the kitchen, after she'd told him her period had come and he'd given her a hug that had only made her angrier. She resented that he was feeling let down, which he hadn't said out loud but he must be thinking. She was suddenly annoyed with the sight of him, let alone his touch.

'I suppose we'll first need to get registered with a GP,' he said. 'You've looked into sperm donors already, I understand. We don't know if it's you or me, but whatever.'

'I haven't looked at sperm donors, what are you talking about?'

He folded his arms, standing there with a face that looked at once smug and nerve-wracked. 'I saw it on your phone. You've been looking it up.' His voice was low and angry.

'I've looked up all sorts of things.'

'*Surely* you can appreciate how it makes me feel?' He opened his eyes a little wider, as if galling her to respond. 'You can be callous, Liz. I think it comes from some emotional damage. I'm serious.'

'Are you really making this about you now?'

'I'm like a fucking… spice. Like fucking paprika. "Oh no, the jar's empty, I'll use some cumin instead."'

'What the fuck are you talking about?'

He pointed at her phone on the counter. 'You've been researching it.'

'I'm not replacing you with cumin. And "emotional damage", what the fuck, John?'

'I don't know, maybe damage isn't the right word.' He folded his arms, leant his hips against a cupboard. 'You have this side to you, though.'

She didn't say anything for a while. He stared at her phone. 'Maybe I looked it up a few weeks ago,' she said. 'If I did, it was just because I wanted to be informed about the process. I wouldn't do anything without talking to you.'

'Informed about the process.'

'Yes, John.'

'We don't know who has the problem. It could be both of us. Or maybe there isn't a problem.'

'Yeah.' Liz caught her breath. The way he looked at her then, it made her sad.

'We should be positive, you know?' He spread out his arms. 'I've been positive, proactive, I've done a lot around the house. The lamps. I've done the garden.'

She met his indignation, tapped the kitchen counter. Through the window, the children were dragging the old cheap set of chairs outside, along a gravel path from the veranda, around the corner and out of view. 'Have you paid me what you owe?'

'I…' He looked uneasy.

'Can you do it today?'

'We said when I have a better idea about work.'

'We didn't say that.'

He stood now with his arms on his hips, looking flustered and awkward. She felt a twinge of pity. He was about to say something but didn't. She could make out the shape of his skull beneath his skin, saw him for the bones, blinked to make it disappear but the impression lingered as she made herself an egg sandwich, and later, as she lay on their deep blue sofa and listened to the faint sounds of voices from other rooms, his face a skull, all her love for a skull. She loved him deeply. It made it worse.

But now was not the time to squeeze, he thought. They'd only just put the lamp up, here at last was the furniture they had ordered. Why bring the money up, to hurt him? Why so sour about things? This month was just the same as the others. They'd taken it all before with a steely determination, it had been a strength of theirs. They could only be practical. What else would change things? It was not his fault, besides, she can't blame him. He'll pay what he owes and he's ejaculated like the best of them. There's more where that came from, all for the taking. He thought then of vines growing over their windows, the house gone to ruin, full of empty bottles and burnt pans.

It was early evening when Monica asked him if he'd seen Finn. Her voice preceded her. He was putting up a dark green shelving unit and had been semi-aware of his nephew's name in the hallway, but it was only when she stood at the threshold that he could see the panic on her face.

'He's not with his sister,' she said.

He wasn't upstairs either, as they soon found out. Together they looked in all the rooms and they didn't find him hiding. Liz got wind that something was up and she stopped cooking to help them search in the attic, just in case, but he wasn't there so she went out in the drizzle with Harrie, who was by then walking to the edge of the treeline, shouting Finn's name.

'He'll be around,' said John. He looked out from the veranda at the water but couldn't see anything except raindrops. Deep breath. Finn definitely wasn't in the kitchen, he hadn't locked himself into the bathroom. In the dining room Ciara was sitting cross-legged reading a book, suspicious enough.

'Are you absolutely sure you haven't seen your brother?' asked Monica.

'I want to read this book.'

'This is important.'

'I don't know where he is.'

She was not telling the truth, even John could see that. When Monica knelt down beside her, placed a hand on her shoulder and asked her again, Ciara buckled, saying that *he* was the one who broke it, not her.

'Where is he, baby?'

Not long after that Harrie and Liz came back to the house with a split piece of wood, part of the antique chair's backrest, the delicate carvings broken just below the head of the shepherd. They'd found it on the shore beyond the trees. The rest of the chair was on its side by the path. Ciara shouted and stormed and had a little cry that Monica had no time for, forcing her daughter to explain herself. 'We won't be angry,' she said, jaw clenched.

The broken backrest was given to John as the parents knelt either side of their daughter, Harrie's hand on her little wrist, and in tears she told them that they had been moving the old furniture outside like they'd been told and when they were finished they had pulled the heavy chair to the trees. There they had played at being the King and Queen of the Seven Seas and she had told Finn to be careful, she had told him to sit still, but he had clambered on the back when it was her turn and it hadn't been her fault at all, she'd been sitting still.

'You're hurting me,' she said.

'Where is he?'

The face of the shepherd was in John's hands, wreathed in wooden leaves. He ran his thumb over the head, the faintest of bumps where a nose and lips once would have been. The wood was a much lighter colour where it had broken away, beneath the dark varnish, jagged beneath the neck of the shepherd. He thought of the first time he'd set eyes on the carving, after his granny had died and they'd taken away the pillows and throws.

Ciara had told Finn that Daddy would shout, that Uncle John and Auntie Liz would also shout at him for the damage he'd done to their precious and expensive chair. He would be taken to the police, she'd told him. So he'd better hide and not come out until she went to get him. It serves him right for saying the deer hated her, which was a lie and a stupid thing to say. She'd found him a place to tuck himself, a hollow tree with big roots. She would have got him before dinner, she said.

All of them went immediately with Ciara outside. The sky was dark with rain clouds and they soon came to the fallen chair on the path. John put it upright. A sad sight, with its snapped arm and broken back. The combined weight of the children must have come crashing down on the carvings, breaking the old wood in two. Liz gave him a sympathetic look. He felt exposed, ridiculous, holding a silly piece of wood.

Finn was not near the tree. Ciara called for her brother, that he could come out, but there was no response. They shouted his name and it was becoming more and more difficult to keep calm about it.

'Wasn't anyone watching them?' Harrie looked at John from below the hood of his raincoat.

'They're your children.'

He felt his chest tighten.

'Are you insinuating—'

'He's not insinuating,' said Liz.

'These stupid fucking woods,' said Monica.

Ciara looked afraid of her parents, didn't want them to approach her. When Harrie asked her if she was telling a fib she screamed that she wasn't. Liz offered to take her back to the house but Ciara refused to go, she shouted *Finn Finn Finn*.

'I don't even know where to start,' said Monica.

'We'll make circles,' said John.

'He could've broken his leg in a ditch, he could've drowned in a puddle. Oh God.'

'Take a breath,' said Liz.

'Take your own fucking breath.'

'Hey!'

'Not now.'

'He could be dead.'

Liz reached out a hand to Ciara. 'Do you want to come back with me?'

'You've already asked her,' said John. He heard the temper in his voice.

'I just don't think this is good for her and it's starting to come down heavy.'

'Finn! Where are you? Finn!' Ciara was getting further away from them.

'You told them to take out the old furniture, Monica, is that right?'

'Don't blame me, Harrie. I'm not going to stand here and have you blame me.'

'Ciara, come back where we can see you, please,' said Liz.

'Don't you fucking blame me.'

'We'll make widening circles around the tree.'

'Let me handle this, John.' Harrie began to point at the others. 'Prune, if you and Monica go that way, we'll go this way.'

'What's wrong with making circles?'

'It'll take too long.'

John felt a red surge. 'No, it's a good idea.'

'FINN,' cried Ciara.

Harrie tripped on a rain-slick root, managed to stop himself falling over by holding onto a tree trunk.

'You know something, you're a joke,' John said. 'You're hopeless.'

Liz stared at him. What was he doing? There was a prickle on the back of his neck, a blood rush, a ringing in his eyes.

'Is he saying that to me? Why are you saying that to me?'

'You embarrassed yourself yesterday, you really made a mess of it.'

John felt a lightness in the sudden anger, as if a weight were finally being thrown from his shoulders in the direction of Harrie. 'You're useless, honestly now. Stop insisting on things. There's no point to you.' There now was the sharp sensation of absence. He was closer to Harrie, then. He was within reach. As if without thought, he pushed him. It caught his brother-in-law by surprise and he tumbled back over the exposed root.

'What is *wrong* with you men?'

'Leave my daddy alone!'

'John!'

'It's the constant fumbling. The constant... The constant—'

'Finn, where are you?'

'And stop calling her Prune. Literally nobody else does it.' John was breathing fast and a terrible thought was telling him to keep on his fallen brother-in-law, to not let him get back up. He should kick him in the teeth, kick them down his throat. Harrie scrabbled to get back up, his clothes smeared with dirt. John was prepared for his fury but there was only alarm on his face.

'I need to find my son,' he said.

'John, leave him.'

Monica strode away from the mess. 'Finn, where are you? Say something. We're not angry with you.'

'John,' said Liz, and her face was pure shock.

He took a breath and walked away, beginning a circle around the tree. The rain was beating down on the leaves and it was making it difficult to hear each other.

'He's acting fucking crazy,' said Harrie.

'You're one to talk,' said Liz.

'I was stopping a fight.'

'You broke a man's finger.'

'Finn! FINN!'

'Can you take her back to the house?'

'No, no. I'm not going.'

'Come here, Ciara. Come here, darling.'

'Finn, Finn!'

'I can't hear what she's saying.'

'Where's Monica?'

'I can't hear.'

'Can you get her, Prune?'

'Don't call her that!'

'Keep walking, John.' Liz held up a hand.

'I can't hear anything.'

'Finn, where are you?'

'I can't.'

'Please.'

'Ciara, please.'

*

Inside, she opened some ready salted crisps and put them in a green glass bowl, told Ciara that her brother would be fine and together they watched *The Simpsons* and Liz thought about the quickness of time and how much had moved in a couple of hours. John the idiot, taking God-knows-what out on a man searching for his son. Is he really so self-involved? Her sister had never looked so scared. Never before had Liz seen the panic she'd seen as Monica searched about the trees, refusing to believe Finn wasn't hiding amongst the roots. Real fear. As it got darker outside her niece came in close to Liz on the sofa. In a heartbeat things could be snatched away. There was no guarantee of anything, she thought.

She rose and walked to the window, listening to the wind and the rain. This wasn't real, you always hear stories, we all know the stories. There was no guarantee. Her sister's face, her fearful face. Where now was Ciara? Still in the middle of the blue sofa. She should go back across the room to her. She peered out of the window but couldn't see much. Monica's voice rattled around. She had an urge to write it down. *There is no guarantee, no certainty of life.* How long until they call the police, she wondered. They'll call them when they get back empty-handed, if empty-handed. No, he'll be fine, found somewhere along the path. No reason to worry, there was a bit of light left. Could it be Sweet? Doesn't bear thinking. Something passed over the lake. Imagine Finn lying in the dirt, fallen down a ditch, his little shoes with their slippery little soles. Imagine him face down. She felt a nasty cramp and excused herself. Ciara didn't respond, watching Marge Simpson throw a bowling ball into the gutter.

She sat on the toilet, bent forward in pain. She felt her eyes well up and she thought she might cry but it didn't come and she was left on a threshold, the emotion large and unwilling to be moved. Home, she wanted to go home, where their mother used to call their grandma on the phone and they would dwell with each other's voices, even the magpie on the balcony with its chittering. Her eyes were closed and she listened to the sound of the TV, loud enough to be heard from upstairs. She wanted to write her sister's voice. *Here is how you sound, here is how I hear you. I do hear you. Don't you think I do?*

When she went back downstairs Ciara was gone.

John trod on. They had at first stayed close to the spot his niece had taken them, but gradually they edged further alongside the path, passing like a comb through the undergrowth. They made less of a circle than a wide constellation that moved further into the woods. At what point would they call the police? It hadn't yet been said but it wouldn't be long, John thought. The whole thing felt remote, at arm's length, as if they were playing a game of hide and seek. John shouted his nephew's name and listened for a reply, could hear the parents doing the same. Finn was probably hiding in the house, he assured himself. His nephew was in a cupboard or a wardrobe or one of the many cardboard boxes they'd emptied of wooden panels and screws. He caught a glimpse of Harrie through the trees. 'I think we should call the police,' he shouted.

'Finn,' cried Monica.

'Finn,' cried Harrie.

Were they ignoring him? Hadn't they heard? They were walking in the opposite direction, the light from their phones passing in and out of the trees. John walked on, his own torchlight on the wet forest floor. Without it, he could not grasp his feet as they trod on leaves and branches. The look on Liz's face after he'd held her in the kitchen. Perhaps she had been hoping more than he'd realised. What had possessed her to hope? His eyes were for a moment closed and he listened to the rain and the calls. Had he hoped too? Would it have made a difference? Here was the feeling that it was impossible, there would never be a small warm body between them. What had possessed her to hope? There now was their light through the trees, still further away. There had never been children. They had never existed on the face of the earth.

Liz was away, in the kitchen, in the hall. 'Ciara,' she called. Where could she have got to? Her heart was left behind as she rushed about the house in search of her niece, who was not downstairs and not upstairs, and these were only quick checks because Liz had a strong feeling the girl had run back into the woods. A nasty cramp coming on strong. Had she tried everything in her power? No point worrying now about the name and the weight. Mother. It wasn't for her, clearly not meant to be. 'Ciara,' she called, flinging open the back door and hoping to see her niece in the open, but there was only the darkening lake and the drenched landscape, not a soul in sight. We have spent our lives with the promise of life to come. She put on her coat and hurried away from the house. 'Ciara,' she cried. It is not yet my turn, she thought. I have not even begun the brutalities. There is no worm in the apple, no strike of lightning. I am less and less certain. He will leave me one of these days. Imagine a golden strand stretched to breaking. 'Ciara,' she cried. I have not even begun to suffer, there is no guarantee. A drop in a steel bucket below a leaky roof. In the years to come the house would fall into disrepair, only their furniture to rot. Black mould on the walls. I will not allow it. I will not allow it.

There never was a hope of life, he thought. There was a pain, the ache of his urinary infection. 'Finn,' he called. There was no great continuance, no big picture. They were phantoms, they had been there for a hundred years. Where are the others? 'Finn,' he called. How long had they been at this? Liz was angry and whose fault was that? No, I am still young, a prime specimen, all things considered. There had never been the hope of children, what a selfish hope to have. Whose voice is this speaking? What bitter words. There never were any children, I have not done enough to earn them. There is a shepherd wreathed in leaves, listening at the window. I am listening, always listening, speechless, unmoving.

Imagine a golden strand running between us, she thought. What more would it take to snap? I will not allow it. 'Ciara,' she cried. I have not even begun to suffer. 'Ciara,' she cried. I have been doing this for the longest time. I know him well, better than he knows himself. He will be satisfied with the voice I give him. Imagine a golden strand. We have not been fruitful, she thought with sudden and enormous pain. There is no guarantee, no promise that life will go on. The sooner we accept that, the easier it will be to spend our days with one another. I am falling to pieces, as my father before me. 'Finn,' he cried. I have been here for the longest time and nothing has changed. There is only a stirring every now and then. It comes to nothing. What had possessed her to hope? What had possessed her to hope? What had possessed her to hope? 'Finn,' he cried, the only word left to say.

*

We went out until we had reached the centre of the lake and there my love stopped the engine so we could enjoy the stillness and the silence, the water calm and giving only a gentle motion. Perhaps he had a different intention, perhaps calmness was not what he felt when he stopped the engine, rather exhaustion, and I thought to ask him about whether his legs ached, but the words would not come. We sat opposite one another and I must have become used to floating because I felt stable in a way I hadn't before, accustomed to the movement and no longer so mindful of the caverns winding deep beneath us, trusting in the boat to keep me afloat. I noticed then that he was not looking off into the waters or at the opposite shore, but studying me with an expression that took me aback with its attention, not hard but delving in the way his eyes seemed to consider each part of my face, my eyes, my cheeks, my lips. It was difficult not to feel a little intruded upon, but at the same time his eyes were sensual in their search, his eyelids heavy and the hint of a smile as he looked at my neck. I was surprised by my body's reaction. He had not moved but his eyes were enough. Why did I feel then that this was some form of revenge?

I moved to him, sitting on his side of the boat and there I kissed him. I put one hand on the back of his head and pulled him against me. He made me stand with his breath against my neck. I forced him to lie down in the middle of the boat and I straddled him, kissing him with an intensity that I tried at first to withhold. Then, as he pulled my knickers aside, I was elsewhere, in the green parlour, a glass decanter in my hand, and I poured myself a measure as my love sat facing the fireplace, our sleeping baby in his arms. On the mantelpiece above the fire lay a hammer, its handle pointed in my direction. A single swipe to break the leaking windows and let in the full weight of the water.

A house was floating nearby, its roof and top floor bobbing close to the boat. With two hands on the hooked pole I snagged the roof and pulled it towards me, lifting it up from the lake. It was heavy but became lighter as water poured from the front door. I set it on the deck. My love seemed reluctant to be near the doll's house and he returned to the shelter of the boat's wheel. Let him do as he wishes, I thought. I inspected the object dutifully. It was crafted from wood, the exterior unpainted or perhaps the paint had worn away. Through the small windows I could see rooms and, running my fingers along the edge of the facade, I found a metal latch that allowed me to open the front entirely, like the cover of a book.

Inside the small rooms were items of doll's furniture, heaped together where they had been tossed about. One room upstairs had a wooden bed and a chest of drawers, another had a metal oven and a couple of tiny chairs. There were no dolls. Perhaps they were still in the water. I glanced around and I could see that my love was watching me from his position by the wheel. He was interested in what I would find, I thought with some satisfaction. He wanted to know whether there would be a small crown and a small pair of crutches, a miniature accordion and a doll's cup, no bigger than a fingernail. I searched the rooms for these things. I longed to see them together. But there were only damp pieces of furniture, even in the parlour with the dark green walls, where the embers of a fireplace faintly glowed.

TWELVE

THE PARENTS DOWNPLAYED THINGS. They'd found Finn sometime before midnight, walking in the woods. He'd been going to the campsite to find Tariq, that's what he'd told them between sobs. When he realised he was lost he'd tried in vain to come back and had ended up somewhere on the opposite edge of the lake. Ciara had been caught by Liz not too far from the broken chair, searching desperately in the rain for her brother. They'd soon been taken back inside and Harrie had carried on with his assembly like nothing had happened, fixing one panel against the next, and it was only when the children had gone to bed that Liz saw the parents holding each other in silence on the blue sofa, a new coffee table in front of them.

In the morning, the first day of September, the atmosphere had a dizziness to it. Conversation was a little too easy over breakfast and both Harrie and Monica were quick to laughter, an infectious sort that came first with talk about the Scare but soon ran into late deliveries and interior design, buoying them up, thought Liz, as her sister spoke thrillingly about the end of summer, how warm it would be well into October. It was a bad thing, they agreed, a terrible thing, but at least it would be nice for days out. The children themselves were a little quiet, both had the beginnings of a cold and they sat around like they were still half asleep, as if the scene around them was playing without their presence.

The family were due to leave and, while the fact itself hadn't been mentioned, the talk turned to motorways and it seemed that the plan was still the plan. Liz listened on with an awareness that she was not herself, not quite, and it was as if her family had already left and this scene around her was only a memory. She ate a big orange, the juice stinging her thumb. A small cut, she supposed. John looked bashful. Good. Where was Alma now, she wondered, imagining her in Newcastle, in a cramped room with Richard. Their time in the countryside would already feel distant, a gap in the summer, already behind them. She would be sitting on the bed, her legs crossed on the sheets. Richard would be washing in the bathroom, she would be waiting for him to finish. She'd be aware of her waiting, that he was the one who had made plans. He would have been secretive, alluding in only the most oblique way to a meeting with friends. Her thoughts would be dark. She would not want them to be so. It was not their split with Tariq. No, she felt very little about the fact he had returned to Glasgow, less than she'd been expecting. Alma looked at the door to their room. Her thoughts were losing their solidity, that is what she disliked. It was making her weak. She would try to find in herself the certainty that had brought her there, the love and anger that together had moved her across the summer. She was still angry, she still wanted him. But she was unable to hold her ideas as she had once done.

She would look at the door to the hallway. She would listen to the shower running.

Harrie took the children outside to get them moving while Monica did their packing. There was a Frisbee thrown between the three of them close to the shore, which seemed to John like it was asking for trouble but what did it matter to him if they lost their Frisbee? What did he care? Ciara asked if he could join, asked her father as if it was his decision to make. Nothing had been mentioned of their clash in the woods, neither of them had properly spoken to the other since then.

'I'm not sure Uncle John wants to,' said Harrie but John stepped forward and so they made a square and threw the blue disc from one corner to the next.

He wasn't as good as he thought he would be. Almost immediately it went over Ciara's head and landed in the lake. Apologetic, he waded out, shoes and socks on the stones, going only as far as his shins to grab the floating Frisbee. Turning back he was met with the sight of the house and the others, struck by an awareness of time passing. He stood in the lake outside of it, the viewer of a photograph on a wall. He felt as if a catastrophe had occurred. Why then were the leaves still green on the trees? The children and Harrie were looking at him. In a couple of hours they would be gone.

They kept playing but soon stopped again when Finn fell on the pebbles, one of his little shoes flung away. John was the closest and he helped the boy to his feet, no blood or grazes, only a bit of dirt on his hands. Harrie was near. He took over, nudging John aside, knelt beside his son, lightly squeezed the sides of Finn's foot and made a honking sound. But it was Harrie's other hand which brought about an emotion in John that ambushed him with its strength, a tender circle drawn on Finn's back by his father's flat hand that drew a line between that moment and a moment years before, less than a moment, more, his own father's body gigantic and close, as if in a timeless expanse, less a body than a sensation of being contained, as if in a great hollow tree. Yes, there it was, the hollow tree, holding him close, as if in the knowledge that the embrace would one day cease. The fear his father felt of losing him. Harrie showed Finn he was listening to everything the boy had to say about his shoes. He looked at his son talking as if it were a miracle. Daily, the fear his father must've felt, cancer or no, that the small body in his arms would not long be contained. He in turn would fear the same, if not for the nothing, the fact there was nothing, not yet, nothing, no. John saw then the loops on a chain that stretched back, the metal pulled tense, pulled not by some unseen hand but by the weight of the chain as it dangled above the dark.

Later, he checked his email and found a message from Total Translations. His old manager was apologetic for the delay in responding. They were still interested in working with him in the future but the truth of the matter was that the bread-and-butter bottom base, his exact words, were turning to AI translations for their copy. In his opinion, which he was sure John shared, the translations you get from these things are riddled with errors. No nuance. But it seemed these clients didn't care. Here the tone became exasperated. These clients would rather have it done for free than have it done well. As long as some sense could be made, a smidgen of sense. It wasn't personal and not a reflection on John's work, the manager said. There was another Hungarian translator on his books who'd been with the company for much longer. He was sure John understood. John had done good work, he was proud of the work they had done together. And he felt bad about this, the manager said. He was sorry. It was no one's fault. It was a long time coming. Hopefully things would turn around.

*

Monica was packing the children's things. Liz was near the doorway, her eyes on the wall where John had scrubbed away the two pencil outlines. The patch was dry. You couldn't tell there had ever been anything drawn there.

'I swear they've thrown about clothes I didn't even know we owned,' said Monica.

'We've been struggling to conceive,' said Liz.

Monica stood with a small pile of Ciara's T-shirts folded over her forearm.

'Oh, Liz.'

Her face had fallen. She looked uncomfortable. Liz regretted saying anything.

'It took us a while.' Monica glanced beyond her to the corridor. 'How long have you...'

'Coming up to two years.'

'Have you been using ovulation sticks? They were a game changer for us. Oh Liz, I remember how it felt.' She placed Ciara's T-shirts in the suitcase. 'Sorry, I just wasn't expecting—'

'No, I appreciate it.'

'I thought you might not want children.' Monica hesitated. Her eyes were scanning Liz's face. 'I'd put you off?' She smiled nervously.

'We'll be talking to a GP, I expect. They'll give us some options.' She thought about her two days of pregnancy at twenty-two, whether it was real or whether she was mistaken. 'Whether it's John or me or both of us,' she said. 'Because that could be it as well. Both of us.' She was reluctant to stop talking. 'Sperm rates are falling. Did you know that? I think it has to be air pollution.'

'There could be a lot of different reasons.'

'Yes.' Breathe. 'You've had yours.'

'I can help,' said Monica, as if she hadn't heard her. 'You should've seen my spreadsheet when we were trying with Ciara.'

'The doctor will give us some options.'

Monica nodded enthusiastically, then she stopped, as if she no longer wanted to fight her sister's mood. They stared at each other, the house quiet. Monica's eyes were heavy but they were not hard. 'You don't need to have children,' she said.

It would've been easy for Liz to take it the wrong way, but she didn't.

'You don't need to have them.'

Liz came further into the room. There was a good amount of light from the high window. She wondered what the previous inhabitants had used it for, if they had used it at all. The walls were painted white and aside from the pencil outlines there had been no scuff marks to suggest where furniture had been placed, no worn sections on the floorboards. 'Did they like it here?' she asked.

'The kids? Loved it.'

Monica went back to picking up the clothes.

'They wanted to get up to the window. If you had a bunk bed or something it would be perfect.'

Liz thought about Alma in a room much like this, almost a cell. She would be looking up at the high window, waiting for Richard to return. Liz helped to pick up some of the children's things, some dolls, a plastic costume crown, and she placed them on the fold-out mattress. She wanted to have a child. She at least wanted the possibility.

'Daddy's hogging the bathroom,' said Ciara in the hallway as she stood with her arms folded and she already looked to Liz like an older girl. Was it her face? The way she moved her lip into a sneer, which looked more adult than child in the dimness of the space. It was strange, as if years had passed since they'd last seen each other. Liz thought to tell her that Daddy was doing his business but Ciara's eyes were imploring so she found herself knocking lightly. 'Harrie,' she said. 'Harrie, I think Ciara needs the loo.'

There was no answer.

'Harrie.'

She tried the door but it was locked. When she knocked a third time to no response she tried not to show her concern, smiling to Ciara and telling her to go downstairs, she'd fetch her when the toilet was free. Where was John? Monica was still packing and she didn't want to scare her.

'John,' she called down the stairs.

'John,' she said more softly as she descended.

'What?' He had come, his hand was already on the bannister.

'Harrie's in the bathroom.'

'Yes?'

Monica was now standing at the top of the stairs, listening to them. Perhaps she understood what Liz meant because she turned to knock at the bathroom door.

'Harrie?' Bang bang bang.

Liz felt a wash of guilt, as if she had caused this.

'Harrie, are you in there? Are you okay?'

Monica waited for a response. When one did not come she banged again at the door. Liz reached the upstairs landing, John behind her. Monica was now gripping the handle and rattling the door, trying to force it open. 'Call an ambulance,' she said. The children were looking up at them from the bottom of the stairs. 'John, can you try?' she asked and stepped out of the way, perhaps expecting him to immediately throw himself at the door, but instead John knocked and called again for Harrie.

This time, there was the sound of something shuffling on the other side.

'Open the door, Harrie,' shouted Monica.

There was the sound of the door unlocking. 'John can come in,' said Harrie. His voice was weak. Monica looked as if she might force the door but John's hand was on the handle and he made a motion to show that everything was fine, that he'd go in and see what was what.

Inside, Harrie was sitting on the toilet. He looked like death. John closed the door behind him. There was blood, his right sock was soaked in it. The colour had washed completely out of his face.

'Your foot.'

Harrie looked around him.

With John's help he stood up and hobbled to the bath, sat himself on its edge so he could pull off his bloody sock. He inspected the bottom of his foot, the scab that had split open, turned on the hot tap and let the water run over his skin. 'About yesterday,' John started, but Harrie shook his head and waved a hand, as if it wasn't worth discussing.

'No, it wasn't right,' said John. 'I was overwhelmed, we all were.'

Harrie gave a little hum. He turned off the bath tap and dabbed his foot with a rolled-up piece of toilet paper. This done, he searched in his pocket for something, pulled out a plaster. 'I've never felt so feeble,' he said. 'It's not a pleasant sensation.'

There was a prickling in John's cheeks, a bloom of shame. 'You'll be alright,' he said. The wound in Harrie's foot was bleeding again. Put on your plaster, he thought.

'I want to at least finish the paper I'm writing,' said Harrie.

He was looking at the sink. 'Did you hit your head?' asked John.

'I'm being dramatic, it's sickening.' Harrie looked scared, embarrassed. His plaster was in his hand, the blood now dripping off his heel. The shame again. Cover your cut, John thought. I can't stand to see it. Harrie's eyes were fearful. Was he expected to meet this fear, was he invited to say a kind word, he who had been cruel?

'I'm not a joke,' said Harrie.

'No.'

'I'm putting things out in the world. Real things. They'll be there after I am gone.'

Harrie's eyes were sunken deep in their sockets, he stared straight at John as if searching. Why this suggestion of death? Nothing had happened, only another failure. For what was he searching? An answer to this outpouring, this consuming sadness? Cover up your cut. Please, for the love of God.

'I am laying down precious jewels. Just because you don't understand my work. It doesn't mean, doesn't mean...'

'Honest, ignore what I said. It wasn't really about you.'

'I have made a fool of myself, but you drove me to it.'

'Ah now, it wasn't all that bad. Your foot, Harrie.'

'My work will be done,' said Harrie, his eyes searching still, hard and searching. 'There are people I know who would be devastated if this paper is left unfinished. That's not an exaggeration.'

The blood was stark against the white. 'It's a relief about Finn,' said John. He had to change the subject, there was only so much he could take of this selfish fear. At the mention of his son, Harrie appeared for a moment bewildered. He turned his attention to his foot, raised above the bath. Good, right, shamed out of this mad self-pity by love.

'He's a funny boy,' said Harrie. There was a faint smile. But then he shook his head, as if focusing back on what truly mattered. 'I'm so close,' he said. 'I'm almost there.' His eyes were shut. John felt a wave of disgust. Is this what it boils down to, this desperate and self-serving need to enshrine the self? He thought of Finn walking in the dark and the rain in search of Tariq. He felt something in himself tear, a belief fall quietly away. I am no different, he thought, and saw in Harrie's vanity his own despair.

'I've nearly put it down,' said Harrie. 'This one, it matters the most, it pushes things forward, yes, it'll keep, there are readers waiting, colleagues across the Atlantic and they care, yes, they do, this is important, it will stick, it will stay.'

His lips still moved, as if he were talking in his own head, but nothing more was said. John plucked the plaster from his fingers, peeled off the wrapper and pressed it on the open cut. Despite the blood it stayed in place.

'Did you faint again?' Monica demanded to know when they exited the bathroom.

'How are we getting on with the packing?' asked Harrie, clearing his throat.

Neither of the sisters moved. They were blocking the men in the bathroom doorway. 'Is anyone looking after the kids?' Harrie asked. 'Someone should look after the kids.'

'Did you faint?' Liz asked.

'No.'

'Did he, John?'

'Prune, do you mind checking on the children?' Harrie asked. He looked like himself. It was dignified, Liz thought, the way he picked up his washbag and pushed with purpose between them, out of the room.

'Come on, the day is moving.'

Liz went downstairs with John behind her but Monica stayed where she was, staring into space. Later, John came back upstairs and she was still there, sitting alone at the top of the stairs. She had seen him approaching. Her face looked heavy but she was not crying and as he reached her she leant to one side to let him through. When he asked her if she was okay she said she was collecting her thoughts. He did not pass but sat beside her. The staircase was only just wide enough for the two of them. Their thighs were touching. She stayed where she was.

'It'll be nice to be home, I expect,' he said.

There was the sound of Harrie's voice from somewhere else in the house, indistinct but loud enough to carry. She laid her head gently on his shoulder. He listened to the distant voices, listened for Liz.

After a while he shifted his shoulder, moving it away. Monica sat back upright. He felt ashamed and she must have seen this because she turned from him. 'It'll be fine,' he said but she did not care to hear it. She stood up and walked down the stairs.

'See you soon, Prune,' said Harrie as he hugged goodbye. The car was loaded. He felt large and strong in Liz's arms as he squeezed her, and she told herself that he was a walled garden, stone piled on stone, incapable of falling. Monica put her hand out of the passenger window and Liz ducked into the car to hold her one more time. Her sister whispered into her hair that it wouldn't be long until they saw each other again. The house was beautiful. She was jealous. Liz kissed the side of her head as if she were an old friend.

'Byeeee,' she cried to the children in their seats.

'Byeeee,' they called back.

*

Soon after they were gone she carried her small desk into the room with the high window and placed it beneath the window, a few feet from the wall so that she could look up and see a square of sky. She was content with her decision. It was as if the desk had always been there. She liked the spareness of the room, the blankness of the white paint. She went and fetched a chair, one of the cheap ones that had been moved outside, it didn't matter which one. She got her notebook and a few other things and John followed her back from the bedroom to see what she was doing.

She put the white glove on the desk next to her pencils and pens, and then she carried on with her writing.

John dragged the remains of the antique chair from where it had lain overnight towards the house, and then further in the other direction along the shore to the bonfire heap. It made track marks in the pebbles that he followed back to the woods, to collect the broken backrest and other small fragments of wood that had splintered away. These things gathered, he walked once more to the pile of dry leaves and roots. This time he wedged the broken chair into the bonfire where it sat like a throne to some sad kingdom of compost.

He felt that words were regaining a firmness. Or maybe he cared less now about their flailing. He liked to think he could take one by the neck and dangle it for as long as he wished. Little mattered. He had fumbled only in overthinking, he told himself. That was all there was to it. Translation was not difficult in the grand scheme of things. A word was not a puff of vapour, it was not a moving platform, not a bag of tricks, not a bend in the river, not a temple in the snow. He looked at the broken piece of wood in his hand, the figure's head, its expressionless face, and he threw it high into the heap.

*

Sweet came around in the late afternoon, just as they were starting to think about food. He said he was passing through the area and that he'd seen the blue Toyota was no longer outside the house. What he actually wanted to talk about was the garden, he later admitted, because he'd been thinking about it all day, what could be done with it. 'The old Palmers had the best intentions but in the end they let it go the way it did.' He looked beyond John. 'I always thought it was a shame,' he said. 'It's a great thing that you're making a go of it. Even if it's a lot to take on, it's a great thing.'

Nothing had been planted in the soil but the flower beds had been raked and the last of the weeds plucked from the tightest nooks in the edges of the masonry. Sweet surveyed the garden with a ready pleasure, smiling fondly as Liz pointed out the trellises that they would attach to the walls for clematis to grow, holding his hands behind his back in a posture that reminded John of a lord or a king. Sweet was impressed with everything they had done, he said. There was still time in the year for marigolds. Liz went inside to make a drink. As soon as she was gone, Sweet's demeanour changed, his smile disappeared and he blew the air out of his cheeks. He sat on a low wall and took off his droopy black hat.

'Did you have any luck finding your dog?' asked John.

Sweet glanced at him. 'No, I have not had any luck,' he said.

The warden reached into his pocket and brought out a pouch of tobacco. He rolled a cigarette without saying a further word to him and John at first thought he had done something to offend the man but Sweet had about him an aura of calm composure. It was as if Sweet was alone in his own garden. He exhaled the first smoke with his eyes closed, his face tilted up to the sky.

'Already it's difficult to picture the house without you,' he told them when Liz returned, his voice warm and welcoming.

Liz had with her three glasses of sherry and they toasted to the end of summer. She'd be back to work tomorrow. Only two days to the weekend, so there was that, then they would be in the routine, good to get back to some kind of routine.

'I have to say I'm relieved,' said Sweet. 'That things haven't had to change all that much.' He sipped his sherry. 'I didn't know what type of people would be moving here. It could've been anyone. I'm relieved,' he laughed. 'You'll find that autumn is beautiful here.' He spoke about the colours they'd see when the leaves turned, how it was his favourite time of the year, a little sad to see the branches become bare but the most beautiful of seasons. 'The evergreens stand out, the yew trees.' They talked about plans for painting the kitchen. 'The Palmers would talk a lot about making the house nice,' he said. 'They had plans for just about every room.' His tone seemed to John to imply that this was a failing. They spoke about inviting him over for a meal. 'I would bring them a good bottle of something every now and then and we'd drink it together.' It would be no problem for him to stay in the guest room if he needed to for work, and in return he had some seeds and bulbs that he would bring around when he remembered. 'They were good to me,' he said. Their presence was a relief, he told them again. He wouldn't have known what to do otherwise, if he couldn't stay the night when he had to work early the next day. 'Change can be terrible and cruel,' he said at one point, as if it was a joke. He rolled another cigarette and when he smoked it he closed his eyes and basked in the low sunlight, and he stayed very still for a very long time.

Even the boat's ripples didn't break the reflection of the stars. I passed across the surface of the lake mindful of the caves far below me, those routes that ran within the limestone rock in all manner of directions. What it would be to plunge into the depths and see them for myself, light their paths with a torch on the shoulder of a rubber diving suit. Where would I go but towards the most inviting, a yawning chasm, and cross into its corridors, and where then but to follow their walls, believing that I would be able at any point to turn around and return the way I came.

Perhaps I thought too much about these things, because I was caught unawares when the boat came to a crashing stop and I was very nearly thrown overboard. The engine made a sound of agony and cut out completely. My mind was tossed into that state of strangeness that happens when a collision occurs, a numbed state of lawlessness that made my body feel as light as a balloon. I moved then as if floating across the small deck and saw for the first time the tree in the water. It was enormous, seemingly on its side although it still had a great many branches full of leaves, jutting out of the water to heights that ran well above my head. It must have been living only moments before, I thought to myself. Could it be living still?

I judged that the boat had become wedged against the tree's trunk. I could reach out and touch the moist bark.

Without the engine, things were quiet. There was only the faint sound of the breeze running through the tree's branches. I considered leaving the boat and climbing onto it, but what would I have done if the boat began to drift away? Still, something in me wanted to go further than just my fingertips so I positioned myself on the bow in such a way that my feet were hanging over the edge of the boat, resting on the trunk of the tree. I was pleased to find that it did not sink into the water. Compared to its size, I was nothing. The bark was gnarled and sinewy, peeling in places. I plucked some leaves from a branch within reach, sharp thin fingers of green. I don't know much about the names of trees. Gradually, carefully, I shifted myself further onto the horizontal trunk until only my hands were still on the boat, gripping the side for balance. The tree did not turn in the water, to my relief, but stayed where it was. Was it actually staying still or were we drifting, the tree and the boat together, on the surface of the lake? I let go of the boat, kneeling, then sitting on the tree. I looked at the branches close to me, wondering if I would find in them the objects that had come to the surface. I searched with my eyes, despite my better senses, for a glint of a mirror or a piece of glass or painted wood or something fashioned from clay. I saw only half-shapes in the branches, the suggestion of handles and legs deep amongst the needle leaves, the sweep of a body moving, a hand, an eye, a pair of lips. I noticed then that the boat had become dislodged and was moving away. My place on the trunk was solid and I longed to crawl further into the depths of the branches, to see where it would take me as it drifted on the water. But my love was waiting for me inside the house and the boat was moving away inch by inch, any longer and it would be out of reach, so I clambered back on board.

There, I stood on the bow and watched the tree float away. The trunk was followed by a vastness of interconnected lines, bare of leaves, and I realised these were the roots. It was as if a giant hand had plucked the tree from the ground and thrown it into the lake.

I managed to start the engine again and headed towards the shore. Back inside, I would tell my love everything. With the others gone, there would be no one to wake with my speaking. I could bring my love to the window and point to the lake, and if the tree was no longer in sight I would describe what had been there only moments before. Two eyes open in amazement. My love's beautiful eyes. I would describe everything in the greatest of detail, leave no word unturned.

THIRTEEN

S HE NEEDED TO BE on a call for nine but John
wanted her to join him, she could tell. He'd been up
since six preparing the heap, he talked excitedly about it
over breakfast, the practicalities of smoke, wind directions.

She was excited too, he could tell. The way she came
outside with her cup of coffee, still in a dressing gown. He
was glad she wanted to see it lit, something they could talk
about later.

He must've chucked a load of petrol on it, she thought,
from the way the wood glistened.

Earlier he'd wrapped an old tea towel around a big stick
and dipped it in the jerry can. When he picked it then off
the ground, she looked at him like he'd lost his mind. This
would be a detail in the story, naturally it would be something she'd mention when she told it back to him.

He looks like a madman, she thought as he set fire to
the torch, loving this a little too much but he does look
handsome with the light of the flame, standing confident
like some ancient man on the side of an urn. There's a
new energy in him, something come back, the torch flung
overhead into the heap.

What did it matter if there was life beyond them? Was he hopeful, he wondered. Surely it was not hope, this dark appetite. He longed to try again with her, knowing it did not matter. The fire had caught the dry leaves, it was too late to stop it from spreading.

The heat was on her face, even from the distance she was standing. He had been right about the smoke, the wind was taking it away from them and towards the lake. They would try again as soon as they could, this time it would be different.

Either there was something in the leaves or he'd been over-generous with the petrol, but the fire was higher than he'd imagined it would be, the smoke almost black and coming off in a great plume against the blue sky. He couldn't do anything even if he wanted to. She was still sipping her coffee, calm as anything.

She'd write something about the bonfire, she thought, how he hadn't looked this content for days. The man she wrote would have eyes that shot about. Not like John's eyes. His eyes then were tender.

He'd go on from there with little care for the depths. He'd speak and trust the words to be under his shoes, as long as the words came and were good enough for the day-to-day. He'd skate on a frozen lake. And there would be all the pleasures of the day-to-day. He would enjoy the pleasures.

There was reason to be hopeful, she thought. Others were on their side, that knowledge alone enough to give a person a push. Autumn would be their season, still warm for a few weeks more.

Nothing beyond the pleasures, that's the way of it, no gain to be had from staring off into the hills, the whole thing meaningless except for the pleasures. The flames were taking the broken chair. The past has shut behind him. There was no dog in the hallway, no more haunting.

The man she was writing in her story would wait with the fire until it was finished, his love beside him, waiting on the shore of the lake until the heap had burnt itself out.

They would hang above the dark, he thought. What did it matter if things continued beyond them? They would hang until they fell, just as they would fall if there were sons or daughters, just the same. Was it hope, this lightness in his chest?

He would take from this scene a sense of occasion, she thought. He would see it as a point scorched in time. As soon as they were done she would write this down. He would squeeze her and they would walk back inside hand in hand.

The past was a shut gate, there was only before them the present, a step to make, what did it matter the direction, theirs to make, what a blessing, plenty of time.

ACKNOWLEDGEMENTS

I'm deeply indebted to the support of my agent, Harriet Moore, and to my editor, Allegra Le Fanu. Thank you to everyone in and around Bloomsbury who worked on this book. Lauren Whybrow, Madeleine Feeny, Carmen R. Balit, Brittani Davies, SJ Forder. Thank you also to Nicola Bell, Peter Cherry, Samuel Gibson, Deirdre Lennon, Matthew Reed, Vaughn Highfield and others who offered feedback on earlier versions of the manuscript. Thank you to the Wild Court Group. Thank you to those at Store 104 for a calm and welcoming place to write. Thank you to Gergő Kovács for checking on my Hungarian sentences. Thank you to my family. Thank you to Lydia. Thank you to Hugh.

A NOTE ON THE AUTHOR

Thomas McMullan is a British writer. His debut novel, *The Last Good Man*, won the 2021 Betty Trask Prize. His short fiction has been published in *Ploughshares*, *The Dublin Review*, *Granta*, *3:AM Magazine*, *Lighthouse* and *Best British Short Stories*, and his journalism has appeared in the *Guardian*, *Times Literary Supplement*, *frieze*, *ArtReview* and BBC News.

A NOTE ON THE TYPE

The text of this book is set in Adobe Caslon, named after the English punch-cutter and type-founder William Caslon I (1692–1766). Caslon's rather old-fashioned types were modelled on seventeenth-century Dutch designs, but found wide acceptance throughout the English-speaking world for much of the eighteenth century until replaced by newer types towards the end of the century. Used in 1776 to print the Declaration of Independence, they were revived in the nineteenth century and have been popular ever since, particularly amongst fine printers. There are several digital versions, of which Carol Twombly's Adobe Caslon is one.